BRUIN CRIMEWORKS

What the [...] DEATH and HATES [?]

"Mayhem in the Hammett manner. It's a lulu!"
--San Francisco Chronicle

"Plenty of rapid-fire action; excellent plot."
--Detroit News

"Fast, snappy, keep-you-up-late thriller."
--Boston Globe

"Hard-boiled, swift-paced."
--Los Angeles Times

"One of the best of the year. (4 pistols)"
--Chicago Daily News

"Plenty of swift, violent action; startling finish."
--New York Times

"Sophisticated, fascinating, speedy."
--Philadelphia Bulletin

"Hard-hitting, well knit; the find of the month."
--Time Magazine

"Tough, but how it moves!"
--Baltimore Sun

"A slick, streamlined story."
--San Diego Union

"Rapid-fire action and the surprise element on every page."
--Minneapolis Sunday Tribune

More accolades for Mr. Dodge....

San Francisco Chronicle, July 20, 1941—

   This department met and liked David Dodge even before "Death and Taxes" was published. Even before we read the book. And we liked the guy, see. He told us a couple of swell stories and we obliged with a few of ours and we downed some lemonades together and we laughed and had a swell time. (We were with a couple of other guys whose wives were away in the country, tra-la, tra-la, tra-laaa. N.B. They're back now, the wives.) Anyway, life was good and the lemonade had a purring quality and we were sure that David Dodge's book would be a good book because it was written by a good guy and the lemonade was good and we felt good and ...   And the next day came as next days will and we were worried. Just suppose, we said to ourself ... Just suppose "Death and Taxes" is a stinkeroo. What on earth will we ever do? Shall we be honest and kick it around and next time we meet him look at the ground? Or shall we weasel and rate it high so we won't have to cringe when we meet the guy? 'Twas the critic's dilemma and we were sad because by that time we were sure it was bad.
   Well, it isn't!
   It's a lulu, it's a honey, it's a good book.
   But you're suspicious, eh? Okeh, read it yourself. Discover why George MacLeod lay "on his back on the vault floor with a small hole in the bridge of his nose."
   There's half a million dollars mixed up in it. A tax refund for Marian Wolfe [sic] whose father apparently hadn't been done right by. Marian was a blonde and MacLeod had "a bankroll, a good looking brunette wife, and a weakness for blondes." Which complicates matters, too. For the reader as well as for James Whitney, MacLeod's partner and our story's hero.
   The story, incidentally, is laid in San Francisco and if you've ever wondered how it would be to travel across the Bay Bridge at 80 miles an hour you can find that out, too.
   Highly recommended.
(Reviewed by Edward Dermot Doyle; "AAAA"=Excellent)

TIME Magazine, August 4, 1941—

A huge tax refund on a dead beer-baron's estate motivates the murder of an income-tax expert. The expert's pardner (sic), who likes liquor, ladies and a good scrap, helps California police clean up a tricky case. Hard-hitting and well-knit--the "find" of the month.

New Yorker, July 12, 1941 —

George MacLeod, reputedly the best tax consultant in San Francisco, gets into trouble when he tries to smooth out the difference between a blonde and some G-men. By trouble it is meant that George gets killed and stuffed into a vault. Fine, meaty story involving bootlegging and a half-million dollars in taxes.

New York Herald Tribune, July 20, 1941—

This rapid-fire affair should give you some new ideas on refunds, blondes, murder in various forms, bootlegging, heavy drinking and that sort of thing. All about how beautiful Marian Wolff got mixed up with the Treasury Department over her inheritance, how a certified public accountant tumbled out of an office vault in a state of rigor mortis, two others got theirs and so forth to a conclusion that satisfies all the requirements of rough-and-ready detection. The opus fairly swarms with questions pertinent to the complex yet lucid plot. Did somebody kill Marian's father on the trip to Washington? Who was the pilot of the plane? Must one always file a return? Did Adolph Zimmerman commit perjury? Where is that envelope? And how would you like to have a million dollars? The story picks up remarkably after a heavy dose of financial details and winds up at lightning pace. Mr. Dodge works overtime to pump alcoholic and fleshly thrills in to a tale that needed no such desperate measures. Fast and easy to read. (reviewed by Will Cuppy)

Books by David Dodge

Novels

Death and Taxes
Shear the Black Sheep
Bullets for the Bridegroom
It Ain't Hay
The Long Escape
Plunder of the Sun
The Red Tassel
To Catch a Thief
The Lights of Skaro
Angel's Ransom
Loo Loo's Legacy
Carambola
Hooligan
Troubleshooter
The Last Match

Travel Books

How Green Was My Father
How Lost Was My Weekend
The Crazy Glasspecker
20,000 Leagues Behind the 8-Ball
The Poor Man's Guide to Europe
Time Out for Turkey
The Rich Man's Guide to the Riviera
The Poor Man's Guide to the Orient
Fly Down, Drive Mexico

DEATH and TAXES

DAVID DODGE

A Whit Whitney Mystery

Introduction by Randal S. Brandt

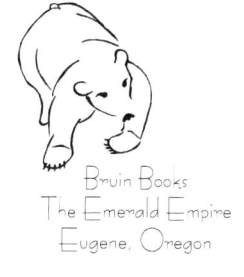

Bruin Books
The Emerald Empire
Eugene, Oregon

Published by
Bruin Books, LLC
July, 2010

© David Dodge 1941
© renewed 1963
Introduction © Randal S. Brandt 2010

All rights reserved. No part of this book may be reproduced or transmitted in any part or by any means, electronic or mechanical, without written permission of the Publisher, except where permitted by law.

This book was designed and edited by Jonathan Eeds
Graphics design by Michelle Roper
Photograph of David Dodge by Ken Watson
1939 road maps courtesy of Shell Oil Company

Special thanks to Kendal Lukrich and Randal Brandt

Printed in the United States of America
ISBN 978-0-9826339-2-2
Bruin Books, LLC
Eugene, Oregon, USA
www.bruinbookstore.com

> For more information on David Dodge visit
> *www.**david-dodge**.com*

"*My Gosh! It's Murder on Montgomery St.*"

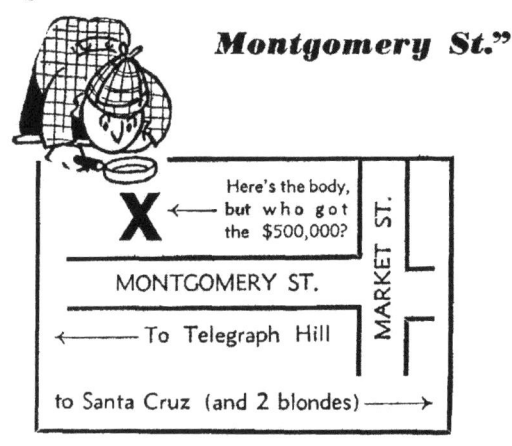

the year's fastest, wittiest mystery

"Death and Taxes"

by David Dodge

It's spicy, it's screwball, and it's the swiftest thing in print. You'll race all over San Francisco with as fascinating a collection of characters as you've ever encountered as they untangle the blonde, the bootlegger, the murder and the $500,000 worth of taxes. David Dodge, a San Francisco tax consultant, has written a hilarious mystery yarn based upon one of the cleverest plots you've ever followed. You'll stay up half the night to finish "Death and Taxes"—then wish it were 200 pages longer. It's a deftly written, wholly enjoyable mystery masterpiece.

$2.00—At All Bookstores

THE MACMILLAN CO.

David Dodge

No Ordinary Public Accountant

Like many authors, David Dodge held a variety of adventurous-sounding jobs before settling down as a professional writer—merchant marine fireman on a South American steamship run, stevedore, amateur actor, and night watchman on the San Francisco docks among them. Yet it was his experience in one of the least-exciting careers possible that defined his first series of mystery novels. At the time Dodge penned his first book, he was working in San Francisco as a Certified Public Accountant. A tax man. And so too is his main character, James "Whit" Whitney. Over the course of four novels, Dodge put his knowledge of the tax code to use and has Whit run down ex-bootleggers, gamblers and con men, German spies, and dope smugglers. While he has no problem bending the rules to keep as many of his legitimate clients' dollars away from the government as possible, he has absolutely no patience with crooks of any persuasion. And, although he would be the first to admit that he is no detective, he certainly does not let a few bullets flying in his direction deter him from protecting his clients and those he loves. Dodge, a creative man in a rule-bound occupation, combined these elements to become, as noted by critic T.J. Binyon, the first author to use accountancy as the "trick" around which to spin detective stories.[1]

David Francis Dodge was born on August 18, 1910 in Berkeley, California. Just before his ninth birthday, his father George A. Dodge, an architect in San Francisco, was killed in an automobile accident. His mother, Maude, relocated with David and his three older sisters to Southern California. At the age of sixteen, he left high school and began working as a bank messenger in Los Angeles, attending night classes at the American Institute of Banking. In 1931, he grew tired of the banking business and shipped out with the Grace Steamship Company, starting out as an oiler and working his way up to fireman on a steamer running back and forth to Chile. Dodge came ashore in San Francisco in 1933 and worked on the docks for a year before taking a job with the San Francisco accounting firm of McLaren, Goode & Co., becoming a C.P.A. three years later.

In 1936, David Dodge married Elva Keith, a Pacific Coast editorial representative for The Macmillan Company, and they set up house at 121 Nineteenth Avenue in San Francisco's Richmond District, near the Presidio. Their only child, a daughter named Kendal, was born in 1940. Dodge's first experience as a writer came through his involvement with the Macondray Lane Players, a group of amateur playwrights, producers, and actors whose goal was to create a theater purely for pleasure and who performed exclusively at Macondria, a little theater located in the basement of a house on Macondray Lane on San Francisco's Russian Hill. A play he wrote for Macondria won first prize in the Northern California Drama Association's 1936 one-act play contest. The prize-winner, "A Certain Man Had Two Sons," was subsequently published and Dodge saw his name in print for the first time.

His career as a writer really began, however, when he made a bet with Elva that he could write a better mystery novel than the ones they were reading. The result was his first novel, entitled—perhaps inevitably—*Death and Taxes*. In the book, Dodge blends a number of elements reminiscent of those found in the works of another San Francisco mystery writer, Dashiell Hammett. Like Sam Spade in *The Maltese Falcon*, Whit Whitney is drawn into a murder investigation because of the death of his partner. Whereas Spade is a private investigator who considers it his professional duty to do something about it, Whit is reluctant to get involved—he is more interested in recovering half of a million dollars in overpaid taxes than in solving his partner's murder. Also, like Spade, Whit deals with a sultry female client—in this case, a blonde with tax troubles—and the alluring widow of his deceased partner. Dodge also smartly borrows from the best elements of another Hammett book, *The Thin Man*, and keeps the tone light—bordering at times on screwball—the dialogue fast and witty, and the alcohol flowing. Venerable San Francisco newspaper columnist Herb Caen was the first to point out the comparison: "Macmillan will bring out (in July) a moiduh mystery with a Thin Mannish S.F. background; it's called *Death and Taxes*, and was written by David Dodge, a local accountant, f'goshsakes."[2]

Unlike *The Maltese Falcon*, though, with its exotic backstory of the search for a fabled jewel-encrusted statuette, Dodge concocts his story around the potentially stultifying intricacies of the Internal Revenue Code, albeit spiced up with a Prohibition-era bootlegging angle. With his background as a tax accountant, contemporary reviewers gave him full credit for getting the financial and tax details right. Fortunately for readers, he does it so effortlessly and authoritatively that it never drags down the plot or detracts from the murder mystery.

Death and Taxes was published in 1941 and David won five dollars from Elva. Three more Whitney novels soon followed: *Shear the Black Sheep*, *Bullets for the Bridegroom*, and *It Ain't Hay*.

After the attack on Pearl Harbor, Dodge joined the U.S. Naval Reserve, contributing to the war effort as a crack member of an elite corps of, as one might expect, accountants. Upon his release from active duty in 1945, and having grown tired of holding down a desk job during the day and writing at night, Dodge packed his family into a car and headed south for Guatemala via the Pan American Highway. He explained the move this way:

> We went to Guatemala to get a fresh outlook on the business of murder. I had shot, strangled, stabbed, poisoned and otherwise knocked off so many people in the vicinity of San Francisco that the well was running dry. Unless I could find a fresh crop of victims, the time was fast approaching when I would have to give up writing murder mysteries and take a job in a shoe store to earn a living. This fate worse than death was precluded when one of my wife's distant relatives left her with a small inheritance. Together with our lifetime savings of $172.50, it gave us enough of a bankroll to follow the swallows south to Central America.[3]

Of course, that statement, while representative of Dodge's humorous prose style, is just a little disingenuous. Many writers have found San Francisco to be fertile ground for fictional murder—and two of Dodge's Whitney novels do not even take place in the city. Nevertheless, the exodus out of San Francisco marked the start of not only Dodge's second detective series, featuring a Latin America-based expat private investigator named Al Colby (*The Long Escape*, *Plunder of the Sun*, and *The Red Tassel*), but also his second career as an inveterate world traveler. A career he successfully combined with his job as a writer and turned into a string of self-deprecating humorous travel books that chronicle the Dodge family's journeys and (mis)adventures in foreign lands. His first "travel diary," *How Green Was My Father* was published in 1947 and landed on the *New York Times* bestseller list. In typical Dodge fashion, he explained that the book started out as a letter to family and friends back in the States, but that it got so voluminous he decided it would be cheaper to publish it as a book than to "make carbons and mail to all and sundry by air."[4]

Always the accountant, a recurring theme of Dodge's travel books is his attempts to extract the last drop of value out of every dollar—or *peso* or *franc* or *drachma*, as the case may be. A self-described "nickel-nurser" and "skinflint," his most successful book was called *The Poor Man's Guide to Europe*, which spent fifteen weeks on the bestseller list and appeared in annual revised editions from 1953 through 1959. Dodge found that travel and writing were the perfect life partners. His travels provided him with backgrounds, settings, characters, and experiences for his novels, travel books, and numerous magazine articles; his books and articles provided him with enough money to continue his travels.

But, if David Dodge is remembered today, it is for his novels—and for one novel in particular. By 1950, the Dodge family's travels had taken them to the Côte d'Azur, in the south of France, where they rented a villa just about the time that a cat burglar appeared on the scene, stealing jewels from the rich and famous. When the thief struck at the villa next door, Dodge, who was briefly suspected of being the culprit himself, saw the basis for a story that was "so much stranger than truth that it cried out to be immortalized between hard covers." *To Catch a Thief*, he claimed, practically wrote itself and was "the easiest eighty thousand words ever put together."[5] Alfred Hitchcock liked it so much he immediately bought the screen rights, and in 1955 Paramount released the iconic film version starring Grace Kelly and Cary Grant.

Following on the popularity of *To Catch a Thief*, Dodge abandoned series fiction and shifted his focus from detective mysteries to taut suspense thrillers in which ordinary characters are thrust into extraordinary situations. His later books consistently garnered favorable reviews and sold well enough that he and Elva could keep on the move. Their travel budget was supplemented by a steady stream of articles written for *Holiday* magazine and a deal with Pan American Airways that provided them with free plane tickets.

In 1968, the Dodges returned to Mexico—the scene of their first adventures on the road—and finally settled down in San Miguel de Allende. A practical guidebook to Mexico, timed to take advantage of the upcoming Olympic Games in Mexico City, soon followed. In the last two novels published before his death in 1974, Dodge returned to plots revolving around financial intrigue, this time featuring a U.S. Treasury Department agent. Sales declined, however, and his final novel, *The Last Match*, remained unpublished until Hard Case Crime resurrected the manuscript and brought it out in 2006.

In all, Dodge wrote over seventy world travel articles and short stories, nine travel books, and fifteen novels, three of which were made into films. Not bad for a C.P.A. from San Francisco. In *It Ain't Hay*, the fourth and final Whit Whitney book, Whit sustains a beating by a trio of dope-smuggling thugs and a doctor is summoned to patch up the patient. Afterwards, he has a conversation with Whit's wife, Kitty:

> The doctor made out a prescription blank. As he wrote, he said, "Was your husband in the army, Mrs. Whitney?"
> "No."
> "Navy?"
> "No. Why?"
> "I never saw a public accountant before with bullet scars in his abdomen."
> "He isn't an ordinary public accountant."[6]

The same could certainly have been said of David Dodge.

Randal S. Brandt
Berkeley, California
May 17, 2010
www.david-dodge.com

[1] T. J. Binyon, *Murder Will Out: The Detective in Fiction*. New York: Oxford University Press, 1989: 31.

[2] *San Francisco Chronicle*, 2 June 1941: 15.

[3] David Dodge, *How Lost Was My Weekend*. New York: Random House, 1948: 4.

[4] *Ellery Queen's Mystery Magazine*, 22, no. 118 (Sept. 1953): 54.

[5] David Dodge, *The Rich Man's Guide to the Riviera*. Boston: Little, Brown and Company, 1962: 8-9.

[6] David Dodge, *It Ain't Hay*. New York: Simon and Schuster, 1946: 58.

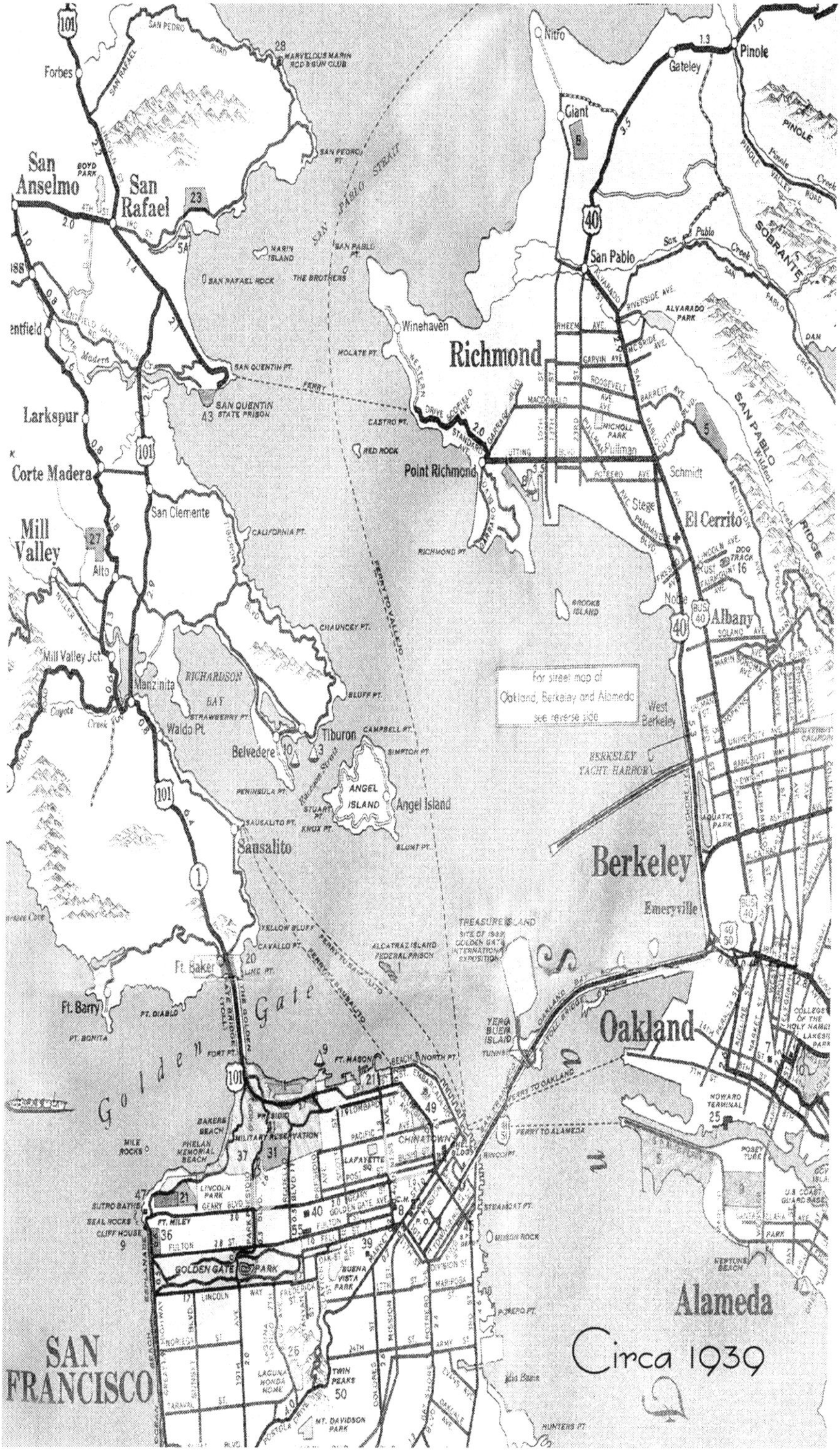
Circa 1939
Richmond
Berkeley
Oakland
Alameda
SAN FRANCISCO
San Anselmo
San Rafael
Larkspur
Corte Madera
Mill Valley
Sausalito
Tiburon
Belvedere
Angel Island
Pinole
Gateley
Giant
Nitro
San Pablo
Winehaven
Point Richmond
Pullman
Schmidt
El Cerrito
Stege
Albany
West Berkeley
Emeryville
Forbes
San Clemente
Alto
Mill Valley Jct.
Manzanita
Waldo Pt.
Ft. Baker
Ft. Barry
Golden Gate
SAN PABLO STRAIT
RICHARDSON BAY
BERKELEY YACHT HARBOR
TREASURE ISLAND
ALCATRAZ ISLAND FEDERAL PRISON
SAN QUENTIN STATE PRISON
For street map of Oakland, Berkeley and Alameda see reverse side
GOLDEN GATE PARK
CHINATOWN
LINCOLN PARK
TWIN PEAKS
FERRY TO VALLEJO
FERRY TO OAKLAND
FERRY TO ALAMEDA

RUSSIAN
HILL
NOB
HILL
North Beach Playground
Coit Memorial Tower
Washington Square
Chinatown
Chinese Playground
Portsmouth
Huntington Park
Union Square
State Building
101
CHESTNUT ST.
LOMBARD ST.
GREENWICH ST.
FILBERT ST.
UNION ST.
GREEN ST.
VALLEJO ST.
BROADWAY
PACIFIC AVE.
JACKSON ST.
WASHINGTON ST.
CLAY ST.
SACRAMENTO ST.
CALIFORNIA ST.
PINE ST.
BUSH ST.
SUTTER ST.
POST ST.
GEARY ST.
O'FARRELL
ELLIS ST.
EDDY ST.
TURK ST.
GOLDEN GATE AVE.
CEDAR ST.
BONITA ST.
WATER ST.
PFEIFFER ST.
VALPARAISO ST.
HAVENS ST.
ALLEN
MOCONDRAY ST.
ALLADIN TER.
WINTER PL.
GLOVER ST.
FALLON PL.
BERNARD ST.
JOHN ST.
TROY AL.
PLEASANT ST.
FRANK ST.
MULFORD AL.
HOOKER AL.
COSMO PL.
MAIDEN LANE
HARLAN PL.
VAN NESS AVE.
POLK ST.
LARKIN ST.
HYDE ST.
LEAVENWORTH ST.
JONES ST.
TAYLOR ST.
MASON ST.
POWELL ST.
STOCKTON ST.
GRANT AVE.
KEARNY
COLUMBUS AVE.
MARKET ST.
MISSION ST.
MINNA
MINT ST.
STEVENSON ST.
JESSIE ST.
FOURTH ST.
WHITE
EASTMAN
MORRELL ST.
McCORMICK ST.
MEACHAM PL.
SCOTLAND
SALMON
WAYNE
EATON PL.
HIMMELMAN
AUBURN ST.
YERBA BUENA ST.
WETMORE ST.
FREEMAN ST.
DORIC AL.
STONE ST.
TRENTON ST.
CHURCHILL ST.
CORDELIA ST.
CARD AL.
JOICE ST.
MONROE ST.
CHATHAM PL.
ST. ANNE ST.
JASPER PL.
BELAIR
TRACY PL.
ROMOLO PL.
BECKETT ST.
FLORENCE ST.
MARION PL.
REED ST.
PRIEST ST.
SHANNON ST.
ANNA LA.

Map of San Francisco Waterfront

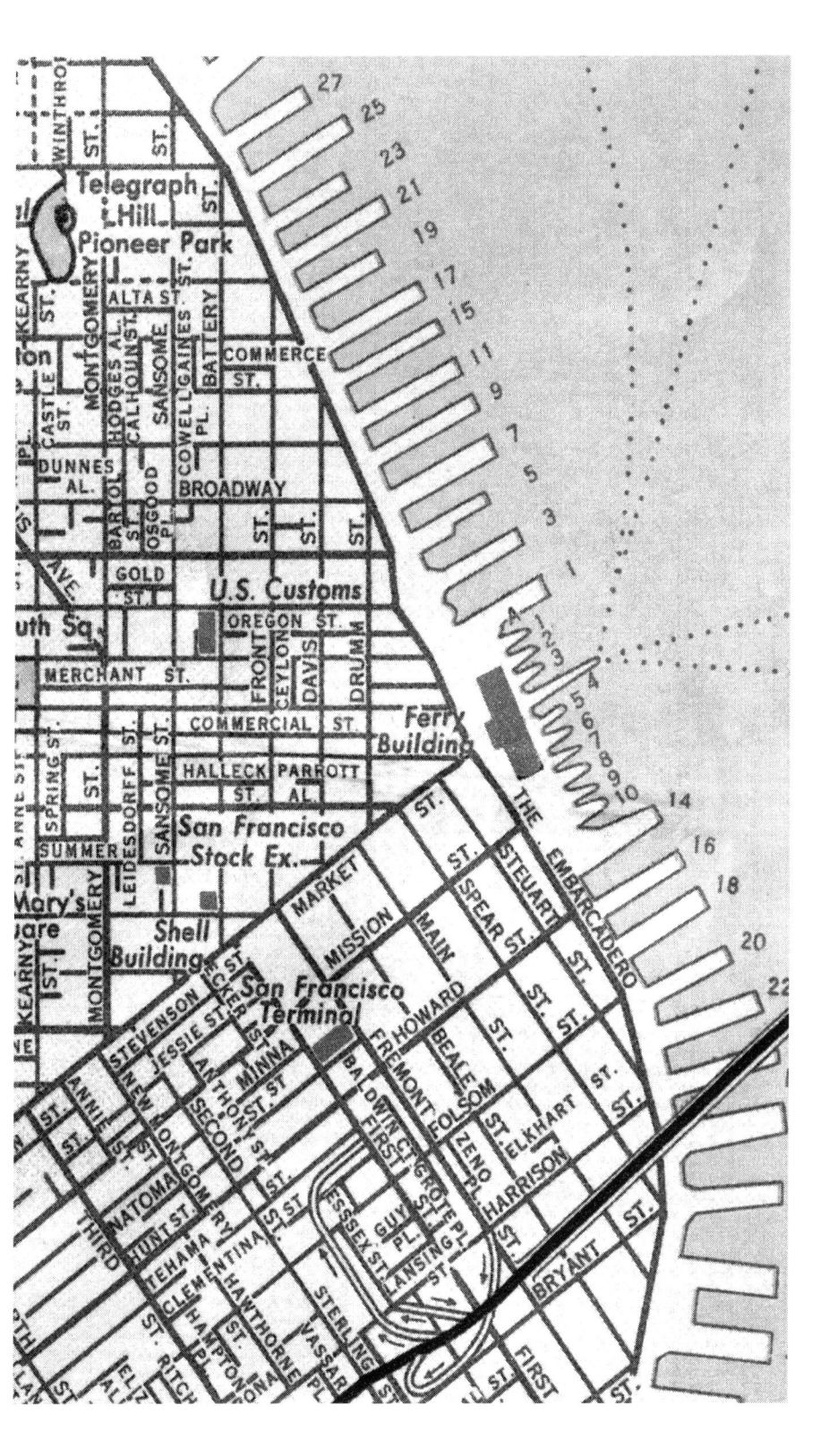

Landmarks:
- Telegraph Hill
- Pioneer Park
- U.S. Customs
- Ferry Building
- San Francisco Stock Ex.
- Shell Building
- San Francisco Terminal
- St. Mary's Square
- South Sq.

Streets (north to south):
- WINTHROP ST.
- KEARNY ST.
- MONTGOMERY
- ALTA ST.
- HODGES AL.
- CALHOUN ST.
- SANSOME
- COWELL PL.
- GAINES ST.
- BATTERY
- CASTLE ST.
- COMMERCE ST.
- DUNNES AL.
- BARTOL
- OSGOOD
- BROADWAY
- GOLD ST.
- OREGON ST.
- MERCHANT ST.
- FRONT
- CEYLON
- DAVIS
- DRUMM
- SPRING ST.
- COMMERCIAL ST.
- LEIDESDORFF
- SANSOME ST.
- HALLECK ST.
- PARROTT AL.
- SUMMER
- THE EMBARCADERO
- MARKET ST.
- MISSION
- MAIN ST.
- SPEAR ST.
- STEUART ST.
- STEVENSON
- ECKER ST.
- JESSIE ST.
- ANTHONY ST.
- MINNA
- FREMONT ST.
- HOWARD ST.
- BEALE ST.
- FOLSOM
- ELKHART ST.
- ANNIE ST.
- 1ST ST.
- NEW MONTGOMERY ST.
- SECOND ST.
- BALDWIN CT.
- GROTE PL.
- FIRST ST.
- ZENO
- HARRISON ST.
- NATOMA
- HUNT ST.
- TEHAMA
- CLEMENTINA
- HAWTHORNE ST.
- ESSEX ST.
- GUY PL.
- LANSING ST.
- THIRD ST.
- RITCH ST.
- HAMPTON
- VASSAR PL.
- STERLING ST.
- BRYANT ST.
- FIRST ST.

Piers (numbered): 1, 3, 5, 7, 9, 11, 15, 17, 19, 21, 23, 25, 27
Ferry slips: A, 1, 2, 3, 4, 5, 6, 7, 8, 9, 10, 14, 16, 18, 20, 22

Oakland/Alameda

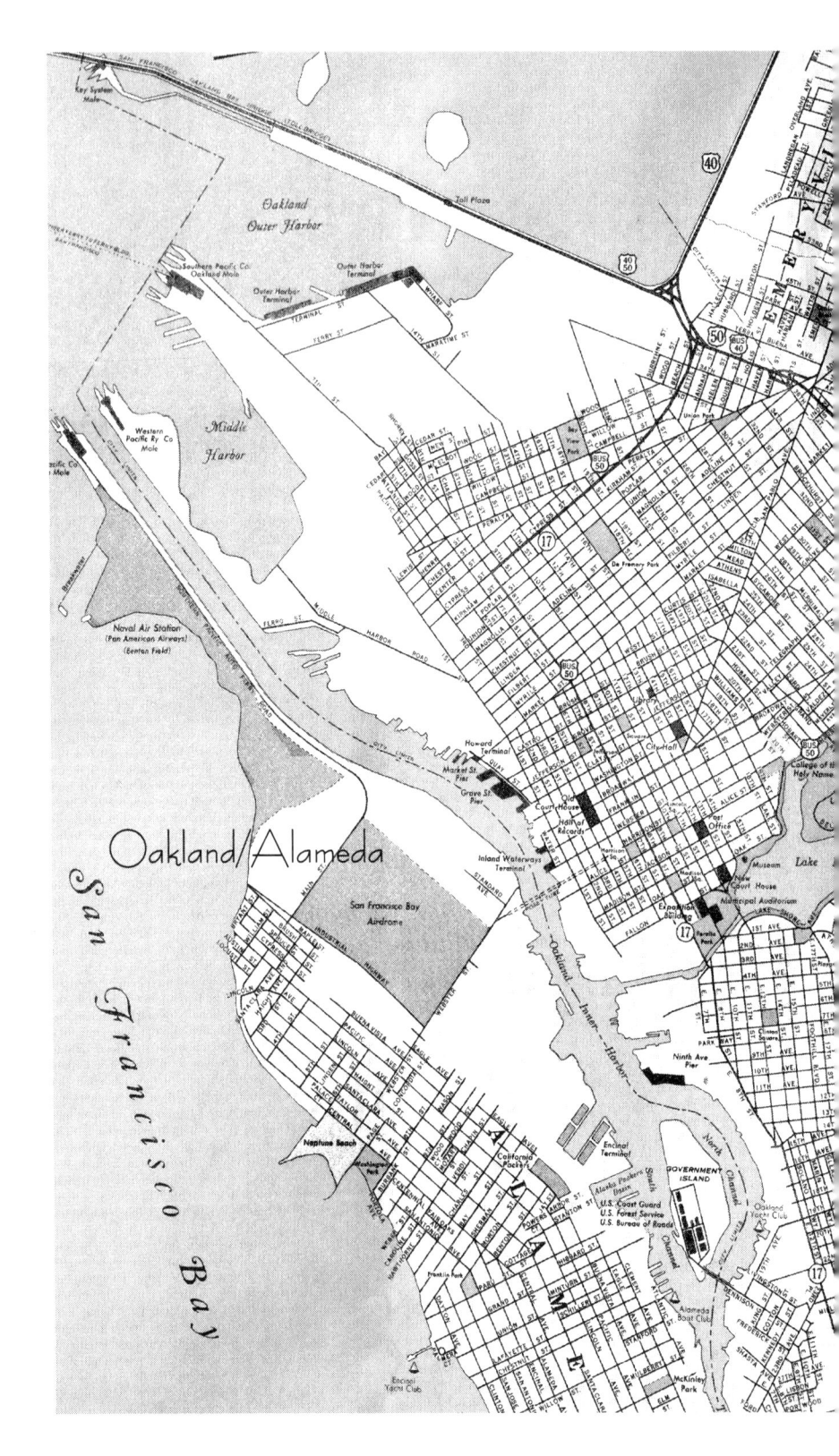

DEATH and TAXES

CHAPTER ONE

GEORGE MacLEOD had a bankroll, a good-looking brunette wife, and a weakness for blondes. He was reputed to be one of the best tax men in San Francisco, and people of means paid him substantial fees to pare their income taxes down as far as they would go without giving the G-men an opportunity to talk about fraud. George was smart enough to keep business and pleasure apart; he did pretty well in both fields until he got involved with a girl who had yellow hair and tax troubles. The combination was fatal to him.

His office was on the eighth floor of the Farmers' Exchange Building. The sign on the door said:

> MACLEOD AND WHITNEY
> CERTIFIED PUBLIC ACCOUNTANTS
> TAX CONSULTANTS

Inside there was a small reception room divided in half by a waist-high partition, and behind the partition was a desk for the girl who answered the telephone and turned away book salesmen. Her name was Miss Kelly. She was not very ornamental, but she was fast at dictation and her typing was superlative. Except during the income tax season she constituted one-third of the office staff. She was forty-five years old, and she had a maidenly crush on James Whitney, the firm's younger partner.

Beyond the reception room several doors opened off a short hall. The first door to the right was marked MR. MACLEOD, and the one opposite, MR. WHITNEY. There were two facing doors a few feet farther down, and the end of the hall was flanked by a washroom and a filing vault with a cast-iron door and a combination lock. A window at the far end opened onto a fire escape.

MacLeod's bad luck began on Friday, May 17, 1940, the day his partner started on a vacation. The vacation was scheduled to begin at five o'clock; at three Mr. Whitney was sitting in Mr. MacLeod's office with his feet on his partner's desk, wearing his holiday clothes: green slacks, brown and white shoes, a coat tailored out of a high-class horse blanket, a yellow necktie, and a panama hat. Mr. Whitney was thirty-three years old, tall, thin, and a pretty good tax man himself when he worked at it. He liked blondes well enough, but he also liked brunettes, brownettes, red-heads, and women with gray hair if they weren't too old.

MacLeod sat at his desk with a pipe in his mouth, his coat off and his sleeves rolled up, scowling at the instructions on the back of Schedule C, Form 706, Federal Estate Tax Return. He was about twenty years older than his partner, and he had a bull neck and the beginning of a belly. Salmon-colored hair grew thickly on his wrists and the backs of his hands and thinly on the top of his head. Pipe-ash decorated his vest.

Whitney took a final puff of his cigarette and threw it out the open window. "It's three o'clock. How much longer are you going to work on that thing?"

"What's the rush?" said MacLeod without looking up. "You got all day."

"I've got better things to do with it than sit around watching you work. If you want to buy me a drink, let's go. You can do that some other time."

"Sure, sure. Just as soon as I finish this schedule." MacLeod kept on reading. Whitney looked at his wrist watch and said something dirty. He let the front legs of his chair to the floor with a thump, crossed to the window, and leaned his elbows on the windscreen. "I'll give you five minutes more. Then I'm leaving."

The French telephone buzzed at MacLeod's elbow. He said, "Uh?" into the mouthpiece, listened a moment, and tipped a switch at the corner of his desk. "Hello," he said. "Hello, honey. How are you?"

Whitney recognized the tone; the caller was female and blonde.

MacLeod said, "You got a what?" The receiver made noises. He said, "For 1938? Did you file a return for 1937?" More noises, and MacLeod rolled his eyes at Whitney and shrugged. "I don't know whether they're right or not, Marian. If you made any money you have to file an income tax return, otherwise no. If you—" More noises from the receiver.

MacLeod scrawled some notes on a piece of scratch-paper. "How much did you get for them?" He listened, nodding, and made more notes. Finally he said, "They've got you, Marian. You should have filed a return." The receiver wailed and he laughed. "It isn't that bad. Bring the notice in tomorrow morning and I'll fix it up for you."

The voice went on talking. MacLeod said, "Well, why don't you come out for dinner tonight? I'll call Kitty and tell her . . . Oh, nuts. She'll be glad to see you." He winked at Whitney. "Sure, any time. I'll call her. Bring the notice along. G'bye." He touched the switch, said, "Miss Kelly, will you call Mrs. MacLeod?" and put the telephone down, grinning.

"Here's one for the book, Whit. This girl had fifteen thousand dollars' worth of securities she inherited back in '35 and she sold them in '38 and made about three thousand bucks profit and didn't file an income tax return. The Treasury Department caught up with her and wants one. It'll cost her fifteen or twenty dollars at the outside, and she's crying her eyes out." He laughed.

"Fifteen bucks is a lot of dough," Whit said. "How about that drink?"

The phone buzzed and MacLeod picked it up. "Kitty? I invited Marian Wolff to dinner tonight. She'll be out there any time." He listened, frowning. "Well, what difference does that make? She isn't expecting a banquet. Tell the cook to put another plate on the table, that's all. . . . No, just Marian. She's alone. . . . What's the matter with the three of us? . . . All right, all right. Who do you want?" He looked at Whit. "Sure, he's here, He won't come, though. He's leaving town. . . . Well, you talk to him."

He put his hand over the mouthpiece. "She wants you to balance the party. Four's company, three's a crowd. You can make it."

"No dice," Whit said. He took the phone.

Kitty MacLeod said, "Whit, will you please come to dinner tonight?" Her voice was a throaty contralto.

I wish I could, Kitty, but I'm leaving for Santa Cruz in about fifteen minutes."

"Business?"

"Some. Mostly pleasure. I've talked George out of a vacation."

"Can't you leave tomorrow morning? George has invited one of his girl friends to dinner and I've got to have a fourth. Please come."

"I can't do it, Kitty," said Whit. MacLeod slapped him across the seat of the pants and made affirmative gestures. "The business end of the trip is a conference tonight with a client in Santa Cruz. I couldn't make it if I stayed for dinner."

"Damn," she said. "Well, that's that. How long are you going to be gone?"

"A month."

"I'd like to see you before you go. You're sure you can't make it?"

MacLeod was still being persuasive. Whit kicked at him and smiled politely into the mouthpiece. "I'd like to see you too. I'll accept the invitation when I get back if it's still open."

"It's always open. Have a good time."

"I will. I'm sorry I can't make it tonight."

"You can do something for me," Kitty said. "Tell George to try to be home on time, and ask him to stay sober until he gets here."

"Sure. I'll tell him. 'Bye." He put the phone back in its cradle.

"You're passing something up," MacLeod said. "This Wolff won a beauty contest at U.C. a couple of years ago. One of those blonde babies that makes your head swim."

"A lot of good she'd do me. Every time I've been to your house I've had to entertain your wife while you took some girl out on the porch and gave her a lesson in the elements of accounting."

MacLeod grinned. "What's the matter with my wife? Don't you like her?"

"Sure I like her. But I'm not coming to dinner, so you might as well forget about it. How about buying me that drink?"

MacLeod leaned back in his chair and locked his hands behind his head. "Any minute now. But you ought to see Marian Wolff, Whit. If there ever was a girl who'd look natural in diamonds, she's it. She was born for the money, and she came so close to having a million dollars it makes her head ache." He rocked gently in the swivel-chair. "She was Harald Wolff's daughter."

Whit looked bored. "Is that so? Fancy."

"I told you about him. The bootlegger. He was one of the first clients I ever had."

"I never heard of him," Whit said. "And if you want to know the honest to God truth—"

"Don't say it." MacLeod raised his hand. "It's an interesting story. The United States of America versus Harald Wolff, or how the Treasury Department caught daddy with his pants down."

"I want a drink."

"Stop bellyaching, will you? You'll get your drink. I want to tell you about Harald Wolff."

Whit sighed and sat down.

MacLeod said, "How long have we been partners? Three years?"

"Two and a half. Honest, George, even if it were interesting I wouldn't want to hear about it."

"Shut up." MacLeod lit his pipe and slid comfortably down in his chair. "This was all wound up before your time, and it goes way back. Old man Wolff and I knew each other when I was just starting in business. We used to go hunting together every season, and I did his tax work. He and two or three other guys and I would bundle our stuff together and go up in the hills the day before the deer season opened and stay there until we had the limit . . . sometimes a day or two, sometimes a couple of weeks. Wolff and these other birds owned a brewery over in Oakland. I audited their books for years until prohibition came along, and then they got along without an auditor.

"Prohibition almost ruined them. It was a nice tight little corporation and they had started on a shoestring and plowed everything back into the business and were making good beer and building up a local trade, when *blooey!*—no more likker. They were cooked. They couldn't make beer and they couldn't get out—nobody would give a dime for the best brewery in the country. So they made near-beer and wondered how long they could last.

"Things got leaner and leaner. Wolff struggled with his honesty all through 1920 and finally gave up and began to turn out the real stuff. He had always run the brewery pretty much by himself, as brew-master and president of the corporation, and he just forgot to tell the other stockholders what was going on. He had the bookkeeper in his pocket—a little bastard called Zimmermann—and the two of them sold beer, real beer, as fast as they could turn it out. Thirty-five dollars a barrel in those days. Zimmermann handled all the receipts; cash on the line and no discount. Near-beer was worth $12.50 or thereabouts, and Zimmermann recorded the sales on the corporation books at the near-beer price, tossed $12.50 in the till, and turned the extra $22.50 over to Wolff, less protection money and a little knockdown, I guess. Wolff was only paying him a couple of hundred a month; I think he had something on him. But whatever Zimmermann got out of it, Wolff didn't miss it. He made almost a million bucks clear in 1921 and 1922."

"And then the axe fell," said Whit. "I know."

"Not then." MacLeod shook his head and puffed hard on his pipe. "They got scared and quit. The big boys began running beer in from the East, the competition got tough, and Wolff had to hire gunmen to drive his trucks. There was some shooting, a few of his boys got killed and it began to cost him more than it was worth. Besides, he wasn't cutting any of the other stockholders in on the gravy and if they found out what was going on it would be too bad. So the Gold Star Brewery went back to making near-beer until repeal."

"I'm a jump ahead of you already. When did the Treasury Department catch up with him?"

"In 1935. The Bureau of Internal Revenue had been sniffing out the bootleggers for years. By the time they got to Wolff he couldn't be prosecuted under the Prohibition Act because it was a dead letter, but evasion of income taxes was something else. Some ex-prohibition agent had to explain where he got his money and he peeped on Zimmermann, and when they sweated Zimmermann he spilled the beans. Wolff and a couple of the other stockholders and I came back from a hunting trip in the fall of 1935 and there was a deficiency letter waiting for Wolff—half a million in taxes, plus fifty per cent fraud penalties, and interest since 1921. It came to a million and a quarter."

"Jesus," said Whit fervently.

"You get the idea. Wolff had dropped me off before he went home, and I was scraping off two weeks' whiskers when the phone rang. It was Wolff—he'd just opened the deficiency letter. He was mad—not scared, just mad as hell, and plenty tough. 'George,' he said, 'some son-of-a-bitch has double-crossed me, and I'm going to cut his throat.' I asked him what it was all about and he told me what the postman had handed him. I thought it was a joke at first—I didn't know anything about the bootlegging then—but he was serious. So I tried to calm him down. I told him to bring his deficiency letter over and I'd see what we could do about it, but he had his own ideas. He'd bought an airplane about a year before so he could get places in a hurry, and one of his ex-gunmen was flying it for him; the guy had been an aviator in the war. Wolff asked me who was the top man in the Department, and I told him the Commissioner of Internal Revenue at Washington, D.C. was pretty high up the line, and he said 'Good, that's all I want to know. Goodbye.'

"I tumbled to it then. I told him not to be such a damn fool, that it wouldn't do him any good, that he didn't know anything about income tax procedure, that he'd have to go about it the right way, and so on. But he said to hell with it, he'd do it his own way, and hung up."

"So he went to call on the Commissioner?" said Whit. "That's one way to file a protest."

"He started to call on the Commissioner. He and his aviator took off that morning and were halfway over the Rockies when the plane changed its mind; they jumped, and Wolff's parachute didn't open. The pilot was picked up after he'd been wandering around in the hills for a week living on his fingernails."

Whit grinned at him. "And then you stepped in and lost the case."

MacLeod shrugged and began rolling down the sleeves of his shirt. "I did what I could but they had him cold. His will named his attorney executor of the estate—a guy called Marston. He was a pretty good criminal lawyer but he didn't know anything about taxes, so he turned the case over to me. The deficiency letter gave us thirty days to protest and by the time I got into the case there was about ten days to go. We filed a protest on the last day." MacLeod smiled. "God, it was some protest. Neither Marston nor I knew a thing about the bootlegging, the corporation's books naturally didn't show anything, and even if we had known that Zimmermann was the key man, which we didn't until later, he was hiding out. I wrote twenty-five pages of stuff that would bring tears to your eyes and it was rejected so fast I don't think they even bothered to read it. And then we had ninety days to pay up or go before the Board of Tax Appeals. So we paid up."

Whit was horrified. "You what? A million and a quarter without going to the Board?"

"It was only a million then. The fraud penalties were automatically withdrawn at Wolff's death. There wasn't any point in appealing. We called in Wolff's daughter—this blonde I was telling you about—and put it up to her. She was sole heir. The estate would liquidate at just about enough to pay the taxes and interest, with maybe a few thousand left. If we appealed, interest would cost almost a hundred dollars a day, even if Marston and I worked for nothing, and I guaranteed that the case would be in the courts long enough to eat up every dime and then some. Furthermore, we didn't have any more chance of winning than a fiddler's bitch and I told her so."

MacLeod lifted his coat from the back of his chair and put it on. She squirmed like hell but there was nothing for her to do. She could quit then and take what was left after the Government was paid or she could throw it all down the rat-hole. So she gave up, and Marston liquidated the estate and paid off." MacLeod looked at the calendar-pad on his desk. "Four years ago this month. The estate was mostly securities and the market was pretty good then or she wouldn't have got a dime. As it was, Marston salvaged about fifteen thousand dollars' worth of the best stocks and turned them over to her. She sold them as soon as the market went up a little, like a chump, instead of trying to live off the income, and she didn't file a tax return. That's what the telephone call was about. Anything to do with income tax scares the pants off of her."

"I can see how it would," Whit said. "What did you get out of it?"

MacLeod shrugged. "I couldn't charge her anything. Marston had a claim against the estate for executor's fees of more than fifteen thousand and he waived the whole thing, so I ate my bill too. Besides—"

"Besides, you thought you could do yourself some good with her," said Whit. "Did you get anywhere?"

"She knew Kitty too well," MacLeod said. "Anyway, that's a hell of a question to ask about a client."

He took his hat from a rack in the corner and beat on the wall with the flat of his hand. "Krebs!" he shouted. "Come in here." There was a noise from the adjoining room and the office door opened a moment later.

The man who stood in the doorway was thin and tall—taller than Whitney's six feet. His coat was off and his vest pockets were crammed with yellow pencils. Short, straw-colored hair stood straight up from his head at odd angles, and he wore horn-rimmed glasses on a beaked nose. His neck was long and lean and his Adam's apple protruded. He said, "Yes, sir," in a surprisingly bass voice, with the shadow of an accent.

MacLeod raked the papers together on his desk. "This is the Jackson estate tax return. I told Mrs. Jackson it would be ready for her Monday morning, and there's a lot to do on it. I want you to whip it into shape so Miss Kelly can type it first thing tomorrow. Everything's right here." He shoved the sheaf of papers at Krebs.

Krebs blinked. "It is almost four o'clock, Mr. MacLeod," he said doubtfully. "I am not sure that I can do it by tomorrow morning."

"You better work on it tonight." MacLeod took Whitney by the elbow and steered him toward the door.

"My wife is expecting me to take her out tonight, Mr. MacLeod." Krebs stepped away from the door, the papers in his hands.

MacLeod grinned at him. "Ah, Krebs. You're not going to let

a little thing like a wife interfere with the firm's success, are you?" He pushed Whit into the hall.

"Wait a minute." Whit shook himself loose. "I've got to get my bags." He went into his own office, picked up two bags and a topcoat, and came out. MacLeod was in the reception room. Krebs stood in the doorway, holding the papers. He looked at Whit calmly and nodded.

"Have a good time, Mr. Whitney," he said. It was just short of being "Haf a goot time."

"Thanks. Take care of yourself, Krebs."

He went through the swinging gate in the wooden partition. Miss Kelly said tenderly, "Good-bye, Mr. Whitney. Enjoy yourself. Are you going to tell us where you'll be, in case we have to reach you?" She beamed at him. He was so handsome, particularly when he wore sport clothes—so much more attractive than Mr. MacLeod in his shiny blue serge with pipe ashes on his vest. She couldn't imagine Mr. Whitney with pipe ashes on his vest.

"There isn't anything important enough for you to have to call me, Miss Kelly. Tonight I'll be in Santa Cruz, tomorrow night in Carmel, Sunday in Santa Barbara, and Monday on the way to Mexico. From there on I don't know."

"It sounds wonderful."

"I hope it is. Good-bye."

The two men went out. Miss Kelly sighed. She would miss Mr. Whitney. He was so much nicer than Mr. MacLeod, so much more considerate and gentlemanly. Mr. MacLeod was occasionally rather coarse, but never Mr. Whitney.

In the elevator MacLeod was having one of his coarse moments. He said, "I'll bet you could take Kelly home with you any time you liked, Whit. Did you ever notice the gooey looks she throws at you?"

Whit shuddered. "Don't talk about it."

The elevator dropped two stories and let off a passenger. Whit said, "George, you don't have to shove Krebs around like that, He's a good man and valuable to the firm. You ought to be a little more considerate."

MacLeod looked mildly surprised. "What are you talking about?"

"Tossing that Jackson return in his face and telling him to work on it tonight or else. You just made him sore. You could have asked him to do it as a favor and he wouldn't have minded, but the way you threw it at him would make anyone mad. Someday he's going to walk out on us."

"So what?" The elevator stopped at the lobby. "Accountants like Krebs come a dime a dozen."

"That's not the idea. He earns his salary and then some, and—"

"Come on, come on," said MacLeod. "I thought you were thirsty."

CHAPTER TWO

MARIAN WOLFF was an ash blonde with cornflower blue eyes and a head-to-toe profile that was a thing of beauty, and she could stop traffic anytime by just stepping off the curb. She sat warming the dimples in her knees at the fireplace in the MacLeod drawing room, and watched Kitty MacLeod at the window.

Kitty never had to bother with traffic signals either. Before her marriage she had been a show girl, and George had seen her first when she was twenty years old singing torch songs in a night club. Now she was twenty-six, a tall brunette with a swell figure. She wore her dark hair parted in the middle and drawn back into a sleek knot at the nape of her neck, and she used brilliant red lipstick to emphasize a perfect complexion. The effect was worth a second glance. She had made George forget blondes for all of six months, and it was some sort of a record. Things had changed since.

Marian looked at her wrist watch. "Do you suppose anything has happened?"

"Nothing ever happens to him except a hangover. He's getting boiled in some bar, damn him. We might as well have a drink ourselves." Kitty dropped the curtain and turned from the window. She folded her arms and looked defiant. "You'll have to excuse the dinner when you get it. The cook still thinks a meal is something to be served on time." She went out to the kitchen.

Marian looked around the room. It was comfortable, pleasant, informal. There were bowls of flowers, reading lamps where they were needed, and bookcases on either side of the hearth. The pictures were good; a couple of water colors, a reproduction of the Flower Seller, and a fine Japanese print over the fireplace. It was a room that showed Kitty's personality; a pipe and tobacco jar on an end table seemed out of place.

Kitty came back with highballs while Marian was looking at the print over the mantel. "That's new. Like it?"

"I like your whole house. I wish it were mine."

"You'd have to take George with it." Kitty handed her a glass. "I don't mind bearing my cross, but when it comes home drunk five nights a week and I have to undress it and put it to bed—" She made a face. "The next man I marry is going to be a Sunday School superintendent."

The front door opened and shut. Kitty put her glass down. "Here he is. You talk to him and I'll plead with the cook." She left the room.

MacLeod came through the archway from the hall. His face was red, the top button of his coat was pushed through the middle buttonhole, and his eyes had a faint glaze. He said, "Hello, hello. Fancy meeting you here. Small world, don't you think?"

"You'd better have an alibi, George. Kitty is mad."

He winked and stumbled down the two steps into the room. "I know," he said in a whisper. "She's always mad. Nice even temper. How about you?"

She smiled and shook her head. "I'm not married to you."

"You can't have everything." He kissed her, filled his pipe, and flopped into the nearest chair, beaming up at her through a wreath of smoke. "I'm drunk."

"I know it. You shouldn't do it, George."

"Business," he said solemnly. "The customer is always right."

From the doorway Kitty said, "Dinner's been ready for an hour and a half. If you can pull yourself to your feet, we'll go into the dining room."

George looked hurt. "That's no way to talk. I had to see Whit off on his vacation, and we had a lot of last-minute business to take care of." He puffed on his pipe. "I got held up."

"All right. Let's have dinner."

The meal was not a success. The cook had put the roast in the warming oven when it was done and said to hell with it. If Mrs. MacLeod wanted dinner at seven o'clock it was ready at seven, and if it wasn't eaten until midnight it was all the same to the cook. She wasn't running no short order joint.

The dried-up roast didn't bother George. He hacked off chunks of meat for the girls, spilled gravy on the tablecloth, and limited his own dinner to highballs. He was full of goodwill, and kept the conversational ball rolling without help. Kitty made an occasional effort to turn him off but Marian and he both thought he was funny so she gave up. After dinner they moved to the drawing room and he switched from Scotch to cognac. His stream of conversation dwindled after the fourth brandy.

Kitty said, "If you want to ask him anything you'd better get him while he's conscious, Marian. I recognize the signs."

"Now why do you want to act like that?" George said angrily. "I'm all right. I feel wonderful." He refilled his glass. "You want to talk to me about something, honey?"

Marian had a premonition that George was not going to be much help. She took a letter from her bag. "This is what I called you about."

George looked blank. He took the letter from her and peered at it. "Oh, sure. Nothing to it. File a return and tell them you've been sick in bed with a doctor for a year and a half, and maybe you won't get stuck with any penalties." He patted her knee and forgot to remove his hand. "Give them the business, honey. If I were a revenue agent and you rolled those big blue eyes at me—" Kitty was watching him and he took his hand away. "Nothing to it."

"You said you'd do it for me. I brought along everything I could find." She took more papers from her bag. "Here are the broker's slips, and these are some dividends I got, and this is my bank book."

George carefully pushed the papers away. "Tomorrow, tomorrow. What are you rushing me for? Let's all be sociable tonight, and tomorrow I'll make you a tax return that'll tear the heart out of the Collector's bosom." He got off the davenport with a struggle, slipped on the hearth rug, recovered himself, and went to fumble with the radio. "Come down to the office in the morning and I'll take you to lunch. Buy you the best lunch in San Francisco."

Marian held the papers in her hand and looked at Kitty. Kitty smirked. "See what I mean? Isn't he cute?"

"George, I told you this afternoon I was going away for the week-end," Marian said patiently. "I'm leaving in the morning. I can't possibly see you tomorrow."

George waved a hand from the radio. "Monday, Tuesday, Wednesday—got all week. Name the day."

A sustained bray of trumpets blared from the loudspeaker. Kitty said, "For God's sake, George!" He turned the current down a hundredth of a volt and began snapping his fingers. He came back to the fireplace, slipped on the rug again, and hauled Marian off her chair. They danced round and round. George's feet got in his way, but he made up in energy what he lacked in finesse.

Marian looked helplessly at Kitty over his shoulder on the third trip past the fireplace and Kitty shrugged. "Slap his face," she said. "It may help."

When the music finally came to a stop Marian broke away looking flustered. George said, "Some fun. Let's have a drink." He closed one eye and squinted at the brandy bottle.

"George, will you please look at these things and tell me if you need anything else? I have to go home and pack and I want to get this off my mind."

"I'll fix it. I said I'd do it, didn't I?" George waved the bottle. "Next week. Never any hurry on those things."

"Please, George."

"What'll you give me?" He leered at her.

Kitty stood up. "I'll take care of him, Marian. He'll do it tomorrow. You run along and forget about it."

Marian looked doubtful, but she followed Kitty to the hall. George came after them with the brandy bottle and found his hat. Kitty said, "Where do you think you're going?"

"Drive the guest home. Perfect host." He had the bottle under his arm. "Let's go, honey. Time's a-wasting."

"Nothing doing," Kitty said. "You're too drunk. I'll call you a cab, Marian."

"I wish you would. Thanks anyway, George."

George grinned amiably and took her arm. "Here we go. 'Night, Mrs. MacLeod. Wonderful evening." Marian said, "It was a lovely dinner, Kitty," over her shoulder as George pulled her away, and the front door slammed behind them.

Kitty shrugged and went back to the drawing room. She heard gears snarl as George got under way, and the scrape of twigs as he wiped the finish off his car on the bushes along the driveway. When the sound of the motor was gone she got another bottle of brandy, poured herself a drink, and sat for a long time looking at the fire. It was after midnight when she went to bed. George had not come home.

CHAPTER THREE

THE SUN was hot and the sky cloudless. The white sand absorbed and held the heat, so that bathers without shoes kept to the wet beach near the water. Big rollers shouldered up a quarter of a mile offshore, marched magnificently toward land, and stumbled at the water's edge in a splatter of boiling foam. A few gulls loafed overhead, balancing against the breeze, and the Saturday afternoon crowd sprawled on the beach. It was a swell day.

Whit lay on his belly in the sand in a pair of red trunks, watching a couple of angels heave a big beach ball at each other. One angel wore a white lastex bathing suit that seemed to have been sprayed on with a paint gun, and the other was partially contained in a pair of flowered pants and a brassiere. They were enjoying the ball game a lot; so were the male members of the crowd lying on the beach around them, including Whit.

He had spent the previous evening with his client, Mr. J. Dabney Dwight. Mr. Dwight owned half of Santa Cruz County and wanted to spread a few hundred thousand dollars around among his family without paying a gift tax. Whit had been late for the conference, slipping down the gray side of the drinks he had had with MacLeod, and Mr. Dwight had demanded some fancy calculations which would have made Whit's head ache at any time, even without a head start. The situation was not helped by the fact that the gift tax had been designed to catch just such transfers as those contemplated by Mr. Dwight, and he had made invidious remarks about Whit's qualifications as a tax man. What Whit wanted now was somebody cute and female to say nice things to him and maybe have a few drinks. He would like very much to stir up an acquaintance with either or both of the ball players.

The gods smiled. The ball got away and came toward him. He stretched for it, hooked it to his chest, and beamed at the angel in white. She was panting a little from her exercise, and her breasts bulged the uplift arrangement built unnecessarily into her suit. Whit said, "Hello. Hot, isn't it?"

"Hello." The other angel joined her. They both smiled, and the first one said politely, "May we have our ball, please?"

"Sure." Whit wrapped both arms around it. "Can I play?"

That was at two o'clock. At five Whit and his angels were perched on high stools in the hotel bar, their heels hooked on the rail, watching the bartender put a professional chill on a bottle of champagne by twirling it back and forth in an ice bucket. The bartender gave the bottle a final spin, took three glasses from the back shelf and ranged them on the bar in front of him. He dropped a sugar cube in each glass, squirted Angostura on the sugar, wrapped the bottle in a napkin, twisted the wire, and eased out the cork. It went *"whup"* into the napkin, and a faint plume of vapor rose from the bottle as the champagne hissed into the glasses. The angels sighed.

Whit admired himself in the mirror over the back bar. He had dug out a turquoise silk shirt to go with his sunburned face, and the combination pleased him. The angels, dressed, looked like tanned movie queens. They were three handsome people. Whit had to admit it. And there was nothing in the wide world to stop him from spending his whole vacation right there in Santa Cruz if he wanted to. The angels were staying for the summer.

He raised his glass. "In spite of a bad sunburn, this is the happiest moment of my life," he began. "It is fitting at this time—"

"Paging Mr. Whitney." The bellhop sounded bored. "Calling Mr. James Whitney. Telephone for Mr. James Whitney. Paging Mr. Whitney."

"Hey." Whit beckoned. The boy said, "Telephone, San Francisco calling. Inna lobby."

The left-hand angel said, "Go on with the speech, Whit. I'm thirsty."

He put the glass down reluctantly and got off his stool. "You go ahead and I'll finish it later. I've got a hunch I shouldn't answer this."

In the lobby he went into the nearest phone booth. It was George MacLeod. George said, "Whit? How fast can you get back to town?"

"About four weeks. Why?"

"No fooling, Whit. I've got something big—something that'll knock your eye out. Can you get here by seven o'clock?"

"Don't be funny, George. I've go something that will knock my eye out right here. Two of them. Anyway, I'm on a vacation."

"To hell with you and your vacation. I want to see you tonight."

Whit said patiently, "Look, George—"

"You know what's happened? The Wolff case is wide open. Right now I'm lining up refund claims for half a million dollars. Five hundred thousand bucks, boy!" His voice trembled. "George MacLeod, the human bird-dog. I always had a hunch about that case and now I've found the bug in it. Somebody did double-cross Wolff, Whit. I haven't worked it all out yet, but if he got more than half of that dough I'll go back to the farm."

"That's just dandy. Even if you weren't crazy a refund would be outlawed. Two years from the date of payment, my boy."

"Four years under the 1921 law," said MacLeod smugly. "I looked it up, so don't argue with me. The estate was framed into paying twice as much income tax as it should have, and we've got to find out who did it right now. You get back here in a hurry."

Whit thought fast. George was pig-headed when he got his mind set on something. "I'll tell you what I'll do. You work on it over the weekend and I'll come in for a while Monday morning. How's that?"

"Monday morning, hell! Listen close, now, because I've got a lot to do and I don't want to talk with you all day. The estate paid off four years ago next Friday. That gives us just six days to get a lot of information, and we've got to work fast. I've made an appointment with the executor to meet us here at seven o'clock, and Monday I've arranged for a meeting of the stockholders of the brewery. We've got to be there with everything under control."

"Why the stockholders? They weren't in on it."

"I'm not so sure of that. I think one of them got the other half of the money. I've stirred up the hive and we'll be there to watch the bees fly." He laughed. "It's the biggest frame I ever saw in my life, and I didn't tumble to it all the time I was working on the case. If I hadn't had to get some security valuations out of the papers for the blonde I never would have looked at the files again, never—and it was there all the time sticking out like a sore nose."

Whit was suspicious.

"That blonde is the heir, isn't she? You aren't cooking up a pipe-dream to convince her she ought to be nice to you?"

"You let me worry about her." George sounded pretty cocky. "I'll tell you what sort of a pipe-dream I'm cooking up. This claim is so good I'm going to take the case for a contingent fee—we get ten per cent of what we recover and no charge if we don't make it stick. That's one of the things I want to talk about tonight. I'll see you here in the office at seven."

"Wait a minute, George. You can handle this without me. I've got a couple of girls on my hands. I'll drive up tomorrow."

"A couple of girls?" George was amazed. "A couple of *girls?* My God, Whit, I'm talking about a fifty thousand dollar fee and you beef about a couple of tarts. You get here by seven. G'bye."

"Hey, wait a minute." The line was dead.

Whit said, "Oh, balls!" slammed the receiver on the hook, and went back to the bar.

Two big brown lads in sport clothes were engaged in an argument with his angels. Whit climbed back on his stool and tasted his champagne. It was flat. His sunburn was beginning to hurt and he didn't like the turquoise shirt now.

The angel on the right said, "Whit, I—uh—this is Eddie and this is Albert. We—uh—sort of had a date with them this afternoon."

"That's nice." Whit was trying to concentrate. "H'lo. Have a drink."

"We don't want a drink," Albert said, looking tough. He was big and young, and hair on a tanned chest showed through his white sweater. "We got a date with these girls, see? A date."

"All right," said Whit irritably. "I see. Go away and leave me alone. I'm trying to think."

"Listen, guy." Albert was standing behind the stool barking in Whit's ear. "All we want is for you to beat it, that's all. Just beat it and leave these girls alone before you get into trouble."

Whit gave up and turned around to find Albert's face glaring at him from the distance of about a foot. His plans were folding up on him, he couldn't figure a way out, MacLeod would probably send the police after him if he didn't turn up in San Francisco by seven o'clock, and his sunburn hurt. He said, "What the hell are you screaming about?"

"How would you like a poke in the nose?"

Whit pushed Albert gently away with his left hand to get some room, braced his feet against the rail, and slugged him as hard as he could on the hollow below his breastbone. Albert went, *"Whoo!"* his eyes protruded, and he sat down hard on the floor struggling for breath.

Eddie said, "Hey," in a surprised voice and rushed. Whit hit him a little lower down, and he landed on top of Albert. One of the angels said, "Oh, goodness."

"Nice shooting, pal," said the bartender critically, polishing a glass.

Whit drank his champagne. "Somebody's always looking for trouble. Fill it up. I have to go back to the city."

"You have to what?" said the angel on the left.

"I'm sorry. I got called back. Just time for another drink."

"That's swell. That's just fine. You sure fixed things up for us." She wasn't so angelic.

"I'm sorry," Whit said patiently. "I can't help it. I'll be back Monday."

"We won't be here."

The angels climbed off their stools and between them hauled Eddie to his feet. His knees were still rubbery but he managed to stand. Albert had some of his wind back and sat up, shaking his head. None of them looked at Whit.

He paid for the drinks. On his way out he said, "Honest, I can't help it. I'll be back Monday." Nobody answered him.

CHAPTER FOUR

BY THE TIME Whit's convertible reached the top of the grade back of Santa Cruz his sunburn had settled down to business and was raising hell. His legs felt as if they had been sandpapered, his neck was sore, and his back yelled every time he leaned against the seat. He could keep his shoulders from touching the upholstery by crouching over the steering wheel, but after a bad moment on a curve he gave up trying to hold the seat of his pants in mid-air. He was well soured on the outdoor life before he got down to the valley.

He stopped for gas at Los Gatos. The station attendant, a young kid in a pair of greasy coveralls and a beanie on which was printed KEEP YOUR SUNNY SIDE UP—DRINK ORANGE SMASH, was on the running board giving the windshield a workout before Whit had set the brakes. Whit looked at the hat and groaned.

"S'matter," the kid said. "Sick?"

"I sure am. That hat of yours doesn't help any either."

The boy took it off and then looked at it. "S'matter with it?"

"Keep your Sunnyside up." Whit got out of the car holding the leg of his trousers away from his skin. "Ow! You ought to see my sunny side up."

The kid grinned and went to the rear of the car. "You're fried, mister. What do you want it filled with, Ethyl or standard?"

"Ethyl, I guess." Whit winced over some new sore spots. "About—" He stopped. "What do you mean, what do I want it filled with? Five gallons is all I want."

"Sales resistance, huh?" The kid slid the hose into the tank. "Make it ten and I'll tell you how to fix that sunburn of yours."

"What a racket," said Whit. "All right, ten."

The kid filled the tank and hung up the hose. "Vinegar."

"Vinegar?"

The beanie bobbed up and down. "Yep. Best thing in the world. Take a piece of cotton and pat it on heavy, and in half an hour you won't know you've been burned. It's a cinch."

"I'll remember that. Vinegar. How much do I owe you?"

The boy took a bill and came back with the change. Whit got gingerly back in the seat and stepped on the starter. "Any special kind of vinegar? Apple vinegar, wine vinegar, tarragon vinegar—what kind do you use?"

"Just vinegar."

"O.K. Thanks." He let in the clutch.

The traffic had thinned by the time he reached the straightaway and he let the car out and began to click off mileage. It was a pleasant day for driving. The long miles of fruit trees on either side of the road were in bloom, some with the new green showing through the flower, some in full blossom. The grass which would burn so brown during the summer was still green and moist, and there were birds in the trees. Whit would have enjoyed it all if he had been aware of it, but there were other things on his mind.

What the hell had George got into, anyway? The firm of MacLeod and Whitney had filed big refund claims at one time or another—maybe not for half a million, but for plenty—and Whit had never known his partner to wave his arms about any of them, win, lose or draw. Even when his client was a good-looking blonde. Still, a fifty thousand dollar fee was a lot of lettuce—if they got it. Whit tried to remember what Mac-Leod had told him about Harald Wolff.

There had been a bookkeeper with a German name. Zimmermann, that was it. Zimmermann had testified that he turned the gravy from the bootlegging over to Wolff, and his testimony had won the Government's case. George and what's-his-name, the executor, hadn't been able to do anything about it while they were protesting the deficiency, yet now George believed he had everything in the bag. What had he stumbled on? Had the blonde told him something? No. George had said the information was in their files all the time. But George wasn't dumb; if he had been able to get anything that morning from a casual inspection of the Wolff papers, he should have seen it four years before when he was searching desperately for something to beat the Government. Something must have changed the picture. Maybe—

Whit looked at the rear view mirror and eased his foot on the accelerator.

A motor-cycle cop pulled out of his hiding-place and took after Whit's car. He was a long way back when he got started, and by the time he began to gain Whit was doing an exact forty-five. The cop hung on for half a mile before he gave up and roared past. Whit nodded in a friendly fashion and waved his arm. The cop shook his head and looked disapproving. Whit let him get a long start and pushed the car up to sixty-five.

George had said there was another stockholder mixed up in the bootlegging, and Wolff had got only half the money. Not more than half. Had Zimmermann committed perjury when he testified that he turned the money over to Wolff? Or had Wolff split with someone afterward? If Zimmermann had perjured himself to save the other man he had been taking a long chance. He must have been paid plenty for—wait a minute. The law said an informer was entitled to ten percent of whatever amounts the Treasury Department collected because of his information. Ten per cent of a million dollars. A man would take a chance for that. But it would have been almost as much if Zimmermann had told the truth and the income had been taxed half and half to Wolff and the other man. So Zimmermann must have got something else out of it if he had lied. Or he might have been promised something bad if he didn't. Bootlegging was a hard-boiled racket.

Whit eased himself from one sore spot to another. The whole business was too involved and too much like a dime novel. He'd wait until he could get the details from George. And he'd tell George a few things himself, while he was about it. George was an inconsiderate bastard. Whit hadn't taken a vacation in the two and a half years they had been partners, and the minute he got away George began yelling for help. It was too bad about him. He'd been running his own business for twenty years without assistance, and now he couldn't file a refund claim by himself. And those two angels were going to waste on a couple of college boys.

Whit got madder and madder.

He was making time. He had reached the Skyline Boulevard on the sea cliffs back of San Mateo. A fog bank covered the hills ahead of him, wisps of mist drifted across the road, and the air began to get damp. The top of the convertible was folded down, but the car was equipped with a gadget operated from the dashboard which hoisted the top into place without human assistance other than a push on the button. Whit pushed it. Nothing happened. He tried again. The top remained neatly folded in its nest behind the seat. The weather was getting worse. Whit stopped the car, put his heel on the button, and tugged at the folded top with both hands. The skin on his back split in a couple of places and the top stayed put. He gave up and drove the rest of the way into the city with water splashing in his face as it condensed on the top of the windshield and flew back before the wind. On the way he rehearsed what he was going to tell MacLeod.

It was dark when he reached California Street, and the street lamps were fuzzy blobs of light in the fog. The financial district was deserted and dead. Cables clattered against pulleys under the car tracks and the foghorns bleated mournfully from the bay. Whit parked his car behind a blue La Salle that stood in front of the Farmers' Exchange, wiped the water from his face and neck, and went into the lobby. The big clock over the deserted cigar stand said seven-fifteen.

The night elevator man looked up from a copy of Snappy Stories. "Hello. Ain't it a little late for you to be starting work?"

Whit glared at him. "No," he said shortly. "Take me up, will you?"

The elevator rose slowly. The operator said, "You're sunburned."

"You're telling me." Whit lifted his shirt collar away from his neck.

"I'll tell you what to do. Best thing in the world. Take a little bicarbonate of soda, mix it up with water, spread it on good and thick, and—"

"Inside half an hour I won't know I've been burned. I know. Vinegar's good, too. You wet a piece of cotton—"

"Nah," said the operator. "I've tried 'em all. Soda's a sure cure."

"I could use one."

The elevator stopped at the eighth floor. Whit walked down the hall practicing his opening remarks. All of the offices on the floor were dark except his own. He opened the door and walked in on a man sitting by the window reading a newspaper. The stranger looked up as Whit came in, folded his paper, and rose to his feet. He was a man of forty-five or fifty with thick, curly gray hair and a brown face. The corners of his eyes wrinkled when he smiled, and his teeth were white against his skin.

Whit said, "Hello. You're Marston?" The other man said, "Yes," and they shook hands.

"Whitney is my name. I'm MacLeod's partner. Where is he?"

"I wish I knew. I was to meet him here at seven." He looked at the watch on his wrist. "I've been here half an hour."

"Come on inside. George has never been on time in his life. On behalf of the firm, I apologize."

"It's all right."

They went into MacLeod's office. Whit threw his hat on the bookcase and sat down behind the desk, being careful of his sunburn. "Have a chair. MacLeod will be along sometime. He's probably out having a drink with himself because he's such a smart guy." He took out a package of cigarettes from his pocket and held it out. "What's it all about, anyway?"

The lawyer accepted a cigarette. "Half a million dollars. Don't you know about it?"

"I know that much and nothing else, except that MacLeod was awfully damn anxious that I get here on time for a man who's half an hour late himself." Whit patted his sunburned face gently with a handkerchief. "I wouldn't be a bit surprised if the whole business were a put-up job. Yesterday I started on the first vacation I've had in two years and a half, and here I am back again. I hate to discourage you, but I'm beginning to think it's a gag."

The lawyer smiled. "I hope you're wrong. I'd have a hard time laughing."

"So would I," Whit said. "Anyway, I'm here. You might as well tell me about it while we're waiting."

"Well, let's see. You've heard about Harald Wolff?"

"What MacLeod told me. Bootlegging, beautiful daughter the sole heir, a million dollars in taxes and interest, no money left for the beautiful daughter, no money left for executor's fees."

"Particularly no money left for executor's fees," said Marston. "I waived about eighteen thousand dollars in a weak moment." He drew on his cigarette. "We paid the deficiencies four years ago next Friday. Today MacLeod called me and said he thought we could get back about half of it. Naturally I was interested, both on behalf of Miss Wolff and myself."

"Naturally."

Marston laughed. "The Government had as a witness an employee of the brewery. He gave the Treasury Department an affidavit in which he set forth in detail what purported to be payments of bootlegging profits to Wolff. He claimed he had kept a record of each payment. We didn't know about the affidavit at first and Wolff was killed in an airplane accident before either MacLeod or I talked to him. We challenged the Government's computations on the grounds that they were unsupported by proof, and they gave us a copy of the affidavit. Then we challenged the figures in the affidavit, and the Government proved that an extra $22.50 per barrel on sales shown in the brewery books would account for all of the money. They had an air-tight case."

"What about Wolff's bank accounts? Had the money been deposited anywhere?"

"MacLeod thought of that at the time. We showed that during the years when Wolff was supposed to have made a million dollars there was no evidence of it in his bank deposits. But the Government dug up a safe deposit box with two hundred thousand dollars in it in bills, and room for a lot more. It just about clinched the case."

"It wouldn't be any material help," said Whit.

"Our big mistake was trying to prove that Wolff had nothing to do with the bootlegging. Neither of us had known anything about it and we were full of honest indignation, so we lost a lot of ground before we discovered that he had actually been in it. By then it was too late.

"Today MacLeod said he had been looking over his files and discovered something he hadn't noticed before. He was convinced they showed conclusively that all of the payments had not been made to Wolff, and he was prepared to file a refund claim for half or more of the tax. He wanted to have you here when he talked to me about it and we made the appointment for seven so you could get here."

"And here we are," said Whit. "All but MacLeod." He reached for the telephone and dialed a number. "I haven't had any dinner and I'm sunburned to medium rare and my vacation is busted all to hell. If he's gone home leaving us here I'll— Hello, Kitty. This is Whit. Is your lump of a husband there?"

"No. What are you doing in town?" Her contralto voice sounded strained.

"It's a long story. I'll tell you all about it later. Do you know where he is?"

"I haven't seen him since last night. He went out about ten and didn't come home."

Whit said, "Oh." They must have been fighting again. George was a damn fool. But it was George's business, not his. He said, "All right, Kitty. If you hear from him, remind him that Mr. Marston and I have been waiting in the office for half an hour, will you?"

"I don't expect to hear from him."

"Well, if you do. 'Bye."

He put the phone down. "No soap. We'll just have to sit." He rose from his chair and grimaced. "This sunburn is hotter than a firecracker. I'll get out the papers and we can go over them while we're waiting."

"Try a little olive oil when you get home," Marston said. "It'll cool you off."

Whit laughed, going through the door. "You're the third today. Vinegar, baking soda, olive oil. I'd look like a potato salad."

He went down the hall to the vault and tried the door. It was locked. He set the combination, swung the door open, and reached inside to turn on the light. Marston heard him say, "Oh, Jesus," and came after him to look over his shoulder.

George MacLeod lay on his back on the vault floor, his head turned to one side, his cheek resting against a filing cabinet. His necktie was twisted to one side and dragged in a pool of blood that had coagulated into a dark brown patch around his head. There was a small hole in the bridge of his nose.

CHAPTER FIVE

IT WAS ten o'clock. Fog-horns still bleated from the bay and the bells of Old St. Mary's on the hill were ringing the hour. George MacLeod had left his office for the last time, in a wicker basket carried by two men in white coats. His picture had been taken by a police photographer who groused because the cramped vault made it difficult to get angle shots of the body, and his last exit had been witnessed by a bored cop who stood in the anteroom with his hands clasped behind him.

Detective Lieutenant Webster of San Francisco's finest sat in a chair in the dead man's office, a cigarette in his mouth, his head cocked to one side to keep the smoke from his eyes. He was a big homely man in business clothes and a trench-coat, with a good-natured face and thick chest and shoulders. In his palm he held something for Whit and Marston to see.

"It was an automatic; there's the shell and the slug that came out of it. Steel jacketed twenty-five. It went right through between his eyes and out the other side."

The other men looked and said nothing. The detective wrapped the bullet and the cartridge case in a piece of paper, put the paper in his vest pocket, and took the cigarette out of his mouth. "It's sort of a light slug, but it did the business," he said. "All we have to do now is find the gun and who shot it. Any ideas, Mr. Whitney?"

Whit had his elbows on his knees and was frowning at the floor "I don't know. Maybe."

"Mind letting me in on them?"

"I'm not sure that they're any good."

"Let's have them anyway. It's my job to figure out whether they're good or not."

Whit went on scowling at the floor. The detective waited. Finally Whit lifted his head and spoke to Marston. "Has it occurred to you that neither of us knows just what MacLeod had on his mind?"

The lawyer nodded. "I've been thinking of that. I hope he wrote something down."

"We might as well find out right now." Whit stood up and started for the door. Webster said, "Where are you going?"

"The vault. I'll tell you in a minute whether my idea is worth anything."

"You'll have to wait. I don't want anyone in there until we've gone over it for fingerprints. MacLeod's shirt was torn and his necktie was twisted; if there was a scrap the killer may have put his hand on something."

Whit came back and sat down. Webster said, "What do you want to see in there?"

Whit rubbed his hand over the back of his neck and winced. He hadn't eaten for ten hours, his head ached, his back hurt, and the long exposure to the sun had left him feeling washed out. He said, "MacLeod was working on a claim for refund of half a million dollars in income tax, and as far as I know he was the only one who knew what it was all about. There may have been someone who wanted to keep him from going through with it."

"That's a lot of money. Whose was it?"

Marston said, "Harald Wolff's."

"Harald Wolff?" The detective frowned. "I know that means something, but it doesn't register. Who—who is he?"

"He's dead. He was an Oakland brewer. About four years ago—"

"Oh, sure," Webster nodded. "I remember. The bootlegger."

"That's right. I'm the executor of his estate."

"Let's hear about it."

Marston told him the whole story—the bootlegging, MacLeod's efforts to defeat the Government's case, the payment of tax, and MacLeod's discovery that morning. When the lawyer finished, Whit repeated MacLeod's telephone conversation as well as he could remember it. He ended by saying, "Maybe you're not familiar with tax law, Lieutenant. The statute of limitations runs against us next Friday. If we file a claim by then, setting forth the exact facts on which we rely to recover the money, we'll have two years to dig up enough supporting evidence to go to court if we have to. If we don't file the claim, or if we file a claim on the wrong grounds, we're out of luck; we couldn't get the money even if the Treasury Department wanted to give it to us. If MacLeod didn't leave anything around to show what he knew, he was the only one with the answer. We'll have to start at scratch."

"I didn't think a bootlegger paid income taxes," said Webster.

"Neither did Al Capone. Bootlegging, white-slavery, or a crap game, it's all the same to the Treasury Department. They get their cut of the income or else."

The detective thought it over. "It's a little out of my line. You think the other man mixed up in it shot MacLeod to keep his mouth shut—is that it?"

"He would have been in the same trouble that Wolff was if MacLeod filed the claim. The Government would go after him whether we got a refund or not. It's something to think about, anyway."

"Sure," said the detective. "But I don't get it. Why should your partner call up these stockholders and tip them off that he knew one of them was a crook? It doesn't sound smart to me."

"I don't know why he'd do anything," Whit said wearily. "I'm no detective. I'm just telling you what he said."

"I think he wanted to start an argument," said Marston. "Apparently there is some animosity among the stockholders. MacLeod told me if he could get them calling names he might get the information he wanted."

The detective nodded. "What about the bookkeeper as a source of information? We could pick him up and sweat him a little. Where does he hang out?"

Whit looked at Marston.

The lawyer said, "I don't know. They discharged him from the brewery when Wolff died and I haven't heard of him since. Hall might know."

"Hall?"

"He's president of the corporation. He was secretary when Wolff was alive, and he moved up."

"Is he a stockholder?"

"Yes."

The detective took the paper-wrapped bullet out of his pocket and tossed it in his palm. "He could be the one that MacLeod was after. We can't rely too much on information he gives us."

"I don't know where else you could get it."

Whit said, "You can't rely too much on information you get from anyone in this case. MacLeod wasn't betting his shirt it was one of the stockholders; he just had a hunch."

"Well, we'll attend this meeting Monday and see what we can get." The detective still played with the bullet. "That gives us one motive. How about some others? This income tax business may have nothing to do with it. Maybe someone was carrying a grudge. Maybe he got into trouble with some woman. A twenty-five is a lady's gun."

Whit had thought of that. "Maybe he shot himself and ate the gun," he said, standing up. "I haven't had any dinner and I want a drink. And I've got other things to do. Let's let it go until tomorrow."

"What other things?"

"For Christ's sake," Whit said angrily. "What do you care? I'll see you tomorrow and answer all the questions you want. Right now I'm tired and I want to get out of here."

"Take it easy," said Webster. "I just like to know what's going on. This is a murder investigation."

"All right." Whit sounded surly. "I'm going to tell Mac-Leod's wife that her husband has been killed."

"Somebody will have to do it." The detective took a notebook and a pencil from his vest. "Where does she live? I may want to talk to her."

Whit gave him the address and picked up the telephone as

the detective was writing. While the bell was ringing at the other end of the line, Whit asked, "How in hell do you tell a woman her husband has been murdered?"

The detective closed his book. "It's not fun. It would be easier for me than it would for you. I'll do it, if you like."

"Thanks. I guess it's up to me."

The receiver clicked. Kitty said, "Hello."

"It's Whit, Kitty. May I come out and see you?"

"Of course, if you like. Is George with you?"

"No."

"Did you see him?"

"I'll tell you about it when I get there, Kitty. In about fifteen minutes. 'Bye." He hung up quickly.

They went into the anteroom. The cop was asleep in a chair with his mouth open. Webster said, "Look at him. Right on his toes," and turned to Whit. "I want to see you tomorrow, Mr. Whitney. I'll have a man take the prints from the vault in the morning and you can get in afterwards. And I have a few more questions—routine stuff."

"I'll be here about ten. That all right?"

"Sure. Any time."

Marston asked, "Do you want me here, Lieutenant?"

"Not unless you haven't anything to do."

The lawyer hesitated. "I was going to play golf in the morning. But of course I'll break it off if—"

"There's no reason for you to turn up unless you want to. Let me have your address and I'll get in touch with you when I want anything."

They made the arrangements. Webster shook the cop awake, threatened to take his badge if he closed an eye all night, and the three men went out to the elevator. The night operator had been questioned by Webster until he was dizzy, and he was impressed with the dignity of death. To Whit he said earnestly, "I'm sorry about Mr. MacLeod, Mr. Whitney. He was a fine fellow." He shook his head sadly. MacLeod had been the only man in the building he actively disliked, but he had forgotten that. He was the last person who had seen MacLeod alive, and it brought them closer together.

"Thanks," said Whit.

"Don't forget the baking soda."

"What was that?" asked Webster, as they got out of the elevator.

"Baking soda. For sunburn."

"A hot bath is the best thing," said the detective. "It kills the burn, if you can stand it."

It was the first time Whit had laughed for hours, "Vinegar, baking soda, olive oil, and a hot bath. I'm making a collection of sunburn remedies."

"I still swear by olive oil," said Marston. "Take it from the burned child. I'll be home tomorrow afternoon if you want me, Lieutenant." He hesitated on the sidewalk. "I'm sorry, Whitney. Let me know the date of the funeral, will you? And if there's anything I can do—"

"Sure." Whit put his hand on the lawyer's shoulder. "Thanks. I'll let you know."

Marston still hesitated. "About that refund. I don't like to mention it now, but it's a lot of money. If there's any chance of getting it back—MacLeod mentioned a fee of ten per cent. If that's acceptable, I wish you would see what you can do."

"I'll work on it," Whit said shortly. "Whether I can do anything for you, I don't know. I'll get in touch with you when I've looked at the papers."

"That's fair enough. Good night" Marston got into the blue La Salle at the curb and drove away.

The detective turned up his coat collar. "You sure you don't want me to talk to the widow?"

Whit shook his head. "I know her pretty well. I'll do it. See you in the morning." He crossed the sidewalk to his car.

A man sat in the front seat of a Chevrolet parked behind Whit's convertible. Webster spoke briefly to him as Whit stepped on the starter. The Chevrolet followed Whit's car as it disappeared in the fog. Webster watched until the two cars were out of sight and then went back up the steps and into the building.

~§~

At Polk Street Whit stopped in a bar and had a slug of whiskey. It felt good on an empty stomach. He had three more, fast. His headache went away. He considered eating some dinner but he was nervous at the thought of having to talk to Kitty and his hunger had disappeared. He had a fifth drink and went back to his car. Before he had driven two blocks the whiskey had taken hold and he was drunk. He felt a lot better.

Kitty opened the door when he rang the doorbell. "Hello," she said. "Where did you get the strawberry tan?"

"Santa Cruz." They went into the living room and he sat on the davenport in front of the fire. Kitty said, "You look tired. Do you want a drink?"

"Not now, Kitty. I—all right, a highball." It would give him more time. He couldn't think of an approach.

She left the room and came back with his drink. He was no nearer an opening than he had been before she went out. He liked Kitty MacLeod. She had carried her own weight all her life, and if she hadn't had the bad luck to marry George—there was no point in his kidding himself. George had not been a bargain as a husband. Dead or alive, he had been a son of a bitch with women.

Kitty was watching him. "Why so solemn, Whit? Bad news?"

"Yes." He took a long swallow of the highball.

"What happened?"

There it was. He looked at the ice in the bottom of his glass and said rapidly, "George is dead. He was shot—murdered."

Kitty said, "Oh."

The silence was uncomfortable. Kitty stared at the fire, frowning. Whit watched her. The fire made his sunburn sting and his head was swimming from the drinks. Kitty said, "Do you expect me to cry, Whit?"

"No."

"Would you believe I was sorry if I did?"

"No. He wasn't a very good husband, I guess."

"He wasn't a good anything. How did it happen?"

He told her. She said, "Do the police think he was killed be-cause of what he discovered?"

"They don't know. I think so."

She was silent again, looking at the fire. Whit closed his eyes. Too much had happened for one day and he felt tired. Kitty said, "I was going to leave him, Whit."

He said nothing.

"I've been thinking of it for a long time. Last night he came home drunk, late. Marian Wolff was here and he kept pawing her whenever he got the chance. She wanted him to do something for her, so she couldn't very well slap his face. He insisted on driving her home, and he didn't come in all night. I called him at the office this morning and asked where he'd been and he laughed at me. I told him he needn't bother to come home at all as far as I was concerned, and he said that was all right with him. That's the last I heard from him."

Whit was quiet.

"I can't pretend to be sorry, Whit. I don't care whether he's dead or alive."

Whit still said nothing. Kitty turned to look at him. His head rested on the back of the davenport, his eyes were closed, and he was breathing through his mouth.

CHAPTER SIX

A NEWSBOY came down Pacific Avenue making the Sabbath hideous with cries of *"Sunnymorningchronicle-examiNER!"* Opposite the MacLeod home he filled his lungs and let go. Whit woke with a start, opening his eyes and closing his mouth simultaneously. The fire in the grate had burned itself out and gray light came through the open window. A blanket had been tucked around and behind him as he sat on the davenport, and only his head protruded from the woolen cocoon. He pushed his arms out of the blanket and stretched. He took full measure of his aches and pains before budging another inch. All of his joints ached, his sunburn stung, and his mouth was full of alum.

The newsboy went down the street bellowing *"Getcha-sunnymorningchronicleexamiNER!"* Whit threw off the blanket and limped over to shut the window. His wrist watch said six-thirty. He went back to the couch and sat down again, yawning and scratching his head. Things began to organize themselves in his mind.

MacLeod was dead and the partnership of MacLeod and Whitney was dissolved. Whit was aware that George's death had done him no financial harm. The partnership agreement provided that he could purchase MacLeod's interest in the business at a price which would be better than reasonable. And there was the potential fee from Wolff's estate. Ten per cent of five hundred thousand dollars—if he could do anything about it. Monday, Tuesday, Wednesday, Thursday, Friday. Five days at ten thousand dollars a day. Or nothing. Or maybe he would get one of those cute little slugs from the twenty-five if he sniffed around too much. Had George really been killed because of what he found in the Wolff file? A twenty-five was the kind of a gun that would fit nicely in a woman's purse, and George could easily have got crossed up with the wrong blonde. What about the Wolff girl? Or Kitty MacLeod? Kitty was through with George, and she had lots of courage. If she was angry enough she'd do it. But not by sneaking up on him; she'd have shot him in the middle of the street and nuts to the consequences. So Kitty hadn't killed him. But if the cop found out that she and George were washed up and had quarreled the night before—

Well, to hell with it. The thing to do first was find out if MacLeod had left a trail behind him. If he hadn't, it was going to be a little tougher for Whit. He would get the Wolff papers out of the vault and—Jesus, what if they weren't there? MacLeod was careless about locking things in the inside safe. If he had been killed because of what was in the papers, the murderer wouldn't leave them around for the next man. It would prove something if they were gone, anyway. And Whit could kiss his share of fifty thousand dollars good-bye.

He yawned again, shivering, and got up and went out to the kitchen. The house was dead and silent. He lifted his heels as he walked across the linoleum. At the sink he drank a glass of water and poured a couple of fingers of Scotch from a bottle that stood on the drainboard. It made him gag, but it woke him up. He got his hat and tiptoed out of the house, closing the front door softly behind him.

The fog was fading. The trees along the curb dripped moisture and the streets and sidewalks were still wet but fingers of sun were beginning to poke through the curtain. It was going to be a fine day. Whit got into his car, mopped up the top layer of water from the seat with his handkerchief, and started the motor. For no good reason he punched the button of the gadget that had betrayed him the night before, and the convertible top unfolded and rose smoothly into place, splattering him with a pint of water. He said disgustedly, "Oh, for Christ's sweet sake," and drove away without bothering to dry his face.

Half a block down the street a Chevrolet was parked under a tree. The man behind the wheel had his hat tipped over his eyes. When Whit's car had gone he sat up, looked at his watch, started his engine and went back to report to Detective Lieutenant Webster.

In his own apartment Whit peeled off his wrinkled clothes and filled the bathtub. His body in the full-length mirror was a lovely pink except for the pale patch around his loins. He turned on the cold water, and when the bath was tepid he lowered himself cautiously into it, let hot water in slowly, and soaked for half an hour. After he had bathed, he went to the kitchen and looked in the cupboard. No olive oil, no soda. There was a bottle of dark red wine vinegar on the shelf, and he smelled it and put it back. He preferred the sunburn.

At nine o'clock he left his apartment, clean, shaved, and wearing a shirt that didn't fit too tightly around his neck. He had breakfast in a joint on Kearny Street and arrived at his office at a quarter of ten. The grapevine had been working. The pimply-faced boy who ran the elevator on Sundays said, "Morning, Mr. Whitney. I'm sorry to hear about Mr. MacLeod."

"He was a nice fellow," said Whit.

"He sure was. Who done it, Mr. Whitney? Have they caught anyone yet?"

"They're working on it." The elevator stopped at Whit's floor.

The cop was still in the anteroom, more or less awake. He had his feet on a chair and his coat unbuttoned. Whit said hello and went through the swinging gate. The cop said, "Where you going?" without moving.

"You remember me. I work here. This is my office."

"O.K. Just stay out of the vault."

"Haven't they finished with it yet?"

"They ain't started."

"Oh, balls. I've got things to do."

"You'll have to wait for the Lieutenant. He'll be here pretty soon," said the cop imperturbably.

Whit waited. It would be nice if he had a daisy. She loves me, she loves me not. The papers were there, the papers were not there. The clue to the whole damn business was in the vault, the clue to the whole damn business had been pinched. He was going to make a fifty thousand dollar fee, he was going to get shot. She loves me, she loves me not. It made him twitch.

After a while he heard the elevator coming up, and the cop bounced out of the chair buttoning his coat. Webster came in with another man who carried a square leather case. The detective was still in his blue serge and trench coat of the night before, he needed a shave, and he looked tired. Whit said, "How about getting after those fingerprints, Webster? I'd like to find out what's in the vault."

"It'll wait," Webster said shortly. "Down the hall, Joe, to the right. Go over everything, inside and out."

"The works," said the man with the bag. "O.K., Lieutenant. You got it." He went down the inner hall and disappeared in the vault.

Webster said, "Let's go inside. I want to talk to you."

In Whit's office the detective closed the door and they sat down. Whit said, "What's on your mind?"

The detective rubbed his eyes with his knuckles. "I've been thinking about the case. I have an idea maybe your partner was bumped off for some other reason beside this refund business."

"Maybe so," said Whit cautiously. "What's your theory?" Had he found out about Kitty's quarrel with George?

"I haven't got one yet." Webster thought a while. "How was he with women? Did he chase around?"

Whit said slowly, "Some. He liked them."

"Get along with his wife?"

"Not too well. He didn't try very hard." It was coming.

"What's she like?"

"Nice. Real nice. He was luckier than most but he didn't have sense enough to know it."

The detective said, "Uh huh," and rubbed the bristles on his chin. He was looking at the floor. Whit said, "You think maybe some woman did it?"

"Maybe. It could have been a woman, it could have been a man."

"A husband?"

Webster looked directly at him for the first time, and Whit wondered what had made him think the detective had a good-natured face. "I don't think so. Have you been sleeping with Mrs. MacLeod?"

Whit let out his breath and stood up. "All the build-up for that," he said. "Get out of here, you son of a bitch."

"Watch yourself," Webster said coldly, without moving. "You're talking to the law."

"Get out," repeated Whit. His face was pale in spite of the sunburn.

"I asked you a question." Webster still sat in his chair. "I had a man on your tail last night, and you didn't leave MacLeod's house until seven o'clock this morning. Maybe you played checkers all night, I don't know. I want an answer."

Whit said, "I'd just as soon throw you out," and moved around the desk. Webster's hands were resting on his knees, and he kept them there. He said, "I'd just as soon throw you in the can if you start something. Sit down."

"To hell with you."

"Sit down. You aren't getting anywhere."

Whit sat down and began to fumble through his pockets. His face was still white. There were lumps at the corners of his mouth. He couldn't find what he was looking for and Webster threw a package of cigarettes on the desk. "I'll put it another way," he said. "Is there anything between you and

Mrs. MacLeod?"

"Go to hell."

"If that means yes, you're in trouble. I can find out if I have to. Just say yes or no."

The color was coming back to Whit's face. He took a cigarette from Webster's package, lit it, and puffed two or three times. "No," he said.

"All right. It looked sort of bad. What were you doing there?"

Whit didn't answer. Webster leaned forward and picked a cigarette out of the package on the desk. "I haven't accused you of anything. If you can explain it, go ahead."

"Why should you believe what I tell you?"

"Maybe I won't. I just want to hear what you have to say, that's all. I can check up." He waited. After a minute Whit said, "I fell asleep on a couch. I had four or five drinks before I got there and I was tired. Kitty MacLeod put a blanket around me and went to bed, I guess. I didn't wake up until six-thirty."

The detective nodded and lit his cigarette. "That's all I wanted to know. How did she take it—the news?"

"Pretty well." Whit was still sullen.

"Pretty well?"

"I told you they didn't get along. She didn't pretend to be broken up. Do you think I killed MacLeod to get his wife?"

"I considered it. Your alibi is pretty good. The coroner's report says he died not later than six-thirty and probably before. And I know you didn't leave Santa Cruz until after five, so you'd have to do some pretty fast driving."

"You didn't waste any time checking up on me."

"It's my business to check. That's why I asked about you and Mrs. MacLeod."

Neither man said anything more for a while. The noise of a cable car rattling down California came up from the street. Webster said finally, "I've got the net out for Zimmermann. We ought to hear something in a couple of days. Of course, we can't rule anyone out yet—we're just guessing about his refund business."

"Sure. I might have killed him to get his wife. Or one of the help bumped him off for his cuff links. There's nothing like being on your toes, is there?"

"Still sore because I have to ask questions, aren't you? What do you think murder is—a game? I don't know you from Adam, and one thing I learned early in this business is not to think a man can't be a murderer just because he has pretty blue eyes. If you want to cooperate, fine. If you don't want to cooperate, that's still fine. Either way you're going to get your feelings hurt and to hell with you."

Whit said, "There's such a thing as being just plain dumb. You admit I have an alibi, so you think I might have done it anyway by remote control. According to MacLeod we stood to make a fee of fifty thousand dollars on the Wolff claim. If I killed him, I threw twenty-five thousand bucks right out of the window. Does that sound smart?"

"Suppose you go ahead and do the job yourself. You make the whole fifty thousand, don't you?"

"I do not. Even if I knew what it's all about, which I don't, and went ahead with the claim, I'd have to do it in five days or not at all. His estate gets half of whatever I make up to the end of the year. That's our partnership agreement."

"I'd like to see it."

"It's in the safe-deposit box. You can have it tomorrow. I can tell you what's in it offhand. I get twenty-five thousand in insurance, and the option to buy his share of the business. His estate—"

"Why do you get insurance?"

"It's customary. He had it on my life and I had it on his; the main reason, as far as I'm concerned, was to take care of the purchase price of the business, or part of it. He had another forty thousand payable to his estate."

"What do you pay for the business?"

"It depends. I buy out for a price based on past years' earnings and so forth. It'll cost me just about the whole twenty-five thousand, maybe more."

"Who gets his estate—the widow?"

"I suppose so. I haven't seen his will. A lot of it is community property and she'll get that. I don't know about the rest."

"What will it amount to—his whole estate?"

"How do I know? A hundred thousand, two hundred thousand, three hundred thousand."

"Pretty well heeled, wasn't he?"

"Yes."

"Whatever happens his widow will get a big piece of change."

"Maybe all of it."

The detective pondered, scowling. "How much are you worth?"

Whit shook his head. "Nothing like MacLeod. He was making money out of this business when I was struggling along in a one-room office on Pine Street worrying about the rent. He got tired of working, I guess. He practically gave me a half-interest. I've got about twenty-five thousand bucks, exclusive of the insurance I'll collect."

"His death didn't hurt you any, financially."

"No. If you forget about the widow, I get more out of it than anyone else. The business is worth a lot more than I'll pay for it."

The detective smiled for the first time since he had come into the office. "We agree that you're the logical suspect, huh?"

Whit laughed. "All right. I'm sorry I blew up. You stirred me the wrong way."

"I didn't put it the way I should have," Webster confessed. "Forget it. I don't really think much of you as the murderer. There just isn't any way you could have got here from Santa Cruz in an hour, without flying, and I know your car was in Santa Cruz at five. You didn't bring it by plane."

"Then why all the questions about Mrs. MacLeod and me?"

"I didn't like the looks of it. You told me what I wanted to know and I've forgotten it."

Whit said, "All right." He didn't believe it, but there was no point in saying so.

Webster reached for another cigarette. "I hear you got into a beef over a couple of girls in Santa Cruz."

"You boys work fast, don't you?" said Whit, "What did I have for lunch?"

The detective grinned. "Champagne. When we check on someone, we cover everything."

"I'm glad I didn't take anyone up to my room."

Webster grinned again.

The fingerprint man put his head through the door and said, "All finished, Lieutenant. Do you want any of the rest of the dump checked?"

"That'll do, Joe. What did you get?"

"The stiff's prints all over the place, three or four other sets, and a couple of smudges. There's a safe inside the vault, and somebody wiped the handle and the combination dial clean. Same thing with the vault door."

"I knew it," said Whit. The other men looked at him. He said, "Those papers are in the safe and someone was after them. If they've been pinched you can stop worrying about why he was killed."

"Uh," said Webster. "Let's have a look. Joe, make me some enlargements of the prints and check them against the records. I don't think you'll find anything but it won't hurt to try."

"O.K." Joe nodded to Whit and left.

Webster followed Whit to the vault. The blotch on the floor was caked and had turned a dirty dark brown. There were smudges of fine gray powder on top of the metal filing cabinets along one wall, and more on the big iron safe that stood opposite them. Whit said, "Here goes nothing," and spun the safe dial.

"I want prints of everyone who comes in the vault," said Webster. He was watching Whit set the combination.

"The staff will be here tomorrow." Whit moved the dial slowly to a final point and pulled up on the handle of the door. The safe opened. Inside there was a central locked compartment and open shelves holding a number of large red paper filing envelopes tied with tape. Whit pulled them out one by one and looked at the gummed labels attached to them. The sixth one was thicker than the others. Whit looked at the name on the label, held the envelope up to his face, and kissed it with a loud smack.

CHAPTER SEVEN

AN HOUR AND A HALF later Webster said, "Well, what do you make of it?"

Whit had his chin in his hands and was staring sourly at the papers in front of him. "Nothing," he said. "Not a goddam thing."

The records of the Wolff case were spread on his desk. He had grouped them roughly in chronological order; a typewritten document of three pages which was headed "Transcript of Memorandum Record Showing Dates and Amounts of Cash Payments Made by Frederick Zimmermann to Harald Wolff—Years 1921 and 1922"; the original report of the revenue agent, asserting income tax deficiencies and fraud penalties for 1921 and 1922, and a supplemental letter withdrawing the fraud penalties; a formal protest against tax, signed by George MacLeod, C.P.A., Counsel, and Frank Marston, Executor of the Estate of Harald Wolff, Deceased; a letter rejecting the protest "after careful consideration" and giving notice that appeal could be taken to the United States Board of Tax Appeals within 90 days at the taxpayer's option; a demand for taxes amounting to more than half a million dollars "with interest at six per cent per annum from the due dates of the returns to date of payment," and finally a slip of paper the size of a dollar bill. It was dated May 24, 1936, and acknowledged receipt by the Collector of Internal Revenue of taxes and interest due from Harald Wolff, deceased, amounting to $952,722.65. On the back of the receipt was a penciled note in MacLeod's writing. It read "1/2 from top brackets=$500,000 plus / 10%=$50,000 plus!!!!!!"

Webster was leaning over Whit's shoulder. "What does the note mean?"

"That's MacLeod's. Eliminate half of the income, and the tax and interest would be reduced by more than five hundred thousand dollars. Our fee of ten per cent would be over fifty thousand. The exclamation points are what he thought of that much money."

Webster wasn't satisfied. "It doesn't look like good arithmetic. If the whole thing is only nine hundred and fifty thousand, half of it would be less than five hundred thousand, not more."

"It doesn't work that way. The tax rates are graduated; the higher the income, the higher the rate of tax. If you eliminate half of the income it comes out of the highest brackets and you save tax at the highest rates." Whit picked up Zimmermann's memorandum and turned to the last page. "This shows about nine hundred and fifty thousand income, and it was all taxed to Wolff. Kick out half—"

"Wait a minute." Webster picked up the receipt and turned it over. He ran his finger down the numbers. "Taxes of nine hundred and fifty-two thou-sand on income of nine hundred and fifty thousand?"

"Taxes and interest. Uncle Sam charges six per cent when

it isn't paid on time. These taxes were due in 1922 and 1923, and they weren't paid until 1936. Thirteen or fourteen years—about eighty per cent added on. It mounts up."

"It sure does. What if I owed them a dollar and they didn't find out about it for a hundred years?"

"If you defrauded them of a dollar they'd take it out of your hide and six hundred per cent interest along with it. If it was just a mistake they couldn't do anything after three years. Do you want a lecture on tax law?"

"Not too much," Webster said cautiously. "I'd like to know about this fraud business. Just in case."

"In words of one syllable, Wolff committed fraud when he didn't report his bootlegging profit. Ordinarily the Government can't collect tax after three years, but if they prove fraud they can get it any time, along with interest and a penalty of fifty per cent of the tax. On top of that, the Department of Justice can slap you in the jug, the way they did Capone."

"I gypped them out of a dollar once," Webster said, "I wish you hadn't told me. Why didn't they collect the extra fifty per cent?" He pointed at the letter which withdrew fraud penalties.

"Wolff was dead. They're personal penalties, and they couldn't be collected from his estate, any more than the estate could be put in jail. Besides, there wasn't that much money." Whit tossed Zimmermann's memorandum on the desk. "A million dollars gone to hell and I haven't the faintest idea how to recover a dime of it. All I can get out of this stuff is that Zimmermann didn't make payments during the first part of August in either year, probably because

Wolff was away deer-hunting." He stood up and stretched his arms. "But I'll find it. If I can't dig up a clue in five days I'll quit the tax business and get a job keeping books."

"How do you know there's a clue to find?"

Whit was mildly surprised. "MacLeod did it."

"That was before anybody played around with the safe."

Whit looked blank. Webster said, "We've been assuming someone was trying to get at the papers. What if those prints were wiped off after somebody put the file away and closed the safe?"

Whit said, "Ow."

"Suppose MacLeod had the papers out and was looking at them when the killer walked in on him. That's possible; he wouldn't sit around sucking his thumb while he was waiting for you and Marston, would he?"

"Ow," Whit said again. "Go ahead."

"The killer took him into the vault and shot him, probably after MacLeod tried to jump him and got his shirt torn. Then the murderer looked over the papers, took out the dangerous ones, and locked the others in the safe so you would think just what you do think. He wiped off the prints, closed the vault, wiped off the vault door—" Webster shrugged. "Why assume he was trying to *open* the safe?"

"Why indeed?" Whit said weakly, "I guess we're ruined."

Webster grinned at him. "Not necessarily. There were two elevators running until six o'clock Saturday. This morning I talked to the operator who left at six. He took MacLeod down at about five and he brought him back here at one minute before six—I guess he was out for dinner. It could have been that he put the papers in the safe before be left and the murderer was waiting for him when he got back. Then it might have happened the other way; the murderer tried to get him to open the safe, MacLeod jumped him and got shot, and the safe was still closed."

"And I'm limp as a rag," said Whit. "Which was it?"

"I wasn't there. But let's be scientific. Whatever happened, if we assume that MacLeod really was killed because of this tax business, we ought—"

"What do you mean, assume? It's open and shut, isn't it?"

"You weren't so sure last night."

"I am now."

Webster looked at him suspiciously. "Are you holding something out on me?"

Whit sighed. "Lieutenant, so help me. I didn't kill MacLeod, I haven't any idea who did, and I don't like anyone enough to cover up for him if I did know. MacLeod found out that somebody had saved himself a lot of money by double-crossing Wolff, and he was going to stir up plenty of trouble. So he was murdered. If it isn't cause and effect it's the strangest coincidence I ever heard of."

"All right," Webster said grudgingly. "Just don't get any ideas about keeping information from the cops if you have any. It isn't smart."

"I believe you."

"All right. Let's assume MacLeod was killed because of this tax business." Whit opened his mouth and Webster hurried on. "He was probably after one of the other stockholders at the brewery, wasn't he?"

"He thought he was. He didn't know for sure."

"But if somebody else was bootlegging with Wolff, it's logical to assume that it was one of the other stockholders, isn't it?"

"I've made my assumption for the day," said Whit. "It might have been a stockholder, it might have been Donald Duck."

"All right, damn it. He was killed because he stumbled on something. How many people could have known what he found?"

"Marston, me, the stockholders of the corporation, and anybody else."

"Who else?"

"I don't know. What about Zimmermann?"

"How would he know?"

"What do you want me to do, solve the case? If you're being scientific, you can't limit the suspects to people you know MacLeod talked with. One of them may have passed it on, deliberately or otherwise. Or MacLeod may have talked to someone you don't know about."

"We'll stop being scientific," the detective said. "Someone shot him with a twenty-five. It probably wasn't you, because you have an alibi. So—"

"Also I never knew Wolff, I didn't know MacLeod until five or six years ago, and I was fifteen years old when Wolff stopped bootlegging. Don't let me interrupt you."

"—so, how about Marston? How well do you know him?"

"I never met him before last night, but he's hiring me to find out what it's all about. I wouldn't pick him."

"It could be a cover-up. If he was the man, he'd have to pretend he was interested in getting the money back."

"Hasn't he an alibi?"

"No. He says he was home until about six-thirty, and then he drove down town alone. He lives by himself."

Whit considered it carefully. "I don't think so, unless you can tie him up with the bootlegging. He was Wolff's friend, he and MacLeod worked together on the case all the way through, and he'll get eighteen thousand dollars if the estate recovers any money. Anyway, it seems to me that if he did it he'd have an alibi fixed up for himself, wouldn't he?"

"Sometimes no alibi at all is the best one in the world. If the murderer had a lot of nerve, the smartest thing he could do would be to wait right here until you showed up, just as innocent as Marston was when you walked in on him."

"I thought you said MacLeod was shot before six-thirty. Marston didn't get here until quarter of seven."

The detective corrected him. "He came up in the elevator at quarter of seven. It's not an alibi for six-fifteen."

Whit had no answer to the argument.

Webster said, "How about the brewery stockholders? Do you know anything about them?"

"No."

"Did anyone in your office besides MacLeod have anything to do with Wolff?"

"Not that I know of. We have only three people here; Krebs, who does most of the work; Miss Kelly, the girl at the desk, and a young kid, Tommy Ward. You can count them out."

"I can't count anyone out. How old is Krebs?"

"About fifty. You're wasting your time if you consider him. He wouldn't swat a fly if it bit him."

"Maybe," Webster said, "It's a German name, isn't it? Wolff was German. Zimmermann was German."

Whit laughed. "Maybe it was Hitler. He's German."

They argued some more along the same lines and the conversation died when Webster ran out of suspects. Whit went back to his desk and Webster prowled around the room gnawing his thumbnail. Whit was trying to make something out of the figures in Zimmermann's memorandum when the detective said, "By God, I know what we can do."

"What?" Whit was marking figures on a scratch pad.

"Trap him. Make him show his hand." Webster was stirred up. "Why, it's perfect. The murderer had to shoot MacLeod because MacLeod found out what was in the papers. Suppose he thought that you knew what MacLeod had found?"

"He'd shoot me," said Whit. "That's easy. He won't get any such ideas if I have anything to do with it."

Webster wasn't paying any attention to him. "All we have to do is spread the word that MacLeod told you what it was all about before he died and that you're ready to file the claims. We could put it in the newspapers. Then the murderer has to try to get you, and we have him in the bag."

"Or vice versa. I get the idea. I don't want any part of it."

"You won't get hurt. I'll give you a bodyguard. And you have to find the answer in five days if you're going to make any money out of it, don't you? This way it's surefire."

"Nope," Whit said firmly. "I'm an honest, hardworking accountant and I make my money with a pencil. As far as being bait for a gunman, you can include me out. I don't want to end up mounted over somebody's mantel."

Webster pleaded with him without getting to first base. Whit was absolutely not going to tell the newspapers that he was ready to file the refund claims. He wasn't ready to do anything, the truth was sacred, and he didn't want anyone looking for him with a gun. He'd go about finding a clue in his own innocent way, without getting a couple of slugs put in him. Nothing would change his mind.

"I ought to pinch you for obstructing justice," said Webster finally.

"Cream-puff Whitney, that's me. I'm going to die in bed."

"You're going to die poor." Webster put on his hat. "Think it over, will you? I'll be in tomorrow morning. I want to talk to your staff and get some finger prints. And we're going to the stockholders' meeting." He went out to the anteroom, woke the cop, and they left. Whit dug into the Wolff papers.

At three o'clock in the afternoon he was up to his ears in them when Krebs came in, dressed in a black suit and a black tie, with a black bordered handkerchief showing in his breast pocket. He stood solemnly in the doorway holding his hat in both hands. "Good afternoon, Mr. Whitney."

Whit said, "Hello. What are you doing here?"

"I heard about it on the radio," Krebs said in his careful English. "I went to your apartment first and then I came down here. I'm sorry, Mr. Whitney. It is a terrible thing."

"You needn't have gone into mourning. Sit down."

Krebs sat down, holding his hat in both hands. "I thought I should wear black. I shall change tomorrow, if you wish."

Whit put down his pencil and looked at him. "Why black? You didn't like him, did you?"

Krebs did not hesitate. "No. I did not like him. But it is still a terrible thing for a man to be murdered, and he was my employer."

"What did you have against him, Krebs?"

Krebs was thoughtful for a moment before answering.

"I worked for him for twenty years, Mr. Whitney. In that time I did as much as he to build up this business to where it is today. He paid me two hundred dollars a month for the last ten years, and I am a good accountant. A bricklayer makes more money than I do. Many times I have considered leaving him, but always I thought perhaps he would make me a partner some day." There was no bitterness in his voice. It was a statement of fact.

"You couldn't have liked it much when he took me in."

"No. I did not like it. But it was not your fault."

"MacLeod ran things, Krebs. I was his partner, but I left it up to him because it was his business to start with. It's different now. You know more about our clients than I ever will. You make three hundred a month starting tomorrow. If I can handle it you'll make more."

Krebs inclined his head. "Thank you, Mr. Whitney. That is fine. Thank you very much."

"You'll earn it. Bring your chair over here."

Krebs put his hat down and moved his chair to the desk. Whit said, "And don't tell the police you disliked MacLeod. They might misunderstand."

"Yes sir. You are badly sunburned, Mr. Whitney. Have you ever used tannic acid ointment?"

"I'll try it," said Whit. "Now listen."

He told Krebs the story of Harald Wolff. The accountant listened carefully and made no comment. Whit concluded by saying, "That's all I know about it. Did you ever have anything to do with the case?"

"I remember when Mr. MacLeod was working on it, in 1935.

He handled it all personally. I knew very little about it, except that there was a great deal of money involved."

"Did MacLeod discuss it with you at all Saturday morning?"

"I saw him only for a minute, when I took the Jackson returns to him. He did not mention it."

"Well, give it some thought, Krebs. We have to do a lot between now and Friday."

There was a racket in the street. Whit went to the window and looked out. A newsboy at the corner of Montgomery had an armful of papers and was holding one at the side of his mouth to get volume. *"Oh, read all about it. Oh, extry. Oh, murder mystery, get your extry paper."* He started up Montgomery Street. Whit said, "Get a paper, will you?"

"Yes sir." Krebs left the office. Whit heard the hiss of the air in the pneumatic stop on the outside door and the click as the door shut.

He went back to his desk and stood looking down at the papers, gently rubbing his sunburned neck. He had hoped that Krebs would have some information which would be helpful, and he felt discouraged. Going over and over the same trail for four or five hours had dulled his mind; his reasoning processes were beginning to repeat themselves. The problem certainly needed a new approach.

The outside door opened and the stop hissed as it closed again. Whit noted it subconsciously. A new approach. So far he had been attempting to solve an income tax problem to find a key to the mystery of MacLeod's murder. Perhaps if he attacked directly the problem of the murder, he could find the clue to the other question. He had been searching for the cause in order to find the effect; if he were to commence with the effect—

The palms of Whit's hands were suddenly moist. Krebs couldn't have got down to the street and back already. It wasn't Krebs who had come into the anteroom. Someone else was out there and was being too quiet about it.

Whit moved his hand toward the telephone and stopped. A man stood in the office doorway. He had a prize-fighter's face; his nose had been broken and was flat across the bridge, and his eyebrow ridges were thick, where they had been split and healed. Both of his hands were in his coat pockets.

They looked at each other for a long five seconds without speaking. The distance between them was too far to cover in a jump, and Whit knew that the killer's hand rested on the gun in his pocket—the twenty-five caliber gun that had killed MacLeod. His heart pounded.

The killer said, "Is your name Whitney?" There was no expression in his voice.

Whit's mouth was too dry for him to speak. It required thought to lie, and he had passed the point of being able to think.

He nodded his head.

"My name's Larson," said the killer. "I'm your bodyguard. You ought to be more careful about keeping your front door locked."

CHAPTER EIGHT

WHEN KREBS came in with a paper, Larson was wondering if he had been assigned to a screwball. Guys who had hysterics when a cop walked in and introduced himself weren't normal. And this guy must be a lush on top of it, yanking a bottle out of a desk drawer and killing half a pint in one gulp.

"Have a drink," Whit said. He put the bottle down and wiped sweat from his forehead. "*Whooey.* I'm glad I had that handy."

"Can't," Larson said regretfully. "I'm on duty. Thanks."

"Too bad." Whit had another. "Krebs?"

"No, thank you." Krebs was disturbed, and his accent was thicker than usual. "This paper says—"

"I can guess." Whit corked the bottle and put it away. I've been framed. Mr. Krebs, Mr. Larson. Mr. Larson is the gentleman who will respond in kind when some one takes a shot at me." Whit took the paper and spread it on top of the litter covering his desk.

Larson said, "H'lo."

"How do you do." Krebs was so upset he forgot to bow. "This is all wrong, Mr. Whitney. The paper has made a mistake."

"The paper didn't make it," Whit said. "I did."

Lieutenant Webster had shot the works. MacLeod's murder made up the headline and two paragraphs of the story; the rest of it was devoted to the Mystery of a Million Dollars, A Race Against Time, and Dead Man's Partner Will Carry On. Even Kitty MacLeod, ex-blues singer and chorus girl, ordinarily worth a column of filler and some leg art, had got little space. Webster had done a good job—from his viewpoint. Behind the *"alleged's," "it is stated's"* and *"presumably's"* of the story lay the trap, with Whit as bait. George MacLeod had been killed to keep him from "recovering a fortune in illegal income taxes" for a client, but his surviving partner, Mr. James Whitney, was in full possession of the facts to go on where MacLeod had left off, and had informed the police that he was grimly determined not to rest until the money was recovered. The story ended with an editorial slap at the administration for cheating honest taxpayers and an implication that the Secretary of the Treasury was not above having MacLeod killed for five hundred thousand dollars. There were pictures of MacLeod and of Whitney. Whit's had been taken two years before at an accountants' banquet and made him look a little bit like Andy Gump, but it was recognizable. It would be a great help to anyone gunning for him. He felt like a piece of cheese in a mouse-trap.

"Do you see what will happen?" said Krebs. "The murderer will try to kill you as he did Mr. MacLeod. You must explain to the papers that they have made an error."

"Uh huh." Whit scowled at the headlines. Webster had set him up like a bottle on a fence. It was a good scheme, too; Whit would be the first to applaud it if somebody else were in the seat of honor. His bodyguard looked tough but not too smart. If the murderer fell for it—Whit shuddered.

"What are you going to do?" asked Krebs.

"Nothing I can do before tomorrow, except get drunk." Whit took out the bottle. There was one big drink left and he finished it and put the bottle in the waste-basket. Drink, drink and be merry for tomorrow and Tuesday, Wednesday, Thursday and Friday he was going to be guest of honor at a shooting gallery.

"I'm going to get the hell out of here before I have callers." He looked at Larson. "What do you do now?"

"Follow you around and keep you from getting bumped off." Larson yawned.

"Any particular method?"

"Nope. Just don't get too far away from me, that's all."

"I won't," said Whit. "This is my first experience with a bodyguard. I'm about to go out and get stiff, and it's up to you to taste everything first so I won't get poisoned."

"I'm on duty," Larson said sternly. "I can't drink."

"That's too bad. I guess I'll have to take my chances. How would you like to go to dinner with us, Krebs? If you don't mind a little shooting now and then."

"No, thank you. My wife is expecting me. I shall look at these papers for a while before I go home, if you will permit me. Perhaps I can find something." He picked up the newspaper. "I wish you would give a statement to the reporters before anything happens, Mr. Whitney."

"I'm going to, first thing tomorrow." Whit took his hat from the bookcase. "If you do find anything, don't advertise it. You might talk to the wrong person."

"I am not afraid," said Krebs with dignity.

"Neither was MacLeod. Lock the stuff in the safe when you're finished."

"I shall."

"Come on, bodyguard."

They left Krebs methodically sorting the papers into neat piles on the desk.

In his car Whit said, "Now, if I were to decide to go to a night club, for instance, and have some dinner and a few drinks, and maybe look at the floor show, there wouldn't be anything you could do about it, now would there?"

Larson smiled all over his prize-fighter's face. "Not a thing but go along and protect you. I hear tell the Frisco Club has the best leg show in California."

"We'll try it. But remember you're supposed to keep me from being shot, so don't get plastered."

"I can't drink nothing." Larson stopped smiling. "The Lieutenant said—"

"A social glass or two at my insistence," said Whit. "The Lieutenant isn't going to be where we're going."

"Well, if you put it that way." Larson leaned back comfortably against the cushions. "This ain't going to be a bad job."

It was early when they arrived at the Frisco Club. They killed time in the barroom waiting for things to start. The place was empty except for a B girl pouring her troubles into the bartender's ear. He broke away when he saw the cash customers.

"Evening," he said, polishing the bar. "What'll it be, gents?"

"Champagne. The best."

The B girl sat up straight and fixed her hair.

"'At's nice," Larson said appreciatively.

"What—champagne?"

Larson shook his head and grinned. Whit said, "Oh. Well, not bad."

The bartender held up a bottle of pink-top for his inspecttion. "How's that?" Whit said, "Fine." The B girl shifted around on her stool so her legs showed. Larson blinked. "Well, well. Look what's going to be calling on us pretty soon!"

Whit looked. "Remember you've got a job. Don't let your mind wander."

"You're safe as a babe in arms," said Larson. "Hiya, toots."

The B girl's name was Gladys, she loved champagne, and she was all alone except for Frances, her girlfriend. She worked a little telepathy and Frances showed up. Frances was mad about champagne. Whit ordered a second bottle. Frances had seen the extras and she thought Whit looked just like the man in the murder case, except that he was better looking. Wouldn't it be exciting to be mixed up in a murder mystery? Whit said it sure would if you weren't the corpse. The girls thought that was awfully funny. The second bottle went fast. Larson put his arm around Whit's shoulder and guaranteed that he wasn't going to be no corpse. Whit said, "Watch the sunburn, chum," and they opened a third bottle. The bar began to fill up and two or three girls tried to crash the party when they smelled champagne. Whit and Larson thought it was a swell idea, but Gladys and her girlfriend put the frost on the interlopers and they faded away. Larson wrung Whit's hand like a dishrag and said that anybody who took a crack at his pal was going to run into a hell of a lot of trouble. He would hunt down the man who killed his pal if it took the rest of his life, pal. Whit was impressed. Gladys wanted to know who would want to kill such a nice man. Larson explained that the Nazzies were after him. Somebody ordered another bottle of champagne.

"I'm hungry," said Whit after a while.

"Dinner," said Larson. "Have to keep your strength up."

"That's right."

"You're goddam right that's right, pal." No one wanted to argue. Whit paid the bar bill of thirty-six dollars and they went in to dinner.

One of the girls had thoughtfully reserved a ringside table for four. It was right on the dance floor, and waiters hovered around it like a flock of sea gulls over a ferry boat. Someone had passed the word about the bar bill. The orchestra started to play before Whit got his eyes focused on the menu. Frances pulled him out onto the floor.

"Don't want to dance." Whit held back. "I'm hungry."

"It'll sober you up. Come on, honey."

"Don't want to sober up."

"You'll like to dance with me," Frances said soothingly. "Come on."

They danced. Frances plastered herself against Whit from knee to collar-bone and he went around the floor in a daze. She was right on one count; it didn't sober him up but he liked it. They danced four numbers without a rest. During the fifth Larson reached out and hauled Whit in as he passed the table.

"Hey," he said. "How about dinner?"

"Not hungry," said Whit. "Leggo."

"I'm hungry," Frances said. "We'll dance some more later."

Whit sat down after an argument and a waiter bobbed up at his elbow. Whit waved his arms grandly. "A bottle of champagne and some food. Make it two bottles of champagne."

"Yes sir," said the waiter. "How about a nice steak?"

"Fine," said Larson. "Four nice steaks."

"Nope." Whit had a craving for something exotic. The condemned man was entitled to anything he wanted—anything. Hummingbirds' wings, barbels' beards,—"Strawberries. Strawberries in December, that's what I want. Bring me a double order of strawberries in December and a bottle of champagne."

"Yes sir." The waiter had been in the business a long time

"You can't have strawberries in December," said Gladys.

"Why not?" Whit was in no mood to be argued with.

"Who says he can't?" said Larson.

"It's May. You can't have strawberries in December in May."

"Lousy service," said Whit. "I'll have the four steaks. What do you want?"

The waiter brought a lot of steaks, a lot of fixings, and a lot of champagne. Between courses Frances gave Whit a workout on the floor and Larson entertained Gladys with the details of the Nazzy plot against Whit's life and his plans for foiling it. After dinner Whit suggested that the champagne was losing its punch on top of all that food. Larson thought he was goddam well right, pal, and they switched over to brandy. It had a lot more authority.

The floor show came on at ten o'clock. Larson discovered that he could applaud louder by slapping his hands on the table top than by clapping them together, and after each number the glasses on the table jumped around like raindrops on a pavement. It was a good show. The chorus went through a routine involving cellophane dresses and a blue spot that temporarily woke Whit out of his coma and made Larson's hands sore. They had some more brandy and some more brandy and some more brandy. Whit passed out.

When he came to he was bumping up and down in midair watching the sidewalk stream by before his eyes. It wasn't sensible. He said, "Hey. What the hell is going on here?" Larson lowered him from his shoulder and propped him against a building.

"How you doing, pal?" Larson was breathing hard.

"Fine. Where we going?"

"Home. You know where you live?"

"Home is where the heart is. What happened to the girls?"

"They decided not to come along when I told them about your wife and kiddies waiting for you."

"Nothing like a wife and kiddies," said Whit. His knees buckled under him and he sat down on the sidewalk.

Larson picked him up again and lugged him to the car, half a block away. Whit's feelings were hurt by the indignity of being carried, but he could drive, by God. Drunk or sober, he was a driving fool. Anybody want to argue about it?

Larson didn't. Whit crawled behind the wheel, started the motor after a couple of attempts, and bounced his car off the fender of the car in front getting away from the curb. The convertible didn't seem to have as much speed as usual. Larson suggested that it would go faster if they took it out of second gear. They argued over it. Whit won the debate when he pointed out that the high gear was over-worked anyway, and the car stayed in second.

They crossed Van Ness Avenue and drove out Washington Street. Larson put a cigarette in his mouth and fumbled with the buttons on the dashboard in search of a lighter, and the top of the car rose into the air and folded neatly back into place behind the seat. Larson said blankly, "I'll be a son of a bitch," and pressed the button again. The top rose into the air and caught the wind like a sail, bellying back in the stiff breeze. The car bucked and slowed down.

"Emergency brake," said Whit, wrestling with the wheel.

Larson experimented. After a little practice he got he hang of it, and they made boulevard stops thereafter by spreading sail. Once they got a good gust of wind and the car went into reverse. Whit had to back into the curb to keep from returning to the Frisco Club. Larson burst into a song with a lot of dirty verses and a rollicking chorus that went:

> *Lower away the main to'ga'ns'l,*
> *Let the good ship roll over.*
> *No young girl is ha-a-ppy*
> *When her true love's at sea.*

They left the car parked in front of Whit's apartment house with the main to'ga'ns'l at half mast. In the automatic elevator Whit sat down on the floor with his back to the wall and went to sleep. Larson said, "Hey, wake up. What's the number of your apartment?"

"Levenhunnerd." Whit kept his eyes closed.

Larson punched the control button and the elevator stopped at the eleventh floor. He said, "Come on, come on. The wife and and kiddies are waiting."

Whit mumbled, "Jussaminnit," fell over the side, and began to snore. Larson picked his pocket for a key, carried him into the bedroom and dumped him on his bed. Whit went on snoring. Larson investigated the apartment and found two things that interested him; a bottle of beer in the icebox and a folding bed in the living room. He used them both.

CHAPTER NINE

WHIT OPENED HIS EYES cautiously and looked to see where he was. A man never knew where he might wake up. Sometimes it was a hotel, if he was lucky, and then he could phone for a bellhop to bring him big pitchers of ice-water. A gallon of that would help. Or two gallons. But he hadn't been lucky this time; it was his own bedroom. He reached out his hand and explored the bed. At least he was alone.

He tried to start the saliva running in his mouth by moving his tongue and working his lips, but all he got was a clacking noise. He was dried out, like a prune. He could lie in bed and die of thirst or he could get up and die of the effort. He tried dying of thirst but it took too long. Besides, his sunburn was still sore, his clothes had contracted longitudinally and were binding him where it hurt, and his feet bothered him. That was a bad sign. It meant he had been too drunk to take off his shoes. He thought of the Indian fakirs who slept on beds of nails. If they could do it, he could. He lay still, and after a while he decided that a bed of nails was a bed of roses compared to being cut in half by his underwear, suffering from sunburn, and dying of thirst all at the same time. With a tremendous effort of will he got off the bed.

In the bathroom he drank a quart of water and took off his clothes. They were past worrying about, so he kicked them into a corner and stepped under the shower. The hot water brought his sunburn to life, but he stayed under the spray for ten minutes. When he got out he was covered with goose-flesh and had the shakes. There was only one thing to do. He wrapped a towel around his middle and went shivering through drawers and closets in the bedroom until he found a half empty bottle of Ten High in a raincoat. He took a deep breath, tipped the bottle up, and let the whiskey run down his throat until his gullet contracted of its own accord. His stomach rose up under his breast bone and he hurried back to the bathroom. Nothing else happened. In a minute the whiskey took hold, the green tinge faded from his face, and he began to remember things again. He took the bottle with him and went to look for his bodyguard.

Larson said viciously, "Get the hell away from me," without opening his eyes. Whit bounced the end of the folding bed on the floor a couple of times and sang, "Good morning to you, good morning to you, good morning, dear body-guard, we're glad to see you." The whiskey was a big help. He had another drink.

"Leave me alone," said Larson ominously, screwing his eyes tight. "Whoever you are, you're going to get hurt. Get away."

"What's the matter? A little champagne bother you?" Whit beat his chest. "Look at me."

Larson opened his eyes a sixteenth of an inch and looked. Whit said, "Sure cure," holding up the bottle of Ten High. Larson gagged, jumped out of bed, and ran for the bathroom. Whit followed him with the bottle.

They skipped breakfast and were at the office at nine o'clock. Miss Kelly was talking in a hushed voice to Tommy Ward, the third member of the staff, when they came in. Tommy was fresh from college and had ambitions to be a C.P.A. His experience hadn't prepared him to cope with a murder.

He said, "Good morning," uncomfortably and shut up.

Miss Kelly dabbed her eyes. "Oh, Mr. Whitney. Isn't it terrible?"

Whit said hurriedly, "Morning, Tommy. Morning, Miss Kelly. I'll talk to you later," introduced Larson vaguely as an officer of the law, and they went into his office. The Ten High had worn off, and he was in no shape to have Miss Kelly sob over him.

He called Krebs in as soon as he had looked at the mail. Krebs reported that he had gone over the Wolff papers painstakingly and had found nothing. What did Mr. Whitney want him to do next?

"Get Miss Kelly and Tommy in here. I might as well have it over with."

The staff assembled solemnly in front of the desk. Larson looked Miss Kelly over, decided against it, and picked up a newspaper. Miss Kelly wiped her nose and yearned to comfort poor, dear Mr. Whitney. Poor dear Mr. Whitney didn't give her a chance to open her mouth. He said, "You all know what has happened. I—"

"Mr. Whitney," interrupted Miss Kelly bravely. "We want to say—"

"I appreciate your feelings, Miss Kelly, and I understand perfectly. Mr. MacLeod's death was a tragedy which we all feel deeply. You need say no more. Right now we have a problem confronting us and I need your help. I want you to tell me everything that you can remember about Saturday morning. The—uh—apprehension of Mr. MacLeod's murderer may depend on what you know. Furthermore, Mr. MacLeod was working on an income tax case involving a substantial amount of money when he died, and for the sake of our client we must—uh—carry on."

Carry on. Why had he said that? Carry on for dear Old Rutgers. Miss Kelly was going to boohoo. He said quickly, "Miss Kelly. Will you tell me what happened here Saturday morning?"

Miss Kelly mopped her nose. Nothing exceptional had occurred. Mr. MacLeod had come in at his usual time and asked her to get a file of old papers out of the vault. She had taken them to him and he had stayed in his office all morning. She had made several telephone calls for him. The only thing that might be considered unusual was that he had still been in his office when she went home at noon. She had left without even saying good-bye to him, because his office door was closed, but if only she had known—. The water ran out of her eyes and down her cheeks. Tommy cleared his throat and looked out of the window, gulping.

"Of course," Whit said desperately. "Please, Miss Kelly. Was it the Wolff estate file that you got for him?"

"Yes, it was."

"That's fine. To whom did he telephone?"

"Several people, Mr. Whitney. Now let me think." She concentrated on it and forgot to cry.

"Anyone across the bay? A Mr. Hall at the Gold Star Brewery in Oakland?"

"No." She shook her head. "They were all local calls, unless he made some himself after I left." The thought of poor dear Mr. MacLeod making his own calls started her off again.

"Did he telephone Frank Marston?"

"Marston?" She brightened, "Yes, he did. We had done some work for Mr. Marston a few years ago, and I remember looking up the number in my book."

"That's fine, Miss Kelly. Anyone else you can remember? Did he call a man named Zimmermann?"

"No, I don't think so. I don't remember the name. He called the garage where he parks his car."

"I'm only interested in someone who may have been connected with the Wolff estate. Can you think of any others?"

"No. I—I—not right now. I'll try to remember."

"Did anyone come in to see him?"

"No. Not while I was here."

Whit was making no progress fast. "Thank you. That's fine. Tommy?"

Tommy said, "I didn't see Mr. MacLeod at all Saturday, Mr. Whitney. I was checking some computations for Mr. Krebs on the Jackson estate tax return and I left about twelve-thirty. Mr. MacLeod was in his office when I went out and the door was closed. He was talking to someone on the telephone."

"How do you know—I mean how do you know it was a telephone conversation?"

"Well, I don't know for sure, I guess. But he was arguing with someone and I didn't hear anyone answer. He must have been telephoning or I would have heard another voice."

"That's right. Did you hear what he was arguing about? Did he throw out a name?"

"No. When I went by his door he was saying that he didn't give a damn what anyone thought, he knew better. He sounded angry and he was pretty loud. He said something else as I went out but I didn't hear it."

Whit got nothing else from him. Miss Kelly made another attempt to break down. Whit soothed her out of the office and sent Tommy back to work.

When they had gone Larson looked up from his paper. "I wish I had a drink."

"So do I. Krebs, what's on your mind?"

Krebs still stood in front of the desk. He had discarded the black-bordered handkerchief and switched from a black tie to a mild blue one. He said, "Have you spoken to the newspapers yet, Mr. Whitney?"

"No. As a matter of fact, I'm not going to say anything to them."

"Oh." Krebs wanted to ask questions but he wasn't sure that it was his business.

"The newspaper story is a frame-up," Whit explained. "The police have an idea that the murderer will make an attempt on me if he thinks I am dangerous, and Mr. Larson is to catch him if he does."

Krebs looked at Larson. "That is very dangerous for you, Mr. Whitney."

"It wasn't my idea. But now that the story is released, I don't think a denial would do any good. And it may be the only way by which we can get somewhere, Krebs. Neither of us seems to be able to find anything in the Wolff file."

"That is so. But you should be very careful, Mr. Whitney." He looked toward Larson hidden behind the sports page. "Would it not be better for you to have more protection?"

"Probably. But if there were too much the murderer would not attempt anything."

"That is so." Krebs hesitated, shook his head, and turned toward the door.

Whit called him back. "You will have to take charge of the office for a while, Krebs. I'm going to be busy on this case and I won't have time for anything else. You will have to do almost all the work. Can you manage it?"

"I do not mind work, Mr. Whitney. I shall take care of everything. If we need extra help I shall tell you."

"Thanks. That's all."

Krebs went out. Larson looked up from his paper and said, "A trap, huh? What's it all about, anyway?"

Whit stared at him. "For Christ's sake. Don't you know?"

"Nope. The Lieutenant says to keep an eye on you, and if somebody starts shooting I get him first, that's all. I'd sure like to know what's going on."

The telephone bell saved Whit from trying to explain. He said, "You just remember what the Lieutenant told you," and picked up the receiver.

"Lieutenant Webster and another gentleman are here," said Miss Kelly.

"Send them in."

Lieutenant Webster had shaved and changed his clothes. He was accompanied by Joe, the fingerprint expert, with his black leather case. Larson stood up when they came in. "Morning, Lieutenant. Hiya, Joe."

Webster said, "Morning." Joe said, "Hiya, Swede," and nodded to Whitney.

Webster looked at Whit and grinned. "Good morning. Have you seen the papers?"

"I have. I'm going to issue a flat denial for the afternoon editions."

"It won't do any good. Anybody who read the story couldn't afford to take a chance on it being true."

"Pretty smart, aren't you? Did you stop to think what will happen to you if I get killed?"

"I'll feel bad," Webster said placidly. "I was thinking about that fifty thousand dollar fee of yours or I wouldn't have done it. I'd hate to have you lose out on fifty thousand dollars."

The telephone rang before Whit could think of anything appropriate. Marston was on the wire. He said, "What's this in the newspapers, Whitney? Have you found anything?"

"No. We're no closer than we were before."

"The newspaper says—"

"It's Lieutenant Webster's idea of a joke. I haven't found a thing."

Webster said, "If that's Marston, remind him of the stockholders' meeting. Two o'clock. Tell him to meet us here at one-thirty."

Whit nodded. Marston said irritably, "What is this, Whitney? Are you doing something I don't know about?"

"I'll explain it when I see you. Webster wants you to meet us here at one-thirty. We're going to the stockholders' meeting."

"All right. I want to know what's going on."

"You will."

Whit put the phone down. "You've got Marston all stirred up."

"That's fine," said Webster. "Fine. The more people we stir up the better. If we stir up the right one you may be helpful in solving this case yet."

Whit said, "You win. Let's not talk about it."

"That's the spirit. Now how about some fingerprints from your staff? Can you explain it so they won't stand on their constitutional rights?"

"A lot of good it would do them," said Whit. "Come along, Joe."

They went out to the anteroom. Whit introduced Joe to Miss Kelly and explained the situation. Miss Kelly was a little upset at the idea but Joe got her prints. Whit asked her to explain to Krebs and Tommy and went back to his office.

Webster said, "I talked to the widow this morning. She doesn't seem to be upset much."

"She isn't."

"No reason why she should be, from all reports. She's a good-looking girl, isn't she?"

Whit laughed. "If I say no, I'm a liar and if I say yes, you'll get suspicious again. Did you get any information from her?"

"She gave me the same story you did about Saturday night. I'm inclined to believe it, unless I hear something that makes me feel differently."

"Thank you kindly. What did you do—ask her if she had been sleeping with me?"

"I use finesse with women. Rough stuff with the men, finesse with the ladies. She likes you. She said—"

"That's nice. What did you get that's constructive?"

"Nothing much. Did you know that MacLeod didn't go home Friday night?"

Whit did some fast thinking. "Yes."

"You didn't tell me about it."

"Why should I?" said Whit, surprised. "It hasn't anything to do with the murder, has it?"

The detective shook his head. "I don't know. He drove Marian Wolff home at ten o'clock and no one knows where he was until next morning when he showed up here. Maybe there was something between him and the Wolff girl, and she shot him."

Whit said, "God, what a mind. First it's Mrs. MacLeod and me, and then it's MacLeod and Marian Wolff. Have you picked anyone for Miss Kelly?"

Webster was serious. "You have to consider everything in a murder case. The doorman at Miss Wolff's apartment house says he left there at ten-thirty, and he turned up here at eight-thirty next morning. I'd like to know where he spent the night."

"Olympic Club, Pacific Union Club, Bohemian Club," said Whit. "He belonged to all of them. He probably got too drunk to go home. What difference does it make? He was killed Saturday afternoon, not Friday night."

"I'll try them." The detective wrote the name of the clubs down in his notebook. "Maybe it doesn't make any difference, but I'd sure like to know where he went when he left that girl."

Joe came in with an ink-pad and some cards. Whit left his fingerprints for the record. Joe gave him a cloth and some benzine to clean his fingers and compared Whit's prints with those he had on the cards. Webster said, "How do they come out?"

"This makes only five sets, including MacLeod's, Lieutenant. There were these and one other in the vault or on the door."

Webster sat up straight. "No fooling. You got a spare?" He turned to Whitney. "Did you hear that?"

"I heard it. You'd better get the janitor's prints. He closes the vault whenever everyone else forgets."

Webster let himself slump in the chair. "Get the janitor's prints, Joe," he said gloomily. "They're probably the sixth set."

"O.K. Where'll I find him, Mr. Whitney?"

"He comes on at eight. You'll have to get him at night."

"O.K Eight p.m. What's his name?"

"Sam—that's all I know. He's a negro and a good boy. Go easy on him."

Joe gathered up his cards and prepared to leave. Webster said, "Wait a minute. I'm going too," and stood up.

Whit said, "Are you going to talk to the hired help?"

The detective hesitated. "Did you?"

"Yes. They didn't know anything. MacLeod stayed in his office all morning, and if he made any telephone calls that meant anything he did it after Miss Kelly went home. All she remembers is a call to Marston."

"I'll let it go for a while. I'm getting discouraged. Talking to them won't cheer me up."

Whit went to the anteroom with the two men. At the door Webster said, "I'm going to see MacLeod's attorney and look at his will. I'll be back before one-thirty. Get that partnership agreement out for me, will you?"

"This noon."

"And I think you'd better talk to Marian Wolff sometime today about this tax business. Tell her I'll want to see her later."

"I'll call her," said Whit. "Anything else?"

Webster put his hand on the doorknob. "No, not yet. We'll see what we can get at the stockholders' meeting."

"Don't give up," said Whit. "Somebody will shoot me any minute and then everything will be lovely."

CHAPTER TEN

BACK AT HIS DESK Whit pushed the papers to one side and concentrated. The Wolff file was a blank; either MacLeod had been a lot smarter than Whit was or the murderer had pinched something. Whichever it was, Whit would get no place by going over and over the same ground. He would have to use a different approach if he were going to file any claims. The easiest way to get information would be to find the murderer and ask him why he had shot MacLeod. Step one—who was the murderer?

The approach through pure reason was not helped by his hangover nor by the steady ringing of the telephone. People he had never heard of called to talk about poor George. Whit said yes indeed and thank you and it certainly was a tragedy until he was tired of the sound of his own voice.

Larson finally went to the gents' room and Whit telephoned Kitty MacLeod. She said, "What time did you leave the other night? I thought you'd still be snoring when I got up Sunday."

"About seven a.m. Thanks for the blanket. If you've been asked any embarrassing questions, Lieutenant Webster had a man shadowing me that night and he saw me leave in the morning. Webster jumped to conclusions."

"He spoke to me about it. Very delicately. I told him what had happened and he apologized for bringing it up."

"Don't misjudge him, Kitty. He doesn't believe you just because he's polite about it."

"I don't care whether he believes me or not. I'm a big girl now. Suspicions about my virtue don't bother me the way they used to."

"It's not only your virtue he suspects. He's toying with the idea that you and I—"

A shadow showed on the glass of the office door and Larson came in. Whit said, "Yes. I'm trying to get in touch with Miss Marian Wolff. Could you give me her telephone number, please?"

"Let's get back to the subject of my virtue," Kitty said. "You switch around too fast."

"I'd rather not say. If you'll give me her number I'm sure she'll be glad to talk to me."

"Don't tell me. Have you visitors?"

"Yes."

"Just when the conversation was interesting, too. Marian is here now. Do you really want to talk to her?"

"Thank you. I'll hold the wire."

He waited. There was some mumbling on the other end of the line and then a voice with a smile said, "Hello, Mr. Whitney."

"Good morning, Miss Wolff. I'd like to talk to you this afternoon, if I may. Could you come down to my office—about one?"

"I don't think I can get there quite that early. Would two o'clock be all right?"

He said, "Well—" The conference at the brewery was set for two. It would take half an hour to drive back from Oakland. If the conference lasted two hours he wouldn't be back before four, and it might be later. "I'm afraid I won't be in after one-thirty."

"Let's make it tomorrow morning. I want to ask you about that story in the newspapers, Mr. Whitney. Is it true?"

"Is what true?"

"About my father's taxes and the refund claim and all that."

Whit began to feel licked. If ever he had been handed a case in which no one knew anything, this was it. He said, "Didn't you talk to George MacLeod about it?"

"Not about anything that's in the papers. I didn't know a thing about it until I saw the extra last night. George didn't even mention it to me."

That was that. Whit wondered what to do next. Marian Wolff had been his hole card, and she had turned out to be a deuce. Wasn't he going to find out *anything* about this case before Friday? Was fifty thousand dollars going to slip through his fingers because nobody knew a thing? Honest to God, if he didn't unearth something soon—

"Hello," the girl said. "Are you still there?"

"More or less. I have to talk to you, Miss Wolff. If you can't come down here, suppose I call on you this evening, about eight o'clock? We can't waste any time."

"All right. Eight o'clock."

She gave him her address, and Kitty came back on the line. George's funeral would be the following day—Tuesday. Whit made arrangements to meet her and, hung up.

When the noon siren sounded he was nibbling at his finger nails and thinking about getting the hell out of the accounting business. Larson stood up and sat down a couple of times without getting any action, and finally said, "Excuse me. I hate to interrupt, pal, but it's twelve o'clock and I've got a katzenjammer that's tearing my head off. If I don't get a drink soon I'm going to fall apart."

"So am I. I've got to think. You run down to the corner and get yourself fixed up."

"The Lieutenant would love that. He'd think it was real nice if somebody came in here and put a couple of slugs in you while I was out leaning against a bar."

"I wouldn't want you to get in trouble just because someone shot me," said Whit. "Let's go."

They went down to the alley and had a few gin fizzes and some corned beef and cabbage. The gloom began to lift a little. On the way back to the office they stopped at the bank and Whit got some papers out of his safe deposit box for Webster. Larson bought some gum in the lobby, just in case.

The detective was waiting for them when they returned. He sniffed and looked sharply at Larson. Larson kept as far away from him as possible.

"You get those papers?" Webster asked Whit.

"Help yourself." Whit handed them over.

The detective struggled through the *whereases*, *hereinbefores* and *notwithstandings* of the partnership agreement, looked at the insurance policies, made some notes in his little black book, and handed the lot back with a sigh of relief. "That cleans up the legal end of it," he said. "I went over to see MacLeod's lawyer and looked at his will. For a man that didn't get along with his wife he treated her all right."

"What did he leave her?"

"Everything, free and clear. The lawyer says it'll come to a hundred and fifty thousand dollars, not counting what you pay for the business. I wouldn't want to think anything nasty about someone as nice as Mrs. MacLeod, but she had plenty of reason for doing the job. Plenty."

"She didn't do it."

"How do you know? Your womanly intuition?"

"She isn't the type, that's all."

"There aren't any types. I'm not saying she killed him, but there isn't anyone in the world who wouldn't commit murder if the circumstances were right."

"The old psychology kid," Whit said. "Tell me more."

Webster scoffed at him. "All you amateur detectives are full of ideas about types that do and types that don't."

"I'm not a detective. I'm just telling you that Kitty MacLeod didn't kill her husband, and you're wasting your time if you've got her on the list. You know as well as I do it was someone mixed up with the tax case, and she isn't."

"Maybe."

"Oh, for Christ's sake," said Whit. "You're not going to be convinced until somebody fills me full of lead, are you?"

"It might prove your point, anyway. If she isn't the one who does it."

"I'm sure going to have to show you the hard way. What else do you know that's cheerful?"

Webster didn't know anything, cheerful or otherwise. He had sweated the elevator operators, the girl at the cigar stand in the lobby, and tenants of offices on the seventh, eighth and ninth floors. His score was still zero. Saturday afternoon was a slack period in the building, and with only two elevators running it had been easy to check on comings and goings during the afternoon. Besides Marston, who had come in not earlier than a quarter to seven, and MacLeod, only two clerks returning from lunch had got off at the eighth floor during the afternoon, and they had left early. Both elevator operators were sure that if anyone but Marston had been in the building who wasn't a tenant, he hadn't used the elevators.

"I didn't expect to get anywhere with the elevator boys, anyway," Webster said. "There's a stairway at the back of the lobby. A herd of elephants could have gone up without attracting any attention. The girl at the cigar counter closed up at three, and after six there was only one elevator going. So anybody could have got to the stairs while the elevator was up. If he didn't take the stairs he could use the fire-escape."

"That's what I call real progress," said Whit.

"Nobody knows anything. If I could get a little cooperation I'd hang the murder on Marston just to get rid of it. He was the only one on the eighth floor within two hours of the shooting."

"What's stopping you?"

"The coroner. He won't budge an inch. MacLeod was dead before six-thirty, that's his story, and I'm stuck with it. Marston got here at ten or twelve minutes of seven."

"My heart bleeds for you," Whit said. "Did I tell you I telephoned Marian Wolff? All she knows about the case is what she reads in the newspapers. MacLeod didn't even mention it to her."

Webster said, "I quit. If we don't get something from those stockholders this afternoon I'm going to resign from the force."

They went to the meeting in a police car when Marston arrived, and on the way Webster explained to the lawyer the purpose of the newspaper story. Marston was not enthusiastic about it; if Whit got killed there would be no refund claims filed. Whit asked if anybody had considered his viewpoint and a three-way argument developed which lasted until they arrived at the brewery.

The stockholders' meeting was presided over by Mr. Elwood Hall, president of the corporation. Mr. Hall had a long horse-face and the manner of an undertaker cheering the bereaved. At two o'clock sharp he took a gold turnip from his vest pocket, checked the time, and rapped on the table.

"Gentlemen," he said. The gentlemen included Whit, Marston, Webster, Larson, and two of the other stockholders—Mr. DeWitt, a slick young man with a hairline mustache who had been introduced as the secretary and treasurer, and Mr. Harrigan. Mr. Harrigan was about sixty and very sporty with spats, a walking stick, and a boutonniere. He seemed to be the only human being of the three. It didn't take any of Whit's womanly intuition to see that Mr. Hall and Mr. DeWitt hated each other's guts. He couldn't blame either of them.

"Gentlemen," said Mr. Hall. "This meeting was arranged at the request of Mr. George MacLeod, at one time auditor of our corporation. You are all aware that Mr. MacLeod has—ah—passed away, and I feel that we should extend our sympathy to his associate, Mr. Whitney." He bowed to Whit.

Whit inclined his head reverently. Hall was a natural for an undertaker; all he needed was white gloves.

Mr. Hall continued. "Lieutenant Webster of the San Francisco Police Department has asked that the meeting be held despite Mr. MacLeod's death, in order that he might ask us certain questions. I shall turn the floor over to Lieutenant Webster." He sat down. Mr. DeWitt yawned loudly.

"Thanks," said Webster. "You've all read the papers so you know why we're here. I'm going to ask Mr. Whitney and Mr. Marston to do the talking, but I'd like to know a couple of things first. What did MacLeod say to you Saturday, Mr. Hall?"

Mr. Hall folded his hands. "I don't remember the exact conversation, Lieutenant. He identified himself—I had not seen him for some time, several years at least. Let me see—it was—"

"Never mind. What did he say?"

DeWitt snickered. Mr. Hall did not look at him. "He asked me to arrange this meeting. Naturally I was surprised at the request, and I asked him the reason for it. At first he was reluctant to tell me anything but I declined to act unless he did, and he finally said that he had discovered evidence pertaining to Harald Wolff's income tax—ah—difficulties which would be of great interest to all of us. He was very insistent and I finally agreed to call the meeting for this afternoon."

"Was that all of the conversation?"

"That was all."

"I see," said Webster. "What time did he call you?"

"Shortly before one. I had just returned from lunch."

"How soon after that did you call the stockholders?"

"Immediately, those that I could reach. I felt that they should be given as much advance notice as possible."

"Those that you could reach," Webster repeated. "How many stockholders are there, Mr. Hall?"

"Five. Mr. Harrigan, DeWitt"—he didn't bother with the Mister—"Mr. Swift, Mr. Putnam, and myself. Mr. Putnam has been in the East for some weeks. Mr. Swift—ah—declined to attend."

"Why?"

"He is an invalid, for one thing. He—"

Harrigan said, "That's not the reason. He's an old man with an ingrowing disposition. He wouldn't come because Hall couldn't tell him what it was all about and because he thought Wolff was a crook and he wouldn't have anything to do with him, even after he was dead."

"Is that so?" said Webster. "How did you feel about Mr. Wolff, Mr. Harrigan?"

"He was a crook and I liked him." Harrigan beamed at the detective in a friendly fashion. Whit thought he was a nice old guy.

"Fair enough. One thing more, Mr. Hall. You had a man named Zimmermann working here a couple of years ago. Do you know where he is now?"

Mr. Hall had no idea. "He was discharged shortly after Mr. Wolff died. I don't know what happened to him."

The detective questioned DeWitt and Harrigan. They had no idea either. Webster began to look irritated. Whit said, "May I ask a question, Lieutenant?"

"Go ahead."

Whit said, "Didn't MacLeod ask about Zimmermann, Mr.

Hall?"

"No."

"Are you sure?"

Mr. Hall looked at Whit down his nose. "Positive."

Whit explained. "I'm not questioning your statement, Mr. Hall, but Mr. MacLeod had been looking at some old records in our files, and one of the papers was a record of Zimmermann's payments to Mr. Wolff. I think MacLeod may have been interested in getting in touch with him."

"Mr. MacLeod did not mention his name, Mr. Whitney."

Whit tried another approach. "Zimmermann's list showed that he made no payments during the first part of August, either in 1921 or 1922. Does that mean anything to you?"

"Mr. Wolff frequently went hunting in the fall. He was quite a sportsman. I imagine that the—ah—blanks in Zimmermann's record were the periods during which Mr. Wolff was away."

"You can think of no other reason for them?"

"No."

Whit said, "All right. Thanks."

DeWitt had been slouched in his chair fiddling with a pencil. He pointed the pencil at Whit and frowned. It was a perfect picture of the keen-minded business executive. He said, "Now then, Mr. Whitney. We've all read the papers, but I'm frank to confess this is a little deep for me. Just what is it all about?"

Mr. Big Shot, thought Whit. It's a little deep for you, all right. He said, "Well, it's a little deep for all of us, Mr. DeWitt. Wolff paid—or Mr. Marston paid for him, as his executor, a million dollars in income taxes. My partner discovered something that proved the taxes were twice as much as they should have been, and he was murdered before he could do anything about it. We're trying to find out what he knew."

DeWitt nodded, pursing his lips. "I see." He sounded dubious.

Marston had been writing on the back of an envelope. He handed it to Whit and said, "Mr. Hall, there were six stockholders who formed this corporation in 1913, if I remember correctly. One was Mr. Wolff, you were another. Can you tell us the names of the others?"

"I was one," Harrigan volunteered. "Buster's father here was one."

DeWitt winced at "Buster." Larson snickered. Harrigan nodded appreciatively at him.

"Mr. Wolff, Mr. Harrigan, Mr. DeWitt, senior"—there was an implication that Buster didn't like— "Mr. Putnam, who is now in New York, Mr. Roberts, and I. Mr. Roberts died in 1920 and Mr. Swift purchased his stock. DeWitt inherited his stock from his father in 1929, I believe."

"So there are three of the original stockholders left— you, Mr. Harrigan, and Mr. Putnam?"

"Yes."

Whit had been reading Marston's note. He said, "I understand there was an agreement among the stockholders that those living should have the option of purchasing the shares of a deceased stockholder, or that any stockholder wishing to sell should make a first offer to the others. Is that right?"

"It is."

"But Mr. DeWitt's stock went to his son, and Mr.—the other

man—"

"Mr. Roberts."

"Mr. Roberts' stock went to an outsider."

"Yes." Hall looked gloomier than usual. He had guessed wrong on that stock and it still hurt. "Mr. Roberts and Mr. DeWitt died at a time when the brewing business was—ah—not a prosperous one. None of us wished to exercise his option and the stock passed out of our hands. When Mr. Wolff died in 1935 we were a little more far-seeing. We each acquired one-fifth of his interest."

Buster had been doing some heavy thinking. He aimed the pencil at Whit's chest again. "Mr. Whitney, am I correct in assuming that you believe Mr. Wolff did not receive the money from his bootlegging in 1921 and 1922?"

"We're inclined to think he got only part of it, Mr. DeWitt." Whit almost said "Buster."

"The papers said that there was strong evidence that he did not actually receive the money."

Whit shrugged. "Well, you know the papers. We think he got about half, and someone else got the rest."

"Whom have you selected for the other culprit?"

Webster didn't like Buster any more than Whit did. He said, "We haven't got any favorites, yet. Maybe your old man."

DeWitt was indignant. "See here, Lieutenant—"

"Hey," interrupted Harrigan, pounding with his cane. "You can't leave me out. And what about Hall over here? He always liked money."

"Mr. Harrigan!" Hall was also indignant.

Harrigan said, "Why don't you confess, Elwood?"

Larson leaned over and whispered in Whit's ear, "Screwballs." Whit nodded.

Webster said, "We're not leaving anyone out. Someone murdered MacLeod, and it could have been one of you." He looked around the table. "Eventually we'll find out who it was. In the meantime I want each of you to send me a statement accounting for your time from one o'clock to seven Saturday afternoon." He took his hat from the floor under his chair and stood up.

Mr. Hall said, "You're implying—" and Webster shut him off. "I'm not implying anything, Mr. Hall. If you can establish a satisfactory alibi I won't have to consider you a suspect. I'm trying to save myself trouble."

Buster had his last idea for the day. This time he pointed the pencil at Webster. "Have you considered the possibility that Wolff may have been murdered, too?"

"Wolff wasn't murdered." Webster was turning to go. "He jumped out of an airplane and—" He stopped abruptly and looked at DeWitt with his mouth open. "Sweet Jesus," he said. "I never thought of that."

CHAPTER ELEVEN

WHIT'S SUNBURN had reached the itchy stage. Going back across the Bay Bridge in the police car he scratched himself absent-mindedly and wondered how he could be so dumb.

It disgusted him that he had given so much thought to the Wolff case without picking up something obvious enough for DeWitt to see. There was no doubt but that Buster had rung the bell. Wolff had been murdered; it had to be true because it explained so many things.

Zimmermann's testimony had been given before Wolff's death, not afterward, which meant that Zimmerman had not feared a day of reckoning. So Wolff's murder had been planned in advance. Mr. X had anticipated the day when the Treasury Department would be asking questions, and against that time he had prepared himself by bribing or bullying Zimmermann and Wolff's aviator into line. When the time came, Zimmerman had thrown Wolff to the sharks and Wolff's pilot had killed him before he could talk. Everything had been lovely until MacLeod poked his nose in, and then it became necessary to shut MacLeod up. Even if he hadn't been able to make the refund claim stick he would have brought the Government into the case, and if the G-men got interested it would be all up with Mr. X, Zimmermann and the aviator. Were they two people or three?

Whit broke a long silence in the back seat of the car. "We certainly were smart about that airplane accident."

"You don't have to argue with me," said Webster sourly. "I've been kicking myself for half an hour. Can you imagine someone like DeWitt figuring it out for us? It makes me want to go back to pounding a beat."

The conversation lapsed. Larson, in the front seat, told a dirty story to the driver in a low voice and they both guffawed. Marston said, "I suppose the thing to do now is find the aviator."

"Carpenter," said Webster. "I'm going to enjoy working on him. Jimmying a parachute strikes me as being a nasty way to kill your boss."

"Where are you going to look for him?" asked Whit. "Nobody has heard of him since Wolff was killed. You've at least got a description of Zimmermann, but all you know about Carpenter is that he could fly a plane."

"That's enough. If he was a licensed pilot I'll get all I need from the Department of Commerce. Sooner or later I'm going to catch up with him and Zimmermann too, and when I do—" He rubbed his hands. "I'll cram that phony airplane accident down their throats."

"Sooner or later," said Marston. "That's the trouble. There's no doubt in my mind that you'll catch them some day, Lieutenant, but if you don't do it by Friday it isn't going to help." He looked at Whit. "You understand me, Whitney. I want to see MacLeod's murderer brought to justice whatever happens. But—"

"We're all in agreement," Whit said. "I'd like to make that

fifty thousand dollars. As it looks now, if we can't find the murderer our claims aren't going to be worth a damn." No one disagreed with him. He said, "I'd like to file them anyway, just to stir up trouble for somebody."

"What are you worrying about?" Webster asked. "It isn't Friday yet."

"It's getting there too fast to suit me."

The conversation died again. The police car turned off down the First Street ramp, and its tires sang as the driver pulled it around the curve. At the bottom of the ramp they turned left, crossed Market and started up Front Street. Whit said, "Tell your driver to drop me at my office, will you?"

"Sure." Webster leaned forward. "Up California, Jack." The driver nodded. Webster said, "Where can I let you off, Mr. Marston?"

"I'll get out with Whitney. It's only a couple of blocks to my office."

"I wish you'd come up and look at my papers," said Whit. "Either something has been stolen or I'm overlooking the clue. I've been through the whole file twice, page by page, and I can't see a thing in it. You might have better luck."

"All right. But I'm not a tax man; don't rely on me to find anything that you can't."

"DeWitt humbled me. Come and look anyway."

The car stopped in front of the Farmers' Exchange and they got out. Marston said, "What are you going to do now, Lieutenant?"

"Wire the Department of Commerce. If Carpenter is still flying a plane they'll know where he is. When we catch up with him we'll get somewhere. Are you going to see Marian Wolff, Whitney?"

"Tonight."

"I hope you get something from her. Swede, you keep your eyes open, and remember what I told you about drinking. You smelled pretty ginny to me this afternoon."

"I wouldn't drink on duty, Lieutenant. You know me." Larson was full of honest indignation.

"Sure I know you, but I'll take a chance. Just remember what will happen to you if Whitney gets shot and you don't bring in the man who does it."

"It's perfectly all right if I get shot so long as he gets the guy, isn't it?" Whit asked.

"You can't expect everything," Webster said. "Let's go, Jack." The police car pulled away.

At the office Miss Kelly had a sheaf of memoranda for Whit—telephone messages. He shuffled through them and handed them back to her. "I don't want to be bothered with anything that isn't absolutely essential. Stall everyone you can until next week and let Mr. Krebs handle anything that has to be done. I'll be free by Monday."

"I'll take care of everything, Mr. Whitney," said Miss Kelly "You needn't worry a bit. It's a terrible strain, isn't it? You poor dear."

"Terrible," said Whit.

Marston still looked surprised when Whit led him into the office and closed the door. "Is that your regular office procedure . . . you poor dear?"

"She has a maternal complex. I can't fire her because she wants to hold me on her lap, can I?"

"I would," Marston said. "Like a shot. Let's see your papers."

Krebs had made a list in his careful handwriting of all the

documents which had come out of the folder, and it was clipped to the front of the envelope. Whit said, "That's what is here now. We found the file inside the locked safe in the vault, but someone who was careful about his fingerprints had either closed the safe or tried to open it. Webster has an idea that he may have got at the file and pinched whatever was dangerous. Can you think of anything that should be here and isn't?"

The lawyer looked at the list and went carefully through the pile of papers on the desk, checking against the list as he examined them. When he had seen them all he shook his head. "I'm afraid I'm not much help. It's been four years since I thought about these, and some of the documents don't even look familiar. If anything is gone I couldn't tell."

"Four years is a long time," Whit said. "Why were these papers left with us? Don't they belong with your records?"

"I suppose they do. MacLeod had always handled Wolff's tax work and he really was in charge of this case. I was glad to turn everything over to him, and when he finished with these I suppose he automatically put them in his files. You might let me have them when you're through."

"After Friday I'll lose all interest. You can have them then."

Someone knocked on the office door. Whit said, "Come in" and Krebs entered with the sheaf of telephone memoranda in his hand. When he saw Marston he said, "Excuse me. I thought you were alone."

He turned to leave.

Whit called him back and made introductions. Krebs shook hands with the lawyer. "I remember Mr. Marston. We have met before."

"Yes, of course." Marston was politely blank.

"Several years ago. You were in to see Mr. MacLeod."

"Oh, certainly." The lawyer nodded. "On the same business that brings me here now."

The three men talked for a few minutes and Marston left. Whit said, "You didn't tell me you knew him, Krebs."

"I did not think to. I saw him only once or twice." He held out the memorandum blanks. "We shall need help, Mr. Whitney."

"Can't you handle it?"

"No. It is too much for one man. Without you or Mr. MacLeod, there is more work than can be done. Tommy is a good boy but he has not the experience."

"I'll be back on the job in a few days. I'm going to concentrate on this case until Friday, and if I don't get somewhere by then—" He spread his hands out, palms up. "I'll go back to being an accountant."

Krebs looked doubtfully at the slips of paper in his hand. "We shall still need help. Someone must take Mr. MacLeod's place."

"All right. Hire a C.P.A.; hire a couple of men on a temporary basis and we'll keep the best one."

"You wish me to do it?" Krebs had worked twenty years for MacLeod and MacLeod had never let the reins out of his own hands.

"I told you to take charge, Krebs. Your judgment is good enough for me."

Krebs said, "Thank you, Mr. Whitney." He left the room.

Whit had three hours to go before his appointment with Marian Wolff, and he did not feel like spending them mousing over the Wolff file. He still had the remnants of his hangover, his head was fuzzy, and for the sake of his clients he needed a clear mind. He said, "Come on, Swede. Bodyguard me down to the bar."

They had a couple of highballs and went to an Italian restaurant in North Beach. The bottle of wine that came with their dinner was a help, and the coffee and rum they had for dessert was the final touch. Larson said, "This is the first time I've felt human all day. That champagne last night almost stopped my clock."

"A big tough guy like you, too," said Whit. "Maybe you ought to remember what the Lieutenant said about drinking. You don't want to be stiff when the shooting starts."

"I'm never too stiff. Shooting is one thing I can do drunk or sober."

"Like my driving."

"No. I'm real good with a gun."

"You don't say?"

Larson finished his coffee, pushed the cup to one side, and moved his chair back against the wall of the booth. "I'll show you something." He put his hands on his knees. "Watch me and figure what you'd do if I wanted to plug you."

Whit watched and felt better about his chances of survival. Larson was really fast. He could put his hand inside his coat and take a gun from under his arm while Whit was waiting for him to start moving. He performed two or three times, beaming at Whit's surprised appreciation.

Whit said, "You are good. How are you when it comes to pulling the trigger?"

"I usually hit what I shoot at. I worked in a carnival for a while, shooting cigarettes out of guys' mouths. I never spoiled any faces."

"I thought that only happened in the movies. Where did you pick up these parlor tricks?"

"I haven't been a cop all my life."

"I could have guessed that. What else were you?"

"A lot of things," Larson said shortly. He wasn't giving out information and Whit didn't ask any more questions. But he was curious. He decided to speak to Webster about Larson.

They killed time at the restaurant drinking rum and playing the nickel piano. It was a quarter of eight when they left for Marian Wolff's, and the fog had come in from the ocean. Whit turned on the windshield wipers. Larson said, "Sort of wet out tonight. Let's leave the main to'g'ns'l alone."

Whit laughed.

They drove up the Union Street hill and turned over to Green. Whit slowed down and peered through the fog at the house numbers. He spotted Marian Wolff's apartment house on the other side of the street and parked under a street light across from the building.

Larson belched, getting out of the car. "I like a good wop dinner. It stays with you."

"It's all right once in a while. Too heavy for a regular diet."

They stood in the street waiting for a car to pass. It was a big shiny Buick. Light from the street lamps was reflected from its slick wet hood. It wasn't going fast. Whit said, "Come on, come on," under his breath and moved forward a step. The Buick drew abreast of him and a man in the back seat leaned forward and put his hand through the open window. Larson said, "Hey," and jerked Whit backward as the gun went off. The slug hit Whit in the side and the shock turned him around so that he was facing Larson. His knees buckled, and he caught at Larson to save himself. Larson bellowed, "Let go, god damn it. Let go!" from a long way off. Whit heard guns roar as he went under.

CHAPTER TWELVE

A MILLION YEARS later Whit woke up. Someone had hit him in the ribs with a meat-cleaver and he tried unsuccessfully to remember when it had happened. The pillow in his mouth bothered him; he turned his head to one side and a stab of pain made his ears ring. He said, "Ow!" His memory returned.

He was lying face down on a bed and somebody was fussing with his back. A brisk voice said, "Just hold still, please." A hand came over his shoulder and pressed a piece of adhesive tape against his collar bone. The voice said, "Now. Let's turn him over." Hands took hold of him and rolled him on his back.

Light glared in his eyes from a floor lamp drawn up beside the bed. The brisk voice belonged to a fat man who was bent over him sticking more adhesive tape to his ribs. Larson stood at one side of the bed, cramping the fat man's professional style, and the most beautiful blonde in the world was on the other. She looked anxious.

Whit said, "Hello," and smiled at the blonde. "I'll bet you're Marian Wolff." George's description of her had been a fair statement.

"Yes. How do you feel?"

"Terrible. Will I live?"

The fat man answered him. "You're going to be all right. Just relax and be quiet." He tore pieces of tape from the roll in his hand.

Whit looked at Larson. "Did you get him?"

"Nope." Larson shook his head gloomily. "There were two. I'd have nailed them both if you hadn't of tied me up. You almost took me down with you."

"Blame it on me," said Whit. "Did you recognize them?"

"They didn't look like anyone I ever saw before. I got the license number, though, and I hit the car. I may have winged somebody."

"Does Webster know about it?"

Larson scowled. "Not yet. I was waiting to see how bad you was hit."

"You know now. Go call him. Tell him I just proved my argument."

"He's going to be sore." Larson was unhappy.

"Is it my fault? Go on, call him."

Larson reluctantly left the bedside. The doctor finished his bandaging job and took a hypodermic syringe from his bag. Whit said, "What's that for?"

"Stop the pain and put you to sleep." The doctor pinched the flesh of Whit's arm between his fingers and aimed the syringe.

"I can't go to sleep here." Whit looked at the girl. He wouldn't mind sleeping there some other time, without a bullet wound, but this night even if he were welcome it would be a waste of hospitality.

"Stop arguing," the girl said. "Go ahead, doctor."

The doctor hadn't waited. He withdrew the needle and wiped Whit's arm with a piece of cotton. Whit said, "How bad is it, Doc."

"Not serious. There's a big hole in your side and you've lost a lot of blood, but the bullet didn't penetrate the abdominal cavity. You'll be laid up for a while."

"What sort of a bullet was it?"

"I couldn't say; it didn't lodge in your body. It slid along your rib for six or seven inches and came out in back."

"Could it have been a steel jacketed, small caliber bullet —about a twenty-five?"

"Oh, no." The doctor was quite positive. "I'd say it was a large bullet and definitely soft-nosed. The cut indicates that it mushroomed. A steel jacketed bullet wouldn't have done that."

"Oh" Whit said. "Thanks." Now what the hell? Two murderers?

Larson came back, very red in the face. The doctor questioned him and Whit about the circumstances of the shooting, took down names and addresses, filled out a report, and picked up his bag. To Whit he said, "You'd better stay in bed for a couple of weeks. Do you want me to send you to a hospital?"

"A couple of weeks? I have to go to work tomorrow."

"Out of the question. You should lie flat on your back for a week at the very least."

Whit was stubborn. "I can't do it. I'm not going to any hospital and I'm not going to stay in bed."

The doctor shrugged. "It's your bullet hole. I'll come by your home tomorrow morning and look in on you. If you get up and wander around before that wound heals you're going to have trouble. Good night."

Marian Wolff went to the door with him. When she came back to the bedroom, Larson had propped Whit up with some pillows and was lighting a cigarette for him. Larson said unhappily, "The Lieutenant is coming out here. He was mad as hell."

"I'll make it as easy on you as I can," Whit said. "Miss Wolff and I want to talk business. Why don't you go into the other room and relax?"

"Is it private?"

"Not particularly."

"I'll stay here. I can't take no more chances."

Marian Wolff said indignantly, "I like that."

"I didn't mean you, ma'am," said Larson. "I was thinking of someone trying to finish the job through the window or something. I got to keep an eye on him."

Whit looked at the open window. "Maybe you're right. If you don't mind, Miss Wolff, he can stay. I have a nervous temperament."

"I don't blame you." The girl pulled up a chair and sat by the bed. "What is it all about, Mr. Whitney? First George MacLeod's murder, and now an attempt to kill you—" She shivered. "It's horrible. I don't understand it."

Whit had planned originally to spare her sensibilities as much as possible, but after his entrance she should be immune to further shock. He said, "It starts with your father's death, not MacLeod's. Your father was murdered too."

The girl had a lot of control. She looked at him for a moment and said, "What makes you think so?"

"That airplane accident was a fake. He was on the way to Washington with information which would cost someone a lot of money and a few years in jail. The someone fixed it with the pilot so he never got there. MacLeod was killed because he discovered what had happened, and I was shot because I'm supposed to know, too."

"Don't you?"

"No. But I'm going to find out."

Whit looked around for an ashtray. The girl handed him one from the bedside table. He said, "Thanks. I'll skip the technical side of what I do know, Miss Wolff. The million dollars that your father's estate had to pay in tax was about twice what it should have been. He got only part of the bootlegging proceeds. Whoever shared with him fixed it to look as if your father had got all the money, and then had him killed. MacLeod found out about it and was going to get part of the tax back and incidentally get the other man into a lot of trouble. So he was murdered—before I found out what he knew. I wanted to talk to you because I thought he might have told you something."

"He didn't. We didn't even discuss my father."

"What did you telephone him about Friday?"

"My own income taxes. The Government sent me a notice that I should have made a report for 1938 and I didn't know what to do about it."

"You saw him Friday night?"

"I went to dinner at his house and gave him the information so he could make out my report."

"He drove you home that night?"

"Yes."

"What time was it?"

"Ten or ten-thirty."

"Do you know where he went when he left you?"

"No. Kitty asked me that. He came up here for a few minutes and—he was drunk." She blushed. "I had a hard time making him leave."

It sounded like George all right. He wouldn't let a young beauty like Marian get away from him without a struggle, particularly if he was tight. Whit said, "I can believe it. I'd like to know where he went."

"Does it have any connection with his murder?"

Whit shook his head doubtfully. "It's probably only a coincidence. From what he told me on the phone and from what you say, he didn't suspect anything until Saturday morning. There wasn't any reason to kill him until then."

"Did he suspect anyone, Mr. Whitney? I mean anyone in particular?"

"I don't think so, except that it may have been one of the brewery stockholders. We know now that there were several people involved in your father's death—the bookkeeper at the brewery was one, and the aviator who piloted your father's plane. The police are looking for them now." Whit yawned. "Excuse me." The hypodermic was beginning to take effect.

"Why did he—they—try to kill you, if you don't know anything?"

"They think I do. You see, we only have four more days in which we can get back the money that was paid to the Government, and we need some action. The story you read in the newspaper was a trap—the theory was that the murderer would have to try to kill me and Larson would catch him. The trap worked all right, but—well—"

"Go ahead," Larson said. He was sitting by the window. "I dropped the ball"

"It wasn't your fault. Things didn't break right."

Larson grunted. "I hope the Lieutenant thinks so."

Marian said, "Mr. Whitney, may I ask you something personal?"

"Depends. How personal?"

"Why are you doing this? I mean, why are you risking your life this way when you could let the police worry about it?"

"I always wanted to be a detective. Lieutenant Webster is going to give me a badge so I can—"

"Please."

"Risking my life wasn't my idea, Miss Wolff. I'd rather go about it some other way. But I'd like to catch the man who shot my partner, and I have to make my living." He yawned again. "Mr. Marston offered me ten per cent of whatever I can get back from the Government. My share would amount to about fifty thousand dollars—if I get anything at all."

The girl was silent. Whit looked at her. "That's a reasonable fee in the circumstances, Miss Wolff. If you don't approve of the arrangement I'll be glad to retire from the case."

"Oh, no. It seems very fair. Only—I don't like Frank Marston making arrangements without consulting me."

Whit said, "Oh. I see." He was learning a few things, anyway. Marian Wolff did not like the executor of her father's estate.

"What if you fail?" Marian asked.

"If I fail, I'm out of luck. You haven't any money, have you?"

"No." She smiled at him. "I'm sorry."

"It's a chance I have to take." He yawned again. "Sorry. That shot in the arm is putting me to sleep. As soon as Lieutenant Webster arrives I'll get out."

"I don't think you ought to be moved, Mr. Whitney. You're perfectly welcome to stay. I have an extra bed."

"No, thanks." He shook his head, yawning. "I'd be in the way."

A siren screamed up the street and choked off in front of the house. Larson got up and went reluctantly into the front room. Whit grinned at the girl. "Comes now the music," he said. "This bullet hole is going to hurt Larson more than it hurts me."

"Poor man. He was terribly upset when he brought you in here. He carried you all the way up from the street, and when I answered the bell he was standing there with a pistol in his hand and you over his shoulder, all covered with blood. I almost slammed the door in his face and screamed."

"We must have been pretty." Whit yawned again. The throbbing in his side was less and he was having trouble keeping his eyes open.

"You were." He saw her smile through a pleasant mist.

The buzzer sounded as Whit was sleepily considering turning the conversation to personal subjects. With a girl like Marian, it was a shame to discuss anything else. But it was just too much trouble to talk.

She got up and went out of the room to answer the door. Whit closed his eyes happily . . . nice pair of legs . . . if he lived through this job he might . . .

Webster's angry voice in the other room dragged Whit back into semi-consciousness. Larson was paying for his sins.

Webster said, "Well, lamebrain. What's the alibi this time?"

Larson mumbled something in response. Whit started to drift off again, and Webster came into the bedroom. He said, "Wake up. How do you feel?"

"Wonderful." Whit kept his eyes closed.

"How bad are you hit?"

"Going to die," mumbled Whit. "Go away."

"Wake up. Are you hit bad?"

Larson said, "The slug glanced off his rib. It wasn't a twenty-five, Lieutenant. The gun sounded to me like—"

"Who asked you?" said Webster. "I wouldn't trust you to tell me the time."

"Wasn't his fault," Whit said dreamily. "Good man, the Swede. Saved my life."

"Nuts." Webster was soured on Larson. "You want to go to the hospital?"

"He's not supposed to be moved, Lieutenant," Marian Wolff said. "The doctor told him to lie flat on his back for a week or two. Any moving around now would be dangerous. And he won't go to the hospital."

"You don't want him lying flat on his back in your bed, do you?"

"I don't want him to die."

"He isn't going to die. I'll get an ambulance and a stretcher and take him home."

"Rather stay here," Whit said indistinctly. "Do my best work in the field. Miss Wolff and I—" He went to sleep.

"Home or the hospital, whichever you like," said Webster with finality. "Swede, get an ambulance."

Larson went to the telephone. Webster said, "I know you

want to help, Miss Wolff, but he has to be some place where I can have a man watching him. If he stayed here, someone else would have to be here with him. Two men would make it pretty crowded for you."

"I could manage if I had to. But you do what you think is best."

"Home's the best place for him."

Webster went into the other room. Larson was hanging up the receiver. Webster said, "All right, Swede. What happened?"

Larson told him.

"What were you doing when this torpedo poked a gun out of the window—looking at the moon?"

"It happened too fast. I tried to pull Whitney out of the way and he fell into me. The car was half way down the block before I could get loose."

"You trick shooters give me a pain in the pratt. You look like a million bucks on the target range and when the money's up you couldn't hit the wall if you were locked in a closet."

Larson's neck began to get red.

"Did you get a look at the guy that did the shooting?"

"Not much. He didn't put his face in the light."

"Did you get the license number?"

"Yes. And I plugged the car a couple of times before it got around the corner. I may have winged somebody."

"You probably winged somebody in the next block."

Larson wasn't enjoying himself. Webster thought for a while and said, "It wasn't the twenty-five?"

"No. It sounded like a forty-five. Anyway, it was a soft-nosed

nosed slug; it spread out on his rib."

"It couldn't have been a steel jacket?"

"God, no. You should have seen the hole in him. It wasn't no steel jacket."

"Oh, for Christ's sake." Webster was disgusted. "Nothing in this whole case happens the way it should."

The buzzer sounded and Marian came out of the bedroom. Three men came in when she opened the door. One of them had a camera mounted with a flashlight bulb. The shortest one of the three said, "'Lo, Lieutenant. I hear tell there was some more shooting. What's the story?"

He was talking to Webster but his eyes were on Marian. So were those of the other reporters, and the one with the camera moved into the room to get a clear shot. Maybe the girl didn't have anything to do with the story, but that was someone else's lookout. A good-looking blonde was enough for the photographer.

Larson said, "Lieutenant, maybe if I told these guys—"

Webster said, "Shut up." The camera bulb flashed. The gentlemen of the press reluctantly turned away from the girl, and Webster said, "Here's your story. Now for God's sake try to get it straight, will you?"

CHAPTER THIRTEEN

NEITHER the ambulance ride nor being undressed and put to bed disturbed Whit's sleep. He had leaked some in transit, and the ambulance men changed his bandages before they left. When they were gone and Whit was snoring in his own bedroom, Webster had it out with Larson.

"Swede, I put you on to cover this man because you're fast with a gun, not because I thought you weren't dumb. Maybe it takes more brains than I thought. Maybe I ought to pull you off and put on another man with more brains and less speed before something else happens."

"Nothing else is going to happen, Lieutenant. I would of got those guys only—"

"Only you missed the boat. You can't alibi this away, Swede. The only thing that counts is the results. I'm risking Whitney's neck and my own to find out who is after him, and if they get him it's going to be too goddamn bad for everybody. I'll bust you off the force before I get kicked off myself."

"Honest to Jesus, Lieutenant—"

"Never mind. I'll give you a chance to save your neck. If you want to get off the job now I'll put someone else on and you can go back to headquarters."

Larson was hurt. "I wouldn't quit now. I want another crack at those guys."

"It's up to you." Webster buttoned his coat. "Just remember what I said. If anything happens to Whitney— anything at all—God help you."

"Yessir." Larson believed him.

"And don't let the reporters see him. I don't care how you stop them, but don't let him talk before I get back."

"Yessir."

Webster left.

Larson went to look at his charge. The bedroom windows opened on a fire escape, and he closed and locked them and pulled down the shades. He did the same to the other windows in the apartment, examined the catch on the front door, and bolted the door leading from the kitchen to a back entrance. When he was satisfied that everything was secure he went back to the bedroom, refilled the magazine of his gun, pulled a chair around where he could watch the bed, and sat down for the night. Lieutenant Webster had made a strong impression on him.

When the effect of the hypodermic wore off about five in the morning, Whit woke up. His whole side throbbed and the close air of the room had given him a headache. He turned his head cautiously and saw Larson asleep in a chair across the room. "Hey, Swede," he said. "Burglars!"

Larson jumped, lifting the gun out of his lap. The safety catch clicked. Whit said quickly, "Don't shoot. Everything's under control."

Larson relaxed. "You don't want to scare me like that, pal. What's the matter?"

"I'm thirsty. Get me a glass of water, will you?"

Larson brought him a drink from the bathroom. Whit said, "How did I get here?"

"Ambulance."

"Did the blonde kick me out?"

"Nope. She wanted to keep you there, but the Lieutenant said you had to come home. You wouldn't have been any use to her in your condition."

"I'm going to have to speak to Webster. I was all set for a nice long convalescence with the blonde soothing my fevered brow and nursing me back to health. What did he have to butt in for?"

"He figured two of us would cramp her," Larson said. "Your brow would be fevered, all right. If that girl was to lay her hand on me I'd light up like a match." He shook his head reflectively. "Boy, what a twist."

"Not bad. How about opening a window?"

"What for?" Larson looked puzzled.

"Some fresh air. I'm tired of breathing this old stuff over and over."

It took an argument, but Larson finally opened one window six inches, Whit had another glass of water and tried to go back to sleep.

It was no use. The torn flesh in his side throbbed with each heartbeat, and the pain made his head ring even when he was perfectly still. For an hour he lay with his eyes closed and tried to take his mind off himself by hypothecating all possible circumstances which would explain the Wolff case. He assumed that everyone connected with it was guilty, singly and in groups—Marian Wolff, Marston, Kitty Mac-

Leod, Hall, Zimmermann, Carpenter, Harrigan, Buster De-Witt, the two dead stockholders (maybe a spirit had done the shooting), the stubborn one who wouldn't attend the meeting—he even built a case against himself. One suspect was as good as another. Whit arrived at three conclusions—*(a)* Zimmermann and/or Carpenter were the men to find; *(b)* logic did not arrive inevitably at a sound conclusion; and *(c)* there was no use trying to go back to sleep.

He woke Larson, had him make coffee, and drank two cups of it loaded with cognac. He was feverish and had no appetite, but the coffee and brandy made him feel better. Larson brought all the seat cushions from the davenport in the front room to build an inclined ramp on the bed so that Whit could sit up in comfort, and Whit brushed his teeth over a basin, had some more brandy with a little coffee in it, and smoked a cigarette. Larson had coffee, without brandy, and scrambled himself a half-dozen eggs.

Whit said, "Run out and get a paper, Swede. I ought to be getting some more publicity this morning."

"I will not. I'm not taking my eye off of you."

"You don't say? I'm going into the bathroom in a minute and I always close the door. What do you think of that?"

"I'll be there. I got my orders."

They compromised. Whit was weak in the knees and needed help to make the round trip from bed to bathroom, but he escaped the final indignity. Larson telephoned for the morning papers, and Whit was finally propped up again on the cushions with his publicity.

There was enough to make him happy. The wars were resting between air-raids, the president had said nothing of current importance, and the movie stars were temporarily out of trouble, so Whit and the Wolff case got the whole front page. His picture was in both papers (they had dug up a better photograph this time) and most of the space was given over to the shooting of the night before, supplemented by a rehash of the previous day's story. One paper printed a camera-man's snap-shot of Marian Wolff that didn't do her justice but was still worth looking at, and a diagram of the street with X marking the spot where he had been shot down. The story contained a bald statement that Whitney had "fired several shots at the speeding death car before he lapsed into unconsciousness."

"That was smart of me. Where were you all this time, Swede? You're not even mentioned."

"It was the Lieutenant's idea. I'm supposed to stay under cover and knock these guys off when they try it again. I guess he figures they thought I was a tree or something."

"*When* they try it again. Jesus, that's something to look forward to. What's this about me being at death's door?"

"It's the Lieutenant again. He wants you alive enough to be dangerous and dead enough not to be able to talk to the reporters."

"I'm not that dead. I'll talk to them if they come around."

Larson said, "Uh." It could have been interpreted any way Whit liked.

The fat doctor arrived at eight o'clock and was professionally pleased to find no sign of infection in Whit's wound. He changed the bandages, recommended a diet of liver, eggs and milk, emphasized the necessity for staying in bed for at least a week, and left. Whit agreed to everything as a matter of expediency and decided not to get up until the next day. He was still shaky and he could think of nothing that could be done until either Zimmermann or Carpenter was located. But he hated to waste the time. It would leave only Wednesday, Thursday, Friday—three days. The statute of limitations wouldn't wait because he had been shot.

The telephone at the bedside rang as soon as the doctor left. The first call was from the Associated Press. Could Mr. Whitney give their representative a statement if he were to call? It was the dignified approach. Larson answered the phone, said, "No," and hung up.

"Who was it?" Whit asked.

"The Fuller Brush man." It was all Whit could get from him. Whit's office was next. Miss Kelly had been crying again. Was Mr. Whitney still alive?

Whit took the phone. "I'm all right, Miss Kelly. Honest. You should know better than to believe what you read in the papers. I'll be down tomorrow."

"Oh, Mr. Whitney." She could hardly talk. She wept some more into the phone and put Krebs on the line.

"Hello," Whit said. "How are things going?"

"Are you all right, Mr. Whitney? The papers—"

"I've seen them. I'll be down tomorrow, Krebs."

"That is good. We were worried."

"Did you get any help?"

"I have some men coming in for interviews this afternoon. One man I know and he is very good and reliable. I shall select two that I think are the best, and you can let one go at any time. Is that satisfactory?"

"Fine. Has anything else happened?"

"No. Everything is running smoothly. You needn't worry."

"Is anyone going to MacLeod's funeral?"

"We should all like to go. If you do not mind we shall close the office for the morning."

"Sure. That's fine. Order a lot of flowers and send some in the firm's name and some in mine."

"I shall take care of it, Mr. Whitney."

"Swell. I'll see you tomorrow."

The next call was from Kitty. She had seen the papers, too, and sounded worried. When Whit explained that he was sore but safe, the relief in her voice was so apparent that it made him glow. It occurred to him that Kitty was the nicest girl he knew, with the possible exception of Marian Wolff. He said, "Kitty, you're a wonderful woman. You were really worried about me, now weren't you?"

"Of course I was worried about you, you fool."

"You like me, don't you, Kitty?"

"I can tell nothing is wrong with you. I'll see you after the funeral."

"I'm sorry I can't make it."

"I'm glad there aren't going to be two funerals. I'll stop in this afternoon. You stay in bed and act sensibly."

"O.K. Bring Miss Wolff along, will you? My bodyguard has a yen for her."

"How about you?"

"I prefer tall brunettes. She's just another client to me."

"I'll bring her for your bodyguard's sake. Good-bye."

Whit put the phone down. Larson said, "That's real nice of you, pal. Maybe you're fooling somebody."

"Maybe I am."

They played cribbage for a cent a point and double for skunks. Larson didn't know the game and Whit fancied himself as an expert, so he taught Larson the rudiments and lost three dollars and a half in the first four games. In the fifth game Larson started off with a twenty-four hand and held another two hands later while Whit was creeping up to the thirty hole. Larson said, "Why didn't I ever get on this gravy train before?"

"Beginner's luck. Anyway, I'm lucky at love, and you know how it goes."

"I wouldn't mind losing money if I could be lucky with that blonde frail."

"She's over your head, Swede. She's going to have half a million dollars if I live until Friday."

"You hope," Larson said. "It's your deal."

The doorbell rang when Whit was trying to peg three points to keep from being skunked. Larson put down his cards with the comment, "No funny business with the pegs, now," and went to the door.

The gentlemen of the press had arrived. They were leg men, old hands at the business of getting what they wanted. Four of them came crowding in when the door was opened. Larson was caught off guard for a moment, but he got between them and the bedroom, closed the door, and put his back against it.

"You boys go on home," he said. "Mr. Whitney can't see anyone today."

Whit yelled through the door, "Who is it, Swede?"

One of the reporters raised his voice. "The press, Mr. Whitney. We want a statement about the shooting."

"Let them come in, Swede."

The reporters moved forward in a body. Larson shook his head. "I'm sorry, gents. He's delirious. Run along like good boys."

A reporter said, "Look, fellah. All we want to do is speak to him for a minute and find out what this is all about. We're not going to hurt him."

"That's right. You ain't going to see him, either."

Whit yelled. "Swede, don't be a damn fool. Let them in."

Larson stayed where he was. The reporters looked at each other and back at Larson. Larson wiped the palms of his hands on his pants, grinning, and the fourth estate moved in on him.

There wasn't much to it. It was the first time Larson had had a fair chance to do a job he was fitted for, and he went about it with his whole heart. The reporter who had done the talking was in front; Larson banged him in the mouth with a left hook and caught the man behind him with a round-house swing. They both lost interest in the news of the day. The third reporter slugged Larson once in the eye before he was knocked flat on his back, and the fourth man fled from the apartment while Larson was stumbling over bodies to get at him. The whole thing took thirty seconds.

Larson lugged the bodies out of the apartment, dumped them in the hall, and went back to the cribbage game dabbing at his eye. "Them amateurs," he said. "Imagine a bunch of college boys like that starting a fight."

"Listen," Whit said frostily. "This is my home. In case you don't know it a man's home is his castle and he can have anyone he likes in it. Even reporters. Did you ever hear that?"

"I don't know," Larson said, feeling his eye. "You'll have to ask the Lieutenant. It's my lead." He picked up his cards.

CHAPTER FOURTEEN

BY NOON Whit had lost nine dollars and seventy-six cents and regained his appetite. Larson ordered supplies from the corner grocery store by telephone and made lunch for him—fried liver, soft-boiled eggs, and a glass of milk. Whit wouldn't have liked the liver even if it had been well cooked, but he was bullied into eating it. Larson had a literal mind. The doctor had said liver, eggs and milk, and Whit was going to get liver, eggs and milk until they ran out of his ears.

Lieutenant Webster arrived while Whit was brushing egg shells off his chest. Larson thought the reporters were back again when the buzzer sounded and went to the door ready to pay them off for his eye, which was beginning to turn green around the edges. Webster greeted him with a bawling out for not asking who wanted to get in before he opened the door, and Larson stayed away from the bedroom while Webster was there.

"How are you feeling?" the detective asked Whit.

"Pretty good. I'll be up tomorrow. Did you find the boys who did the shooting?"

"Not yet. We found the Buick—it was a stolen car. There were four bullet-holes in it, so I guess the Swede wasn't entirely asleep."

"Lucky for you he wasn't. You'd have had a hell of a lot of explaining to do if I had been killed because of your bright idea."

Webster grunted noncommittally. Whit said, "I don't know why I let you talk me into it. I've been lying here thinking of a lot of ways to get information without being a clay pigeon. Did you think of sweating the hired help at the brewery? One of the old-timers might know something about Zimmermann."

"That's where I spent the morning. The old-timers weren't talking. Nobody was talking. They were the worst bunch of clams I ever saw."

"How about Carpenter? Did you get anything on him?"

"I'm still waiting to hear from the Department of Commerce. They take their own time about answering wires. Another murder more or less doesn't bother Washington in these days."

There was a note of gloom in the detective's voice that Whit had not heard before. He said, "Cheer up. You've learned a few things, anyway. You can write some of your suspects off the list."

"Who?"

"Well, me. And Kitty MacLeod. And Marston. The shooting last night proves that MacLeod's murder was connected with Wolff's income taxes, doesn't it? That cuts Mrs. MacLeod out. Marston knew about the trap, so he wouldn't have fallen for it, and I'm out because I was damn near killed."

"The shooting seems to pin the murder down to the income tax business," Webster agreed. "But I still don't know who was involved in it. I can't see any connection between Mrs. MacLeod and Harald Wolff, but it could be there, and trap or no trap, Marston might want you out of the way enough to hire someone to get you. Nobody is clear until we find the right man—or woman."

"Marston could get rid of me by firing me off the job," said Whit. "Where do I stand? Am I still a suspect?"

"You're not at the head of the list," Webster said cautiously. "I've known men to shoot themselves or get themselves shot just to be free of suspicion, but not with a soft-nosed slug. I think if you had picked a gun you would have used the twenty-five. It would have been a lot less painful."

"Thanks. I'm glad to know you won't be after me if I live. Who's your new favorite?"

Webster shook his head doubtfully. "I haven't any. That slug that hit you complicates things. We're looking for two guns now, and probably two killers. Maybe more."

"Zimmerman and Carpenter?"

"Your guess is as good as mine. But there must be more than one. The twenty-five wasn't the kind of a gun a professional would have. Not enough smack to it. The gunman who shot you probably used a forty-five. He sounds more like somebody who knew his business."

"Or vice versa. MacLeod's dead and I'm alive. How about one man and two guns?"

"Not likely. No one who had a forty-five would use the popgun; you have to hit a man just right to stop him with a steel-jacketed bullet. There are at least two men and maybe three."

"Three?"

"Both of the men in the car were shooting at Larson when they got away. Neither one used a light gun, according to the Swede."

Whit said, "Oh," and changed the subject. He was tired of

worrying about the number of men who wanted to kill him. "Did you tell Larson to keep the reporters away from me?"

"Yes. I didn't want you to say anything until I had a chance to talk to you. Did they get here?"

"They sure did. They went right out again, too."

Webster smiled. "The Swede has his uses. How many of them?"

"They didn't get close enough for me to count them. Three or four, I guess."

"Anybody hurt?"

"It sounded like it. Your watchdog is getting a mouse under his eye."

"It had to be done. When they come back Larson will let them in and you'll have a story for them."

"O.K. What do I feed them this time?"

Webster looked uncomfortable. "Tell them you're still going ahead with the refund claims before Friday. We'll see what happens."

Whit stared at him in amazement. "For Christ's sake. You mean I'm supposed to suck those gangsters into taking another crack at me?"

"There's nothing else to do," Webster said angrily. "We've got to find out who is doing the shooting. Do you think I won't be busted off the force if anything goes wrong? It was your idea to solve this case in three days, and how else are we going to do it if we don't trap somebody soon? Our only other hope is Zimmermann or Carpenter, and Christ knows how long it will take to find them."

Whit said, "You're crazy. I won't do it."

"If someone is after you he won't stop now, anyway. All this will do is make him move faster."

"No," said Whit. "I'm goddamned if I will. There's not enough in it for me."

Webster stood up and put on his hat. "All right. You can kiss your refund claims good-bye. I'll break this case my own sweet way in my own sweet time."

"Wait a minute." Whit was getting angry. "You want me to stick my nose in the wringer again, and because I won't do it you're going to throw me overboard. Is that it?"

"I'm not throwing you overboard," Webster said irritably. "I just can't break the case in three days unless you want to take a chance. I can't make you do it if you don't feel like it."

"I don't," said Whit. "I don't feel like it and I won't do it."

The buzzer sounded while they were glaring at each other. Larson went to answer it. This time he had his gun in his hand and carried on an argument through the door before opening it. Mr. Harrigan came in, looking very natty in a dark suit and pearl gray spats. He had a gray Homburg in his hand and a walking stick over his arm. When he saw Webster with his hat on, he said, "Good afternoon, Lieutenant. Are you coming or going?"

"Just leaving."

"Don't go yet. I want to talk to you."

"What about?"

"The murder."

"What about it?"

"Let me observe the amenities first." Harrigan smiled cheerfully at Whit. "Mr. Whitney, from your appearance I gather that the morning newspapers exaggerated the imminence of your death. I was at Mr. MacLeod's funeral this morning, and I am happy to see I shall not be attending yours for a while. Accept my congratulations on your escape."

He sat down on the foot of the bed. Whit said, "Thanks. If I have my way nobody will be going to my funeral for a long time."

Webster said, "What did you want to see me about, Mr. Harrigan?"

"I wondered if there were any developments in the murder mystery Have you caught Mr. Whitney's attackers?"

"No. Not yet. We'll get them."

Mr. Harrigan nodded his head cheerfully "That's fine. Sit down, Lieutenant I have some information for you."

Webster hesitated and sat down, still with his hat on. Harrigan said, "Now, first of all, where does the case stand? How far have you gone toward solving it?"

Webster scowled at him. "It's sewed up. By Thursday at the latest we'll have the loose ends gathered together."

"Have you found the killer?"

"I can't say yet. In a day or two you'll know the whole story."

"You wouldn't deceive an old man, would you Lieutenant?"

"I wouldn't give away any more information than I could help," the detective answered. "You're a suspect, Mr. Harrigan. I haven't yet got a report on your alibi for last Saturday."

Whit thought that Webster could have pulled his punches a little, but Harrigan took it well. He said, "A man from your office has checked it, I believe. He questioned me, my house-boy, and several friends whom I entertained Saturday, and he seemed quite satisfied. This is my boy's day off, but I went so far as to tell him to stay home so that you wouldn't be inconvenienced if you wanted to question him about my alibi for last night."

"Nothing like being prepared in advance. Where were you

last night?"

"Entertaining friends. Would you like me to obtain their affidavits?"

"It wouldn't hurt—if you had enough of them."

Things were getting out of hand. Whit said, "Let's all have a drink and forget the alibis for a while." He raised his voice. "Hey, Swede. Make some highballs, will you?"

They talked about the weather until Larson brought in the glasses.

Webster said, "Don't get any ideas in your head just because I'm having a drink, Swede. Remember what I told you."

Larson said, "Yessir." The swelling under his eye had developed into a full-blown shiner.

Harrigan said, "My, my. That's a fine eye you have there, Mr. Larson."

"You ought to see the door I ran into." Larson grinned and went back to the kitchen where the whiskey bottle was waiting.

Harrigan sipped at his highball, and began to question Webster. The detective headed him off with yes-and-no answers, but the old man was politely persistent. Webster finally said bluntly, "You sound to me as if you were after information more than you're giving it."

"I'm a curious man, Lieutenant. Since I retired I like to poke my nose into other people's business. And I should like to know if any of my business associates are criminals. I've even been doing a little investigating on my own."

"What kind of investigating?"

"Just looking around and asking questions. It would please me tremendously if I solved this case before you did. I've always fancied myself as an amateur detective."

Webster snorted, "I can't stop you. But this is no case for amateurs, Mr. Harrigan. People who know anything seem to get hurt."

"Amen," Whit said earnestly. "Ignorance is wonderful."

"I've been thinking of that. I'm not quite sure whether to keep what I know strictly to myself or to tell as many people as possible so there will be no point in anyone shooting me. What would you suggest, Lieutenant?"

Webster sighed heavily. "Just what is this big secret of yours?"

The old man smiled at him.

"I know where to find Zimmermann."

He had a good sense of the dramatic. Webster almost dropped his glass, and Whit choked on a mouthful of whiskey and seltzer. Mr. Harrigan leaned back in his chair, clasped his hands around his stock, and nodded pleasantly at them. "I thought you would appreciate it."

Whit was still strangling over his drink.

Webster said, "You what?"

"Yes." Harrigan nodded. "I've found him—that is, I know where to look for him. It's probably not as important as I thought it was first, if you have all the information you need to solve the mystery, but I was quite pleased with myself."

Webster held himself in with an effort. "Let's forget about that. Where is he?"

Mr. Harrigan shook his head. "I'll trade with you, Lieutenant. You tell me—"

Webster interrupted him harshly. "This is a murder case, man. If you have information, spit it out. Where is he?"

"Be reasonable, Lieutenant," pleaded Harrigan. "I'm not asking for professional secrets. I just want to know—"

"I can get it if I want to be nasty. Where is Zimmermann?"

Mr. Harrigan sighed, took a notebook from his pocket, and thumbed through the alphabetical tags. "Sacramento. He owns a restaurant called the Busy Bee, on J Street."

The detective wrote it down in his own book. Whit got his voice back. He said weakly, "Where did you get it?"

"I asked questions. I went around to all the men in the brewery until I found one who had some information. For ten dollars he told me what he knew."

Whit looked at Webster. "I thought you said you had questioned the boys at the brewery this morning."

"I did. What was the name of the guy who took your ten dollars, Harrigan? I'm going to talk to him."

"You can't have, it," said Harrigan firmly. "I got the information in confidence. Some of those men were bootleggers at one time, Lieutenant, and they don't like policemen. That's why you couldn't get anything from them."

The detective did not press him. "Did your bootlegging friends tell you anything about the aviator—Carpenter?"

"Not yet. I'll be glad to let you know when they do."

Webster grunted, picked up the telephone, and called headquarters. He gave detailed instructions to the man on the other end of the line. When he put the phone down Harrigan said, "Now, Lieutenant, may I ask some questions?"

"Ask all you like. You may not get the answers."

"Very encouraging. How far have you progressed toward solving the murders?"

"It's in the bag."

Mr. Harrigan was not discouraged. "Who shot at Whitney

last night? The same person who killed Mr. MacLeod?"

Webster nodded. "That's right."

"Was there actually a million dollars made out of the bootlegging in 1921 and 1922?"

"Ten million," Webster said. "Any more questions?"

"I think you can answer that, Webster," Whit said. "If Mr. Harrigan was in on it, he knows anyway, and if he wasn't it doesn't matter what you tell him."

"Thank you." Harrigan nodded at Whit. "I should like to know how the money was kept out of the corporation. I never did understand it."

Webster said, "All right. You tell him, Whitney."

"Wolff made beer," said Whit. "He sold it for thirty-five dollars a barrel. On the brewery books he called it near-beer and rang up the near-beer price—twelve dollars. The other twenty-three he put in his pants and no one knew the difference."

"I see. Now, what happened when—"

"That's all," Webster said, standing up "When the case is solved I'll tell you anything you want to know, Mr. Harrigan. In the meantime it's safer for everyone if you don't know too much." He looked at Whit. "Forget what I said, Whitney. If we get hold of Zimmermann I'll break this case tomorrow. In the meantime, just stall the reporters along, will you? Don't say anything at all, and stay close to Larson."

"Sure. Have another drink?"

"Nope." Webster shook his head. He seemed happier than he had been. "I've got work to do. Things are beginning to move."

CHAPTER FIFTEEN

TEN MINUTES after Webster left, Kitty MacLeod and Marian Wolff came in escorted by Frank Marston. They were all returning from the funeral. Marston had met Kitty for the first time that morning and was being attentive; he helped her off with her coat, supplied a light for her cigarette, and generally gave the impression of hovering over her. It looked to Whit as if the lawyer had gone off the deep end. Kitty was taking it in her stride.

Whit noticed evidence of something else he had already guessed. Marian Wolff was not tremendously fond of Marston, for some reason, and Marston responded in kind. They spoke to each other with a cool politeness or not at all. Whit would have liked to know what was behind it. Another thing puzzled him; he had never seen Kitty and Marian together before, but he had assumed that they were at least good friends. Now Kitty was being obviously frosty to Marian, and Marian was putting herself out to be friendly. A lot was going on that Whit didn't know about.

Everyone had met everyone else except Larson and Kitty. Whit made the introduction and Larson stood around looking from Marian to Kitty and back again, wondering how a man went about getting one for his own. Two such women in the same room were a new experience for him.

Kitty sat on the foot of the bed and took off her gloves. She said, "Whit, could I have a drink? Something strong?"

"Of course. Swede, fix up highballs for everyone, will you?"

Larson took his eyes off Marian Wolff's legs and went out to the kitchen.

Kitty said, "Are you really all right, Whit? You look awfully pale."

"I'm fine. I'll be back on the job tomorrow. It isn't a bad wound."

"It is too," Marian said. "I saw it. It's a terrible gash, poor dear."

"What did Lieutenant Webster have to say about the shooting?" asked Marston.

"Nothing much. If at first you don't succeed, try, try again. He wanted me to turn the other cheek."

Marston shook his head. "He's a brute for punishment, so long as you have to take it. I hope you turned him down."

"I did."

Kitty looked from the lawyer to Whit. "What are you talking about?"

Whit said, "Didn't you know I was cannon-fodder? Lieutenant Webster planned to have me shot so my bodyguard could get the gunman, whoever he is. Only the plan didn't work except for the first part."

"Whit!" Kitty was incredulous.

Marston said quickly, "It was entirely Lieutenant Webster's idea, Mrs. MacLeod."

"It's the most horrible thing I ever heard of," Kitty said indignantly. "Whatever made you do it?"

Whit shrugged his good shoulder. "I didn't have anything to say about it. Webster put a story in the newspapers and the first thing I knew the shooting had started."

Kitty looked at Marian. "Did you know about it?" she asked coldly.

"Of course not. I wouldn't have permitted it. I'm surprised that Mr. Marston did."

Marston had nothing to say, and there was an uncomfortable silence. Whit was preparing to break it up when Larson came in with the drinks and handed them around. His entrance smoothed things over. Whit said, "If I live through this it will probably be due to Mr. Harrigan. He gave Lieutenant Webster a lead that doesn't call for any shooting." He raised his glass to Harrigan, sitting quietly in the corner. The old man inclined his head modestly and said, "Thank you."

Marston said, "A clue?"

"He found Zimmermann."

The lawyer turned to Harrigan in surprise. Mr. Harrigan said deprecatingly, "Not exactly. I discovered where he might be located. The police still have to catch him."

"Where is he?"

Harrigan explained. Marian said excitedly, "Then if they catch him we'll be able to get the money back?"

"Probably," Whit said. "If he talks."

"What if they don't catch him?" asked Kitty.

"I don't know. Webster will probably want me to paint a bull's eye on my chest. The only other hope he has is to get hold of the aviator who piloted your father's plane, Miss Wolff.

Either he or Zimmermann has the information we need."

"Oh, I hope they find him," said Marian. "Then all this shooting will be over."

"So do I. From the bottom of my heart." Whit tipped his glass and drank to the wish.

Harrigan rose to leave after promising Whit to let him know if he got any more information. He said, "Miss Wolff, some of the men in the brewery knew your father well and still remember the pretty little girl he brought to the plant to see them years ago. The man who gave me the information about Zimmermann did so partly because I told him how much it meant to you." He beamed gallantly at her. "You're not a little girl any more, but you're certainly still pretty. I hope to get more help from the men; if you were to accompany me to the brewery some day it might be easier."

Marian gave him a dazzling smile. "You put it very nicely, Mr. Harrigan. I'd be delighted."

"I'll call you."

Mr. Harrigan said good-bye politely to everyone, and left.

A moment later Marston finished his drink and stood up. "We ought to leave the patient to his worries," he said. "Can I drive anyone home?" He was looking at Kitty. She said, "Thank you. I want to talk to Whit for a minute, and then I think I'll walk. It's not far."

Marston was disappointed. He said perfunctorily, "Marian?" and she replied as perfunctorily, "No, thanks." The lawyer left immediately. When he had gone Marian telephoned for a taxi.

After Marian departed Whit continued to wonder what in hell there was between her and the lawyer. He was going to pin Marston down soon and ask questions. Certainly Marian

Wolff did not treat the lawyer with the tender affection which might be expected by a man who had practically given her eighteen thousand dollars of his own money. Whit was sure that Marston wouldn't do it over again if he had the chance.

Larson came back to the bedroom after letting Marian Wolff out. He was still dizzy from her smile of thanks. Kitty looked at Whit and made a motion with her head. Whit said, "Swede, go out in the kitchen and sneak yourself a drink while I'm not looking. Mrs. MacLeod and I want to talk."

Larson said, "O.K." and went out, leaving the bedroom door open. "Don't close it. I won't listen."

Kitty smoothed her gloves carefully across her knee. Whit waited. He was tired, and the wound throbbed in his side. After she left he would try to go to sleep. He hoped she didn't want to talk about business; he wasn't up to it.

She said suddenly, "Why don't you get out of this, Whit?"

"Out of what?"

"Don't be dense. You know what I mean. Stop being an amateur detective before you're killed. Those murderers aren't going to leave you alone as long as you're dangerous to them."

"Nothing else is going to happen, Kitty. Larson stays with me all the time."

"Larson!" She made a face. "He's a cretin. He wasn't any help to you last night."

"I'd have been dead now if he hadn't pulled me out of the way."

"That's just it. Next time you may not be pulled out of the way." She moved from her seat at the foot of the bed and sat next to him. He saw that she had faint circles under her eyes.

"Whit, please get out before you're killed."

"Damn it, Kitty, I can't. I'm in too deep. I promised Marston and Marian Wolff I'd get the money back for them if it were possible, and I can't drop them now. There are only three days to go."

"What do you care whether they get the money back or not?"

Whit frowned at her. "I thought Marian Wolff was a friend of yours."

"She isn't. Even if she were it wouldn't make any difference. You're just a stubborn fool to risk your life for people you don't even know."

"I'll make fifty thousand dollars out of it if I win. You may not know it, Kitty, but half of that will be yours."

"I don't want it. I don't want anything except for you to stop before someone kills you." There were tears in her eyes and she winked them away. Whit said, "Aw, honey, don't. Please." He put his good arm around her and kissed her.

The kiss wasn't what he had expected it to be. She was pretty, he liked her, and he had kissed her before, but this time it was different. For one thing, there were tears on her lips that had been shed for him, and for another—it was just different. Whit wondered uncomfortably if it were ethical for a man to have ideas about his partner's widow on the day his partner was buried. He had them.

Kitty was sniffling on his shoulder. He patted her back and said, "Quit it. If you—" He stopped. Kitty felt the muscles of his arm tighten. She turned her head to see what he was looking at.

A man was coming cautiously down the fire-escape from the

floor above. Under the blind which covered the half-opened window his shoes and trouser-legs were visible as he quietly descended the ladder. Whit's heart began to thump. Kitty took a long breath and got off the bed as the legs reached the landing. Whit waved her violently toward the door. She shook her head and looked around the room for a weapon. A hand reached between the curtains to take hold of the window shade, and Whit filled his lungs. "Larson!" he roared. "Quick!"

The man on the fire escape jumped for the ladder. A chair fell over in the kitchen, and Larson burst into the room with his gun in his hand. Whit yelled, "The fire escape! Kitty, get away from there!" Larson shoved her aside, slammed up the window and leaned out for a snap shot. The fugitive had made the landing at the floor above and was starting up the next ladder, screened by the metal lattice-work of the platform. Larson's gun roared. The bullet hit a rail and whined off in a ricochet. The man on the ladder screamed "Jesus, don't shoot! I'll come down," and put up his hands. Larson said, "O.K. Keep them up and take it slow and easy."

Kitty's legs had gone back on her and she was sitting down when Larson backed through the window with his captive. The visitor was young, pale and scared. He climbed awkwardly into the room with his hands still in the air. Larson pushed him into a corner, shoved the gun into his navel and frisked him carefully. Nothing turned up. He growled, "Where do you keep it, punk?"

"Keep what?" The punk was white and unhappy.

Larson smacked him across the face with the back of his left hand. "Go on, be funny. Where's the gun?"

"Wait a minute," said the pale young man. "You got me wrong.

All I'm after is an interview with Mr. Whitney. I'm from the Chronicle."

~§~

Two men from the Sacramento police department stood in front of the Busy Bee Quick Lunch on J Street and looked the joint over. It wasn't busy. A truck driver was having a hamburger and coffee, and the counter-man was reading the afternoon paper. They were the only people in the place.

The two cops talked it over on the sidewalk. They looked like Tweedledum and Tweedledee in plain clothes. Tweedledum said, "A fellah called Zimmermann, maybe with another name. No description. Maybe trouble, maybe not. That's a hell of a assignment."

"How about the monkey behind the counter?"

"Come on. We'll try him. Leave me do the talking."

They went in. The truck diver chewed on his hamburger and looked at the wall. The counter-man was tall and skinny, and his sleeves were rolled up on his thin arms. He moved away from the paper. "Afternoon," he said.

Neither cop sat down. Tweedledum scowled at the skinny man. "Your name's Zimmermann," he said. It wasn't a question.

The counter-man shook his head. "He ain't here."

Tweedledum moved around behind the counter and crowded the man back against the wall. "Don't give me none of that stuff, Zimmermann. You're wanted down to headquarters. Come along quiet." He wrapped a paw around the man's thin wrist and dragged him out from behind the counter. The skinny man said, "Hey. What is this?" in a frightened voice and tried to pull away. Tweedledum jerked him forward off his feet. "You want to get hurt? Come along"

The truck driver spoke up. "What's the matter with you guys? He ain't Zimmermann."

Tweedledee said, "Who asked you to sound off?" The truck driver looked up at him and went back to his hamburger. "My mistake."

The counter-man said, "For Christ's sake." He was still struggling to get his wrist away from Tweedledum. "I ain't Zimmermann. I only work in the place. What is this, anyhow?"

Tweedledum said, "Shut up," and scowled at the truck driver. "You know this guy?"

"Sure I know him. I know Zimmermann, too. This guy ain't him."

Tweedledum let go of the counter-man. "O.K. Now we're getting somewheres. Where is he?"

The counter-man moved back behind the cash register, rubbing his wrist. The truck driver finished his coffee and wiped his mouth with the back of his hand. "Ask Doc here."

Doc said, "I don't know. Honest to God. I ain't seen any sign of him for three days. What do you want him for?"

"Police business. Where does he live?"

"Out on P Street. He's supposed to take over at seven o'clock and he ain't been in since Saturday night. I went out a couple of times to his house and nobody wasn't there, so I been closing up at seven. I don't know where he is."

Tweedledee put his oar in.

"Why didn't you report it to the police? Maybe he's been murdered or something."

Doc shrugged his shoulders. "I just work here. I'm paid up to next Saturday night and if he don't turn up by then I'll close the dump and walk out. It ain't none of my business what he does with himself."

"You sure got a fine sense of civic responsibility," said Tweedledee critically.

"It ain't nothing to me what he does," Doc mumbled. "I ain't going to poke my nose into anything."

"Leave us have the address," said Tweedledum.

Doc gave it to them.

Tweedledum said, "You call the department if he comes in or you hear from him, see? And don't say nothing about us looking for him."

"I ain't going to say nothing. It's no business of mine."

The cops went out and got into their car. Doc and the truck driver watched them through the window. The truck driver said, "Them flat-foot bastards. Give me some more coffee."

Doc poured it for him, muttering. The truck driver said, "Maybe you ought to telephone and let him know they're after him."

"I said it wasn't none of my business, didn't I? Anyway, he ain't there. I was out last night and Monday looking for him. I don't know where he is."

The cops cruised along P Street until they found the address. It was an old house and it needed paint. A palm tree grew in the middle of a patch of weedy lawn in front.

Tweedledum said, "You cover the rear," and went up the steps.

The doorbell rang faintly in the back of the house. Tweedledum held his finger on the button for more than a minute. Nothing happened. He tried the door and the two windows opening on the porch. All of them were locked. He went around to the back trying windows as he came to them.

There was a screen door on the back porch. Tweedledee had his nose against the wire, peering into the house. The door was latched only with a hook, so Tweedledum kicked a hole in the screen and reached through to lift the latch. They went in. Zimmerman was there.

The body was slumped on a davenport in the dingy front room. The place smelled. There was a small hole in the corpse's forehead and another small hole in the back of his head. Blood had run down his face and stiffened his shirt front. Tweedledum dug the bullet out of the plaster wall with a pocket-knife and showed it to his partner. "A lady's gun," he said contemptuously. "One of them steel jackets. About a twenty-five."

Tweedledee looked at the body and grunted. "I'll bet it wasn't no woman who done it. Look at that homely puss. No woman ever got interested enough in that guy to even want to shoot him."

"Well, never mind who done it. Frisco wanted us to find the guy and we found him. Let's go."

CHAPTER SIXTEEN

WHIT started Wednesday morning off by having a tremendous argument with the fat doctor, who arrived at eight o'clock to change his patient's bandages and tuck him in. The battle went on for fifteen minutes and ended with the doctor flatly ordering Whit to stay in bed and Whit flatly telling him to go to hell. The doctor washed his hands of the case and walked out.

Whit was in a surly mood. He hadn't been able to sleep, except fitfully, and most of the night he had smoked cigarettes and worried. In the small hours of the morning it had been hard for him to feel hopeful, knowing that two or three people were earnestly trying to bump him off. Until early in the evening when Webster, on his way to Sacra-mento, had stopped in with news of the discovery of Zimmermann's body, Whit had hoped that everything would soon be over. But the death of Zimmermann made things worse than before. Anyone who had murdered three times already was not going to give up the attempt to add Whit's scalp to his belt. Not if he needed it.

The bookkeeper had been shot with the twenty-five. To Whit it was the final proof that MacLeod's murder had been a result of his discovery concerning Harald Wolff's income taxes, and it dissipated his uneasy suspicion of Kitty MacLeod. Still, he would like to know why she disliked Marian Wolff, and why Marian Wolff and Frank Marston hated each other, and a lot of other things. Kitty was too anxious for him to get out of the case. Either she was afraid he would find something which he shouldn't or his safety meant more to her than he had suspected. Was she in love with him? It wouldn't be hard to take. Her mouth was soft, and there had been salt tears on her lips—

He went to work in a Yellow cab, still worrying. Larson looked the street over carefully and waited until there were no cars passing before he gave Whit the sign to leave the foyer of the apartment house. Nobody shot at them during the ride down-town, and nobody was waiting for Whit when he walked quickly from the cab to his office building. But it was a strain. The hair on the back of his neck didn't lie down until he was safe behind his own desk. Larson parked himself in a chair by the door and read the morning paper. Zimmermann's death had made a big splash in the headlines.

While Whit was opening his mail, Miss Kelly knocked on the door, put her head in, and said brightly, "Good morning, Mr. Whitney. How do we feel this morning?"

"Fine, thank you. Back on the job as usual."

She looked at him critically. "You're awfully pale. Are you sure you shouldn't be in bed? We don't want you to overexert yourself, you know. Your health comes first."

"I'm as good as new." Whit studied a circular advertising Personalized Printing for Professional People. Miss Kelly would moo over him for half an hour if he gave her a chance, and he couldn't stand it in his weakened condition. If he looked busy she might go away.

She did. In five minutes she was back to tell him that she had remembered something else about Saturday morning. Mrs. MacLeod had telephoned Mr. MacLeod. Did it help Mr. Whitney any? He said it did, a great deal, and she went away pleased. He dug into the mail.

Running the office took more time than he had realized. MacLeod had always handled the helm and Whit had forgotten how much work was required to keep the wheels moving. Now it was all on his shoulders. He began to appreciate George.

Krebs brought in the two new men and introduced them; Mr. Monroe, C.P.A. and Mr. Prentice, C.P.A. They seemed all right to Whit, except that Mr. Monroe looked like a hard-shell deacon. Whit gathered that he was Krebs' choice. Prentice was about Whit's age and said very little after expressing his sympathy with Whit's poor health. Whit liked him. He always talked too much himself, and he appreciated anyone who could keep quiet when he had nothing to say. Whit told them he was glad to know them and hoped they would get along all right. They hoped so too, and they would do their best. They both shook hands with him. Krebs took them away to start on a couple of audits which were over-due.

There were some letters to be answered, so Whit dictated to Miss Kelly for an hour. Then Krebs came back and brought in a tax protest and two or three reports of examination to be reviewed. Whit went over the first report with him, item by item. After half an hour he said, "Are you satisfied with these things, Krebs?"

Krebs was surprised. "They are all right, Mr. Whitney. Everything has been checked."

"Why don't we just send them out, then? If you're satisfied, I am."

"If you wish. Mr. MacLeod reviewed everything that went out over the firm's name. I thought you would like to do so."

"It isn't necessary. I know you don't make mistakes."

Krebs shook his head. "Everyone makes mistakes sometime. They are your responsibility if they go out with your name on them. I am only an employee."

"Well, forget that you're an employee for a while until we get straightened out. Let me know what you're doing once in a while and if I want to see anything I'll tell you."

Krebs started to say something and changed his mind. "Very well, Mr. Whitney." He went out with the reports under his arm. Whit called after him. "Send Tommy in here, will you?"

Tommy was properly respectful when he came in; a man who had gangsters after him was entitled to respect. He said, "Morning, Mr. Whitney. I'm sure glad to see you alive and kicking."

"Thanks, Tommy. I'll be kicking for a long time yet. Do you want to do me a favor?"

"Sure."

Whit fished a key out of his vest pocket. "My car is sitting out on Green Street, if it hasn't been towed away. How would you like to drive it back to my garage? I won't be using it for a while."

Tommy's face fell. He said, "Whereabouts on Green Street?"

"Near Leavenworth. You know what the car looks like, don't you?" Whit saw Tommy's expression. "There's no danger, Tommy. Nobody will shoot at you. I'll have a cop go along if it will make you feel better."

"I'm not scared. Sure, I'll get it." He took the key.

"Well, what are you looking so sour about?"

"I thought you were going to ask me to do some work on the Wolff case."

"What is there in the Wolff case that interests you?"

Tommy said sadly, "Well, it's getting a lot of publicity. Everybody I know keeps asking me about it and I don't know anything. I'm tired of having to bluff."

Whit laughed, and immediately grabbed his side. "*Ow!* Read the papers, Tommy. They have the whole story."

"I know better than that," Tommy said, grinning. "You don't give away everything you know."

Whit shook his head regretfully. "I wish you were right. I've gone as far as I can with it. There's nothing anyone can do now except pray for a break."

Tommy said, "All right. I just thought I'd ask," and turned away. Whit had an idea. "Wait a minute," he said, "Maybe you can do something."

Tommy said, "Oh, boy. Lead me to it."

Whit got the Wolff papers from the safe in the vault and showed Zimmermann's affidavit to Tommy. "Here's what I want you to do, and if you make the grade you're a better man than I am. This is a copy of an affidavit showing payments which were supposed to have gone to Harald Wolff—the bootlegging gravy. The total amount of the take is about right, but MacLeod found something proving that Wolff got only part of it." Whit tapped the big filing envelope. "He found it in here, Tommy. I've sweated over these papers until I'm cockeyed and I can see only one thing that might be a clue, if you can make anything out of it." He pointed out the August dates when Zimmermann had made no payments and explained what he had learned of Wolff's hunting trips. "There's a possibility that something was stolen from the file and a possibility that I'm just dumb. If you can figure out what MacLeod found in here, I'll—I'll raise your salary fifty per cent. I only want to know one thing—how was MacLeod sure that Wolff didn't get all of the money?"

Tommy took the papers. He said solemnly, "Mr. Whitney, you've come to the right man. If it's here I'll find it. When does the raise go into effect?"

"Cash on the line. Deliver the goods and you start collecting. There's one thing to remember, Tommy. In this case you have to keep your nose clean. If you get any ideas, tell me about them and nobody else. Of course, it's hard on your public, but it's absolutely necessary. Understand?"

"Right," said Tommy firmly. He left with the file under his arm.

Whit went back to work. He was in MacLeod's office cleaning papers out of the desk drawers when Miss Kelly came in to announce that a Mr. DeWitt was waiting to see him. Whit put down a handful of MacLeod's check stubs and returned to his own office.

Buster was as slick as ever. He even had the tips of his mustache waxed. He had read about Mr. Whitney's accident in the newspapers and hoped it wasn't as bad as it sounded. Whit said he was fine, thanks. Buster backed and filled for a while and wondered if he could see Mr. Whitney alone. Whit was sorry but Mr. Larson was his bodyguard and had his orders. Mr. DeWitt would understand the necessity for caution after last night. But Mr. Larson could be trusted not to repeat anything he heard in confidence. Buster came to the point.

"It's about the murders, of course. I tried to see Lieutenant Webster this morning, but he had gone to Sacramento so I came to see you. Unfortunate thing, Zimmermann's death. You were rather counting on him to solve the case, weren't you?"

"We would have liked to talk to him."

"I can understand that." Buster put his finger-tips together. "Perhaps the solution can be reached without him, Mr. Whitney. I wonder if you've given any real attention to the one logical suspect?"

"Who?"

"Understand, I don't want to make any accusations. But if you follow a logical process of reasoning you must arrive at certain conclusions."

"That's right. Who is your suspect?" Whit knew what was coming.

"Elwood Hall."

Whit looked out the window. DeWitt might be perfectly right, of course. He had come through with one idea already, and Hall was as good as the next man. But DeWitt hated Hall's guts. Whit had a hunch that the processes of Buster's reasoning wouldn't have to be too logical.

"What makes you pick him, Mr. DeWitt?"

"Look at the facts. Hall was secretary of the corporation in 1921 and 1922, when the bootlegging took place. He says he didn't know what was going on, but that's preposterous. He and Wolff were the only stockholders actually working at the plant, and it isn't reasonable that Wolff could have made beer right under Hall's nose for two years without his knowing it."

"Perhaps not. But as I understand it, Hall didn't spend much time at the brewery. He only turned up once a week to sign checks."

"Once a week for two years, and he signed every check that went out. He must have noticed that the brewery was pretty active for a near-beer plant."

"There's something to that. What else?"

"Well, here's what could have happened." DeWitt twisted his mustache; he was enjoying himself. "Hall and Wolff were together in it. Hall found out that the government was after them and bribed Zimmermann to say he had given all the money to Wolff. Then Hall had Wolff killed. He got Wolff's job and was out of trouble. Somehow your partner found out that Zimmermann had lied, but he didn't know who really had got the money and he asked Hall to call the stockholders' meeting so he could get them together and find out who it was. Hall saw what was going to happen and shot him before he could ask any questions."

It wasn't a bad piece of reasoning, even if it was colored by wish-fulfillment. Whit said, "Then Hall must have murdered Zimmermann."

"Correct."

Whit looked contemplative. DeWitt watched his face. Whit swung around. "What do you think, Larson?"

"Could be," Larson answered cautiously. It was the first time in three days that he had been asked for his opinion on anything, and he gave the problem proper consideration. "Depends on the alibis. Where was Hall on Saturday?"

"He says he was working at the plant office until eight. We close up on Saturday afternoon, so no one was around to prove he wasn't there."

"Um hum," said Larson judiciously. "According to the paper, the Sacramento coroner says Zimmermann was killed Sunday. Where was Hall then?"

DeWitt shrugged. "He has some kind of a story. A detective came around the plant this morning to question us about Sunday. I don't know what Hall told him, but if you check it you'll find he had time to get to Sacramento and back. Can't you see how obvious it is, Mr. Whitney?"

"I'm an accountant, Mr. DeWitt, not a detective. I'll tell Lieutenant Webster what your idea is. He'll be interested."

He eased Buster out of the office after promising him again that no one but Webster would hear of the conversation. When he had gone, Whit said, "That bastard. He'd sure like to see Hall go to jail."

"There may be something in what he says," Larson said.

"Sure, Hall might have done it. It would be all the same to DeWitt either way, so long as he could get him in trouble."

"He could still be right about it."

"I'd disagree with him on general principles," Whit said. "I'll bet you ten bucks it wasn't Hall, just because Buster picks him. What do you say?"

"No bet." Larson shook his head. "I only said he could be right." He picked up the newspaper. "Listen to this. That reporter must have bruised his fist on me."

He was reading Whit an indignant editorial concerning police brutality and the beating up of innocent newspapermen when Miss Kelly announced Marian Wolff. She came in looking like the spirit of spring in a blue dress and hat, and Larson's eyes took on a glassy look. He sat and watched her with his mouth open.

Marian was upset by the news of Zimmermann's death, both because another murder frightened her and because she knew that Whit had been counting on the ex-bookkeeper as a source of information. She said, "What are you going to do about the refund claims, Mr. Whitney?"

"I don't know," Whit answered. "I'm waiting to hear from Lieutenant Webster. He went up to Sacramento to look around, and if he finds a clue we shall still have a chance."

His tone was discouraging. Marian said, "A chance?"

Whit nodded his head slowly. "I'm not sure of anything, now that Zimmermann is dead. About all we can hope for is that Webster will catch the murderer by Friday, or find the pilot of your father's plane. If the murderer hasn't shut him up too, he may have the information we need. The trouble is that we have only two days to go."

Marian was dismayed. "But isn't there anything you can do to get more time? Couldn't you explain things to the government people?"

"No. Friday is the last day. The law is a peculiar thing, Miss Wolff. It gives us only so much time to recover your money, regardless of circumstances. If we file proper claims within that time and set forth the exact grounds on which we rely to get the money back, we will be given additional time to prove the facts, and when we do the money will be refunded. If the claims are filed too late, or even if they are filed in time but the wrong grounds are relied upon, they will be rejected. There's nothing we can do to change it."

Marian said desperately, "Then you won't even try to get the money unless they catch the murderer?"

"I'll try. I'll file some sort of a claim by Friday, whatever happens, but it won't be worth anything unless I know more than I do now. I can't even tell how much to claim. Without at least that information it's a lost cause."

She looked at him without speaking. He said, "I'm sorry it sounds so bad."

Marian smiled with an effort. "I might as well know the worst. May I see you alone for a minute?"

Whit wondered what was coming. "You'll have to ask my bodyguard. He has strict orders."

Marian turned to Larson. "Please. Just for a minute."

Larson looked helplessly at Whit. Lieutenant Webster's instructions had been as explicit as his threats against Larson if he left Whit for a minute. Whit said, "It's all right, Swede. You can wait outside the door."

Larson still hesitated. Marian walked over to him, put her hand on his arm, and smiled into his eyes. "Please," she said softly. He blushed bright red and went out of the room in a daze. They could see his shadow on the ground glass of the door after it closed behind him.

Marian turned quickly to Whit, She was no longer smiling. "What did Kitty MacLeod say to you yesterday after I left? Did she want you to give up trying to get the money back?"

Whit hesitated. Marian repeated angrily, "Did she?"

"Yes."

"Why? What did she say about me?"

"Nothing. She was afraid I might be killed!"

"So you told her you would quit."

"I told her I would do everything I could for you," Whit said carefully. "I have no intention of quitting."

The girl came closer to him. She had to look up to see his face. "Please tell me the truth, Whit. You're the only one who can help me. If you've given up I don't know what to do."

"I told you I would do what I can, Miss Wolff. Only—"

"Can't you call me Marian?" She was very close to him, and he could smell the faint scent she wore. He had to swallow before he could answer her. "Marian. I'm still on the job. But I had to tell you—" He got no further. Marian put her arms quickly around his waist and stood on her toes to kiss him on the mouth, hard. Her arms were tight around his bandaged ribs, but he didn't feel anything.

CHAPTER SEVENTEEN

LIEUTENANT WEBSTER sat at his desk and stared gloomily at two bullets on the blotter before him. One had a dent in its nose and the other was unmarked, but otherwise they were identical. Both were steel-jacketed, both were twenty-five caliber, and both had been fired from the same gun. Webster looked at them for five minutes without moving. Then he said, "Oh, hell," put them in a cellophane wrapper, stuffed the package in his vest pocket, and pressed a button on the desk.

A man in uniform opened the office door. Webster said, "Is Murphy around?"

"Yes sir. He just came in. Do you want to see him?"

"What the hell do you think I asked for?"

The uniformed man backed out. Webster rubbed his hand over his chin and tried to remember when he had slept last. If he ever got time he would crawl into bed and stay there for three days. But time was too valuable to waste on sleep. It would have to wait.

A neat man in plain clothes came into the office. He was small, unobtrusive and undistinguished. He hung his hat on a stand in the corner and sat down in the chair opposite Webster, pulling his trousers up at the knees.

"What did you get?" Webster asked.

The neat little man took a sheaf of typescript from his inside pocket and prepared to read from it. Webster said, "Never mind the book, Murphy. Save it for the District Attorney. Just tell me what you have."

"Yes sir." Murphy looked at his papers. "I've got them in alphabetical order. Anyone you want first?"

"You can have them classified by the color of their hair if you like. Give me the dope. I haven't got all day."

"Yes sir. Carpenter is first, and we haven't anything on him yet. We're still waiting to hear from the Department of Commerce. DeWitt, not so good for Saturday. He says he went out to dinner by himself at six o'clock and then to the movies. Sunday he was at Mount Diablo Country Club from eleven A.M. to six, and I checked with men who were playing golf or bridge with him all the time. No check that's worth anything before eleven or after six. The steward at the club—"

"Zimmermann was killed after eleven A.M. and before sundown Sunday," Webster interrupted. "A man next door saw him stirring around in the morning and the coroner guarantees the other end. The time in between is all you have to worry about."

"DeWitt is out of it for Sunday, then. Hall—"

"Wait a minute. Mount Diablo is Marston's club. Wasn't he there too?"

"Yes sir. But he and DeWitt don't know each other. DeWitt's a new member, and Marston hangs out with the old guard. I couldn't find any connection between them."

Webster thought it over and Murphy waited. The Lieutenant said, "You better work on that angle. Look up the record on DeWitt's old man and see if he and Marston had anything to do with each other before he died. Might be more than a coincidence that young DeWitt and Marston were at the same place on the same day. What about Marston's time?"

"He's farther down the list." Murphy shifted his papers around. "If you want him now—"

"Never mind. Do it your own way."

"Well, Hall is next. He claims he was at the brewery Saturday until eight. No check on it, and nothing for Sunday. His family was away and he says he was fiddling around in the garden all day, so there's no way to check it unless the neighbors saw him. I haven't had time to talk to them yet."

Murphy turned a page. "Harrigan. He had a houseful of guests from early Saturday until early Sunday afternoon. I talked to a couple of them and they give him an alibi for the time they were there. Nothing doing for Sunday from about two or three, when everybody left, to seven. His houseboy gets Sunday afternoon off and comes back at seven to cook his dinner."

"He could have made it to Sacramento and back between three and seven," said Webster. "He was the one who told us where to find Zimmermann. What does he say he was doing in the afternoon?"

"Taking a nap."

"Give him a little extra attention. Who's next?"

"Kelly. The girl at Whitney's office. No check for Saturday. She went to a movie with a couple of other biddies about seven and she was supposed to be shopping in the afternoon. Sunday she was at the beach with a boyfriend, all day." Murphy smiled faintly. "The boyfriend was tough. He's got a divorced wife on his tail for back alimony and when I talked to him he thought I was working for her. He almost busted me one when I—"

"I got troubles of my own without listening to yours," said Webster grumpily. "Who's next?"

"Yes sir. Krebs. Saturday afternoon he was home and his landlord gives him an alibi from five to six; they were chewing the rag for an hour or so. Sunday he says he was hunting for Whitney from noon until three and found him in the office. His wife alibis him up until noon and after four-thirty, when he got home. The rest of the time he says he was looking for Whitney or talking to him. I haven't checked with Whitney yet."

"You haven't checked with anybody." Webster was disgusted. "What his wife says doesn't mean a thing. As far as you know, Krebs had all day to get up to Sacramento."

"I got everything I could in the time I had," said Murphy apologetically.

"Well, you'll have to get more. Go on with the next one."

"MacLeod. The widow. Nothing doing for Saturday. She says she was home alone all afternoon and that's that. Sunday she's clean; the Wolff girl went to see her and they alibi each other from noon until about four-thirty. A neighbor was talking to her at eleven."

He rearranged his papers and continued. "Marston. He says he was home all Saturday afternoon and drove down to see MacLeod about six-thirty. He lives by himself, so there's no check at all on it. The elevator operator at the Farmers' Exchange took him up to MacLeod's office about quarter of seven. Sunday he was at

Mount Diablo before ten, talked to the club professional about his game, and played eighteen holes alone. He says it took him about two hours and a half and I haven't found anyone who saw him on the course. At twelve-thirty—"

"Hold it," interrupted Webster. "Two hours and a half is too long for a man going around by himself. I've played golf."

"So have I. I asked him about it. He said the course was empty and he spent a lot of time practicing his putting."

Webster grunted dubiously. "Keep working on it. You ought to find somebody who saw him."

"Yes sir. At twelve-thirty he came back to the club house for lunch. Two or three people, including the steward, place him in the grill or the card room all the time up to six." Murphy turned another page.

Webster said irritably, "Damn it, you haven't cleared anybody at all. Every one of them is wide open for either Saturday or Sunday or both. Can't you plug up the holes?"

"I haven't had enough time. In another day or two I'll tighten these up a lot."

"It'll be too late in another day or two," Webster said. "Go on; let's see if the rest of them are as bad."

"Putnam. He's been in New York for a month. Swift,—" Murphy shook his head. "I had a bad time with Swift, Lieutenant. He's half paralyzed, and he keeps a Jap boy to push him around in a wheel chair. I had to argue my way in to see him, and then he blew up as soon as I started to ask questions." Murphy smiled his faint smile and rubbed his elbow. "The skibby took hold of my arm and I went where he pushed me—out. There wasn't any feeling in my funny-bone for an hour."

"Haven't you been back?"

"Not yet. I thought I'd let him go for a while. He couldn't have sneaked up on anybody in a wheel chair."

"For Christ's sake, Murphy. I want an alibi for every one, even if they're stretcher cases. If a Jap houseboy is too much for you, take the riot squad, but find out about Swift."

"Yes sir. This afternoon." Murphy looked at his papers. "Ward's next. He's O.K. for the whole route. Lives with his mother, a sister, a brother-in-law and his sister's two kids."

"Ward?"

"The young fellow at Whitney's office. His clan alibis him from early Saturday afternoon until Monday morning."

Murphy's next page had more typing than the others. He said, "Whitney. I telephoned the clerk at the hotel in Santa Cruz, and he says Whitney left there about five; not earlier and maybe a few minutes later. Marston and the elevator man check him into his office about seven-fifteen. He couldn't have made it up from Santa Cruz in less than two hours no matter how fast he drove, so he's clean for Saturday. Sunday, you saw him at his office in the morning. What time did you leave him?"

"You can forget Whitney. After Monday night he's one man I'm sure about. Who's next?"

Murphy turned the page reluctantly; he had put extra effort into verifying Whit's alibi. "Marian Wolff. Her story is pretty good, but if I were you, Lieutenant, I'd keep my eyes on that girl. In the first place, she's too good-looking to be real. I never saw—"

"You're not me," Webster snarled "I didn't stay up all night working my tail off on this case so you could tell me what your ideas are about Marian Wolff. What I want is her alibi, if she has any. Never mind what you think."

"Yes sir." Murphy hunched his shoulders instinctively to protect his ears. "Saturday afternoon she was in Burlingame with some friends—a guy called Stacy and his wife. They give her a clean bill from Saturday morning until Sunday morning. Stacy says she left there at eleven A.M. Sunday when she heard about MacLeod on the radio. She got to Mrs. MacLeod's around noon and she was with her until four-thirty. The doorman at her apartment house checks her in before five."

Murphy put his papers in order and fastened them with a paper-clip. "That's the list, except for MacLeod. I tried his clubs and he wasn't at any of them Friday night, so I let it go to work on the alibis. It's the best I could do in the time I had."

"MacLeod isn't important. Forget about him." Webster took a cigarette package from his pocket, fished out a wrinkled cigarette and straightened it between his fingers. "But you've got to tighten up the slack in those stories, Murphy. There's still a lot of work to do and you'll have to move fast. Get somebody to help you and keep going." He lit his cigarette.

"Yes sir," said Murphy. "What's all the rush, Lieutenant? I never saw you push so hard on a case before."

Webster took one puff at the cigarette, examined it carefully, and dropped it in the cuspidor. "Five hundred thousand dollars."

Murphy was puzzled. Webster said wearily, "It's over my head, too. Whitney is trying to get a refund of half a million dollars in income taxes that belongs to Marian Wolff, and he has only two days left to do the job. He can't figure out how to get the money unless he knows who killed his partner, and I can't catch the murderer unless Whitney tells me why the money ought to be refunded. Work it out for yourself."

"It sounds like a tough one to break in two days."

"It's worse than that. If I had any sense I'd take my time and do the job right, but I hate to see anyone lose half a million bucks."

Murphy stood up and put his papers back in his pocket. "I'll work as fast as I can on it. There are a lot of people to talk to in two days. How many men can I have?"

Webster had a new idea. "It's just routine checking now, isn't it?"

Murphy nodded.

Webster said, "All right. You can have as many men as you need, but let them do it themselves. You forget the alibis and concentrate on finding someone who saw the murderer. He either went through the lobby to get to the stairs or he went up the fire escape, and he wasn't invisible. Talk to the people next door and in the building across the alley, the cop on the beat, the newspaper boy on the corner—everybody. We're going to end up with so many lousy alibis we can't count on any of them, so we might as well try something else. Don't waste any time."

"Yes sir." Murphy took his hat and went out.

For ten minutes after Murphy had gone Webster leaned back in his chair and stared at the ceiling, trying to think. His mind was fuzzy with fatigue. When he caught himself falling asleep in the chair he went down to the locker-room in the basement of the police station and took a long cold shower that failed to wake him up but made him feel cleaner. His shirt was too dirty to put on again. He went through lockers appropriating what he found until he had gathered together a clean shirt, a pair of shorts and some shaving equipment. After he had shaved he washed out his socks and hung them over a steam-pipe, wrapped a towel around his middle, lay down on a bench, and went immediately to sleep.

An hour later a patrolman came down to the locker-room and woke him.

"Call for you from Sacramento, Lieutenant. Captain Goss."

"Thanks." Webster sat up yawning, cinched the towel around his waist, and went, to the phone at the far end of the locker-room. He was still groggy with sleep. He had trouble keeping his eyes open while he waited for the switchboard operator to give him the call.

There was a series of clicks in the receiver and the line was open. The man on the other end said, "I've got something for you, Lieutenant."

"Good." Webster yawned until his ears cracked. "Did you find the shell from the automatic?"

"Yes. It had kicked into the fireplace. We dug up something else while we were going through the house. Zimmermann was paroled out of Sing Sing in 1920."

"He was what?" Webster woke up.

"That's right. We found his parole papers. He served six years of a ten year stretch for grand larceny."

Webster suddenly felt cheerful for the first time since he had heard of the ex-bookkeeper's death. He said, "God, that's the best news I've had in ten years. Was Zimmermann his right name?"

"It's the name on the papers. Adolph Zimmermann."

"Send them down right away, will you?"

"I'm putting them in the mail, special delivery. You'll get them tonight."

Webster said, "Captain, I'm a new man. If you ever want anything from us, let me know. The city and county of San Francisco are yours."

Captain Goss laughed. "Thanks. Good luck to you. Goodbye."

Webster hung up, went back to his stolen linen, dressed and ran up the stairs two at a time. It took him five minutes to get off a fast wire to the New York State Prison at Ossining, asking for all information available concerning Adolph Zimmermann, parolee.

He left the police station whistling between his teeth. Things were looking up.

CHAPTER EIGHTEEN

WHIT was still punch-drunk from Marian Wolff's visit when Webster came into the office. Too much had been happening all at once, and he wasn't as durable as he had been. The bullet wound had taken a lot out of him.

The detective said hello cheerfully, nodded to Larson, and sat down. Whit asked suspiciously, "What are you so happy about?"

"Oh, clean living has its rewards; I just had an hour's sleep and a bath. How do you feel?"

"Terrible."

"What's the matter? Can't you take it?"

"No. Too many things going on all at the same time."

Webster was interested. "Something new?"

"Well, no; nothing important. Kitty MacLeod has been trying to talk me into quitting the case while I'm still in one piece, and Marian Wolff wants to be sure I'll stay with it as long as there's a chance for her to get her money back. They're both convincing. And Buster DeWitt has a theory about the murder."

Webster took a fresh package of cigarettes from his pocket, offered one to Whit, and lit one for himself. "So Mrs. MacLeod wants you to give up?" he said thoughtfully. "Now I wonder why she feels that way? She must not like Marian Wolff very much."

Whit took as much time as possible to light his own cigarette. He had talked too much. Webster's suspicious mind would make something out of Kitty's anxiety to get him out of the case, and whatever the real reason was, Whit wanted to find it out for himself. He blew out the match and said lamely, "Well, she's afraid I might get killed. She thinks I ought to get out before anything else happens."

"Why is she so anxious about you all of a sudden? I should think she'd want to know who killed her husband, even if she didn't care about Marian Wolff."

"It isn't all of a sudden. I've known her for a long time." Whit was being pushed into a corner and it made him mad. "For Christ's sake, don't go getting any ideas about Kitty MacLeod and me again. We had it all out once before. She likes me, I like her, and she doesn't want me to get killed. Neither do I."

"All right, all right," Webster said soothingly. "There's no need to get excited. I was just asking."

He seemed satisfied to drop the subject, but Whit had a feeling he was not going to forget it. He wished he could learn to keep his mouth shut.

Webster said, "What did Miss Wolff have to say? Does she know how Mrs. MacLeod feels?"

"Yes. She was in here half an hour ago to make sure I wasn't going to quit before the claims were filed. I told her I'd stay with it."

"Must be nice having a couple of women like that worrying about what you're going to do. I wish I was young and handsome."

"Marian Wolff is worrying about her half a million bucks." Whit hated to admit the real reason to himself; the kiss she had given him still made shivers run down his back, but he knew better than to fool himself. Kitty's interest might be genuine; Marian's was not unless she had fallen for him at first sight. He did not have enough faith in his own glamour to believe it.

"Probably," Webster said. "What did you say about DeWitt?"

"He was here too. He has Hall picked for the murderer. The Swede thinks his theory is pretty good, but I have a hunch he's after Hall's blood. A little thing like hanging a murder on Hall isn't going to bother Buster."

Webster looked at Larson. Larson said, "All I said was that it wasn't a bad theory, and just because DeWitt doesn't like Hall doesn't mean his idea has to have holes in it."

"DeWitt came through once for us," said Webster. "Let's hear it, Whitney."

Whit told him what Buster had said. The detective considered it seriously. "It doesn't sound so bad. He's right about Hall having the opportunity. I had a man checking the alibis. Hall is wide open for Saturday and Sunday both."

"I'll give you the same bet I offered Larson," Whit said. "Ten bucks Hall isn't the man."

"What makes you so sure?"

"I'm not sure. I'm just gambling because I think DeWitt is a dummy. His guess about Wolff was a fluke."

Webster snorted. "We need a lot more flukes of the same kind. I think I'll just give Mr. Hall's alibi a special workout. If I could find that he got some of that beer money—" The detective heaved an enormous sigh. "God, I'll be glad when this is over."

"You and me both. What did you dig up in Sacramento?"

Webster stubbed out his cigarette. "Something real interesting. Zimmermann was paroled out of the big house." He told Whit of Captain Goss's discovery.

Whit whistled. "That's the first real information we've got. What does it do for us?"

"Nothing, so far. I wired the warden at Ossining, and when I hear from him we may have something."

Whit was thinking hard. He said slowly, "Maybe there's a lead there. I've got an idea."

"Go ahead."

"Well, Zimmermann was paroled. I don't know just how a parole works but it wouldn't do him any real good to get tangled up with the law again. Yet there he was right up to his ears in a bootlegging racket—one little slip, a little publicity, and back he goes to the pen. Right?"

"It wouldn't help him any if he were picked up," Webster agreed.

"Sure. So he wasn't in the bootlegging business for love, and he didn't make any real money or the Bureau of Internal Revenue would have gone after him. What did he get out of it?"

"You're all right so far. Keep going."

"MacLeod thought Wolff had something on Zimmermann because he only paid him a couple of hundred a month while Zimmermann was doing all the dirty work. Wolff must have known that Zimmermann was an ex-convict and held it over his head. So when—"

"Being an ex-convict is better than being a convict, which is what Zimmermann would have been if they had caught him bootlegging. You're on the wrong track. Zimmermann needn't have got into the racket at all—unless someone had more on him than we know about."

Whit had to agree with that. He said, "Well, then Wolff had him by the short hairs some way, and—"

The detective interrupted again. "Wolff or the man we're looking for. We're accepting the fact that Wolff had a silent partner, and it's more logical to assume that he was the one who had the goods on Zimmermann. He probably forced Zimmermann to double-cross Wolff because of what he knew."

"That's one assumption. The other is that Wolff had Zimmermann over the barrel and Zimmermann got together with Mr. X to have Wolff killed. Their interests were the same—the silent partner saved a lot of money and kept out of trouble with the government, and Zimmermann got rid of the man who knew too much about him."

Webster nodded. "That's right. It could have happened either way."

"When was Zimmermann paroled?"

"1920."

"He was working at the brewery all through 1921. He must have come right out of Sing Sing to go to work."

"By God, now." Webster sat up straight. "He may have been paroled *to* someone. The parole boards are damn curious about what a man is going to do when they let him leave the state. Wolff or someone else may have gone on record as having a job for him. If it turned out to be somebody besides Wolff, we'd have a good idea where to do a little extra-special investigating."

"How long will it take to hear from New York?"

"Tomorrow, if they get right to work. But we don't have to wait for them. Call up Hall and ask him who got Zimmermann his job. If he doesn't know we'll ask everyone who was around in 1920 until we find out."

Whit reached for the telephone. He had the receiver halfway to his ear when he stopped and replaced it. "We'll tip our hand. If Hall is the man we want, he'll know what we're looking for."

"I thought you were sure it wasn't Hall," Webster said. "Anyway, what do we care if he guesses what we're after? If he lies to us we'll get him when we hear from New York."

"Suppose he just skips?"

Webster rubbed his hands. "Jesus, I just wish somebody in this case would do something foolish like trying to get away. All my worries would be over. Go on, telephone."

"All right. But let's call Marston first. He may know something about it and we won't have to take a chance on one of the stockholders dusting out for Mexico."

"We'll have to take a chance on Marston," said Webster.

Whit scoffed at him and picked up the phone. "You get the strangest ideas. I suppose Marston is hiring me to find out that he's the murderer."

"He might be. You seem pretty sure about him. Would you bet he isn't the man we're after?"

Whit nodded his head, said into the phone, "Call Mr. Marston, Miss Kelly," and hung up. "I'll give you four to one on the field. Pick anybody you like and I'll bet forty to ten that you're wrong. I'm a percentage player."

The detective smiled. "You sure are. Those aren't even bookmaker's odds."

"Let's make up the book and see." Whit reached for a scratch pad, wrote down a list of names, and handed the pad to Webster. "Those are the men who had something to do with Wolff in 1920 and are still alive."

The list was short; the names were Carpenter, Hall, Harrigan, Marston and Putnam. Whit said, "I'm putting Carpenter in, but I don't think he counts. He was just one of the stooges."

Webster shook his head as he looked at the list. "What about the dark horses? We might be overlooking someone entirely."

"Five to one," Whit said generously. "Six to one; pick them all and you can't lose."

The telephone rang. Miss Kelly said, "Mr. Marston has been in court all day, Mr. Whitney, and he isn't expected back until after four. Shall I leave a message?"

"Never mind. Call Mr. Hall at the Gold Star Brewery in Oakland." He hung up. "Marston's in court."

Webster nodded.

Mr. Hall was in. His voice over the telephone was as precise and careful as a radio announcer's. He made a sympathetic remark about Whit's unfortunate affair with he gunmen and hoped that everything was all right. Whit said it was, thanks. Did Mr. Hall know how Mr. Zimmermann had obtained his position at the brewery?

There was a long silence on the wire. Hall said finally, "I can't say, Mr. Whitney. Mr. Wolff was the active manager of the plant at the time. Mr. Zimmermann simply started to work one morning and was introduced to me later as the bookkeeper. At that time, my visits to the plant were—ah— infrequent."

Webster lifted his eyebrows. Whit shook his head. He said, "I should like very much to find out, Mr. Hall. I wonder if you would mind looking over the company records to see if you can find anything."

"Not at all. But I'm inclined to think there'll be nothing to find, Mr. Whitney. Most of our personnel records for years prior to 1923 were—ah—destroyed."

"Oh." Whit didn't like that. "Who destroyed them?"

"Mr. Wolff. We employed some—ah—unsavory characters during 1921 and 1922, as you are aware, and I believe Mr. Wolff wanted no record which would connect them with the corporation."

"I see. Do you think Mr. Harrigan would have the information? Or Mr. Putnam?"

"I can't say. You'd have to ask them."

"Would Mr. Marston know?"

"I can't say. I doubt it."

Whit had an idea. "What about Carpenter, Mr. Hall? Mr. Wolff's pilot. I understand that he was employed by the brewery before he worked for Mr. Wolff personally. Do you know anything about him?"

"You mean in regard to the time when he entered our employment? No, nothing at all."

Whit gave up. He thanked Mr. Hall for his cooperation and obtained his promise to call back if anything was in the records. Hall's name he scratched off the list.

Webster said, "One strike. Try Harrigan."

Whit put in the call. He said, "This man Putnam, Webster.

He's supposed to be in New York. Do we know he's there? Suppose he's really hiding out around here. He could shoot everyone in California without being suspected."

"That's right," Webster said seriously. "Except that there wasn't any reason to kill MacLeod until six or seven hours before it happened and you can't get out here from New York in that time. Also, I checked up. He's been in New York since he left town a month ago."

Whit said, "Oh, well. It was only a suggestion."

The phone rang again. Miss Kelly put Harrigan's house-boy on the wire. Mr. Harrigan had left in the morning and the houseboy didn't know when he'd be back. Any message, please?

"No thank you, please," said Whit, putting the phone in its cradle and making a neat check after Harrigan's name. "I'd call that one a ball. Old man Harrigan is out sleuthing around. I'll bet be finds something before you do."

"You're in my alley now. How much?"

"Ten bucks."

"It's a bet. He had a lucky break on Zimmermann, if he didn't shoot him himself. I'm not so sure he didn't."

"Four to one on the field. You kind of favor Harrigan, don't you?"

The detective shrugged. "I haven't any favorites. Harrigan is too interested to suit me, and his alibi for Sunday is no good. Besides, I don't like that story of his about slipping ten dollars to one of the men in the plant and getting Zimmermann's hideout. It smells. I sweated everyone in the plant and didn't get a thing."

"You weren't handing out any money. Also, you're a cop."

Webster grunted.

There were two names left on the list—Putnam and Carpenter. Whit said, "What about sending a wire to Putnam to see if he knows anything about Zimmermann?"

"Go ahead. He's at the Waldorf-Astoria and his initials are S. G. Ask him about Carpenter, too."

"That's a nice spy system you have. Too bad you can't get any real information."

Whit pressed a button on his desk. Miss Kelly came into the office with a notebook and pencil. Larson gave up his chair and leaned against the window. Miss Kelly sat down, pulled her skirt over her knees, poised her pencil and smiled brightly at Whit.

"Telegram to S. G. Putnam, Hotel Waldorf-Astoria, New York City." Whit looked at his watch. "Make it a straight wire: *Have you any information re employment of Zimmermann or Carpenter by Gold Star in 1920 or 1921 question mark. Who recommended their employment question mark.*" He turned to Webster. "What else?"

"Ask him if he knows where Carpenter is now."

"'*Where is Carpenter now question mark. Please wire rush collect. Important.*' Sign it—"

"Sign it *Webster, San Francisco Police,* Miss Kelly," Webster said. "We may get some action that way."

At the window Larson stretched his arms and yawned. "I could use some action. This job isn't as exciting as I thought it was going to be."

Webster opened his mouth, looked at Miss Kelly, and said mildly, "That will be all from you, Swede."

Outside in the reception room the telephone bell rang. Miss Kelly jumped to her feet. Whit said, "Take it in here if you like."

Miss Kelly took the phone from his desk and pushed over a switch. "MacLeod and Whitney... Yes. Who's calling, please? ... Just a minute." She put her hand over the mouthpiece. "Mr. Harrigan for you, Mr. Whitney."

Webster said, "Find out what he's doing." Whit nodded and took the phone. Miss Kelly went back to her desk in the anteroom.

Harrigan's voice was elated. "Hello, Whitney? I've been trying to get hold of the sleuth. Is he there? I've got news for him."

"Yes." Whit winked at Webster. "What's up?"

"I'm calling from the Alameda airport. I've found Carpenter."

"Oh, Jesus. Is he alive?"

The detective jumped out of his chair and said, "Give me that phone." Whit fought him off. Harrigan said, "I think so. He's up in an airplane now doing sky writing. He just dotted an i. You tell Webster to get over here in a hurry and grab him when he finishes his lessons." Mr. Harrigan chuckled. "How am I doing?"

"Wonderful. Stay there and keep an eye on him. We'll be right over."

Whit slammed the phone down and grabbed for his hat. "Carpenter," he said. "Harrigan's found him at the Alameda airport and you owe me ten bucks."

Webster said, "Come on, Swede. Move fast and keep your eyes open."

The phone rang again on Miss Kelly's desk as they ran out. They were half-way to the elevator when she opened the office door and called after them. "Your office is on the line,

Lieutenant."

The detective stopped, hesitated, and went back. Whit and Larson held the elevator at the floor until he came out again and joined them. He looked as if he had eaten something sour. In the elevator he took a bill from his wallet and handed it to Whit without comment.

Whit said, "Thanks. What was the call?"

"My office just received a wire from the Department of Commerce that Licensed Pilot Frederick Carpenter can be reached at the Alameda airport."

CHAPTER NINETEEN

BLOOD trickled from Fred Carpenter's split lip. He wiped it away with the back of his hand and said doggedly, "I'm telling you, it was an accident. His parachute didn't open, that's all."

Webster hit him again across the mouth and the split opened wider. The detective said, "Come on, spit it out. We haven't got all day. Who hired you to dump Wolff?"

The aviator put up his hand to wipe his mouth. Webster knocked it down and slapped him again. Carpenter's eyes flicked up to rest on the detective's face and then dropped. He let his arms rest on his knees.

Whit was watching him closely. He wondered if they had made a mistake in concluding that the aviator was responsible for Wolff's death. For one thing, Carpenter did not even seem frightened, in spite of the beating he had been taking from Webster, and Whit was sure a guilty man would have cracked before then. They had picked Carpenter up when he taxied his plane to a stop at the Alameda field and slammed him into a car before the chocks were under his plane wheels. The strong-arm tactics had started when they reached the police-station, and Whit knew that he would have given himself away before then if he had been in the aviator's place with anything to hide. Carpenter was either telling the truth or he had more courage and more will-power than anyone Whit had ever known.

The aviator sat on the edge of a bunk that stretched across one side of the cell. He was short and stockily built, and he wore brown moleskin pants and a leather jacket patched under one arm with a piece of adhesive tape. His hair was a bleached yellow that made his tanned face seem dark by contrast, and he appeared to be about forty-five. He looked at the floor where the drops from his lips were forming a puddle, and paid no attention to Webster's question.

Webster said, "What's the use of making it tough on yourself? We know that accident was a phony. All we want is the name of the man who gave you your orders."

Carpenter said nothing.

"You. I'm talking to you. Who was it?"

"It was an accident," Carpenter said patiently. "We were over the mountains—" The detective hit him hard with the back of his hand and a new split appeared in Carpenter's lip. Webster said, "We can get it out of you. Some of the tough boys down in the basement will make you think you've been through a concrete mixer. There's no sense in making us do it the hard way. Tell us what we want to know and we'll fix it so you get off easy."

Carpenter continued to watch the puddle on the floor. Webster looked at Whit standing by the cell door. Whit jerked his head. The two men left the cell and walked down the corridor out of earshot.

"You aren't getting any place beating him up," Whit said. "I don't like the idea of having it slugged out of him. How about letting me have him for a while?"

"I'm not going to slug him. The Commissioners won't let you lay a hand on these crooks any more." Webster sucked at his knuckles. "I was just trying to scare him. What's your idea?"

"I'm going to try to make a deal with him."

"What sort of a deal?"

"It's worth a lot of money if he has any real information. I thought I'd offer him a cut—let him know what we're up against and tell him there's a thousand dollars in it for him if he comes through. We can't lose anything and he might open up."

"You'd get a long way with that. Nobody's going to take a chance on a murder rap for a thousand dollars. Anyway, I can't be a party to it. It's bribery."

"Well, five thousand, then, and you don't know anything about it. You fix it with the district attorney to get him off easy and I'll do the bribing without telling you."

Webster didn't think it would work but he agreed to let Whit try. "I want to squeeze him a little more on those Saturday and Sunday alibis," he said. "If I don't get anything constructive you can have him."

A uniformed turnkey stopped them as they walked back to the cell block. He said, "There's a couple of reporters here to see you, Lieutenant."

"To hell with them. Tell them I'm out."

"I told them you were busy. They said they had to talk to you and they'd wait."

"I don't want to see them at all, Pete. Get than out of here."

"Yes sir." Pete turned away. Webster said, "Something else you can do for me." He jerked his thumb over his shoulder. "I'm going to be in the cage down there. In about five minutes I want to get called out to the telephone."

"Yes sir. In five minutes." The turnkey walked on down the corridor.

Whit and the detective went back to the cell. Carpenter still sat on the bunk with his elbows on his knees. His lip had stopped dripping blood and was beginning to swell.

Webster had a notebook in his hand. He said, "Where did you say you were Saturday between five and seven?"

"I was sky-writing until five. Then I went home, changed my clothes and had dinner. I had a date at seven."

Webster looked at his notebook. "This Mabel broad?"

"Yes." Carpenter's swollen lip interfered with his enunciation.

"Will she back you up?"

Carpenter shrugged. "How do I know? Ask her."

Webster said, "I'm getting tired of bruising my hand on you, but don't get flip with me or I'll give you something to chew on. What did you and Mabel do Saturday night?"

"Went to the movies."

"Have a nice time?"

Carpenter looked up. "Screw you," he said.

Webster hit him backhanded and Carpenter's head jerked. "We don't like coarse language here, chum. We'll call on Mabel and God help you if she doesn't back you up."

Carpenter licked his lips and spat on the floor.

Webster looked at the notebook again. "Sunday you claim yo were giving flying lessons. Is that right?"

"Yes."

"Who to?"

"I don't remember their names. The airport sells the time and I take them up. You can look at the field records if you want to find out."

"You didn't fly to Sacramento during the day, did you?"

"What would I want to do that for?"

Webster said, "Shut up. I'm tired of smacking you. How long did you give flying lessons?"

"I was at the field most of the day. I had three students between ten and two-thirty or three, and another one that was supposed to be there at three-thirty. He didn't show up, so I knocked off about four."

"Then what?"

"I went to the Fair."

"With Mabel?"

"Yes."

The turnkey came back down the corridor and stopped outside the cell. "Telephone, Lieutenant."

Webster said, "Thanks. I'll be right there." He frowned at his notebook and put it in his pocket. "Come on, Whitney. We'll let the wrecking crew work on him for a while."

"You go ahead," said Whit. "I think I'll ask some more questions."

Webster said, "Have it your own way," and left the cell.

When the detective's footsteps could no longer be heard in the corridor Whit said, "I'm not going to stall with you, Carpenter. It's worth five thousand dollars to me to find out who engineered that airplane crackup. Cash on delivery." He waited, watching the aviator's face.

Carpenter looked up at him. "What do you guys want, anyway? Who are you trying to frame?"

"We aren't trying to frame any one. We know that airplane crackup was faked. Who arranged it?"

Carpenter shook his head. "You're crazy." His lip was bleeding again. He wiped his mouth on his sleeve, and the blood made a long wet smear on the black leather. Whit gave him the handkerchief from his breast pocket. Carpenter said, "Thanks. What are you in this for? You're not a cop."

"My name's Whitney. I'm working for Harald Wolff's daughter."

Carpenter mopped his lip. "Oh, yeah. I read about you in the papers." He looked at the blood on the handkerchief and put it back to his mouth. "You and the lawyer that got killed the other day were partners."

"He was an accountant." Whit took a package of cigarettes from his pocket and held them out. Carpenter put one carefully in the corner of his mouth, and Whit took one himself and lit them both. The aviator grinned on one side of his face and let smoke stream out of his nose. "The old come-on," he said. "You give me the soft soap for a while and then your boyfriend comes back and strong-arms me again." He shook his head. "O.K. What's next?"

"If you've read the papers I don't have to tell you what it's about. We know you were flying Wolff's plane and we know his parachute was fixed. I want the name of the man who hired you to crack up the plane, and I'm willing to pay for the information. I'll guarantee you'll get all the breaks when it comes to a trial."

Carpenter felt tenderly of his mouth. "I've read the papers enough to know they're full of hot air. What's the real lowdown?"

Whit hesitated, wondering how much to say, and decided that since he knew nothing himself there was nothing to be lost by talking. "You know about Wolff's tax troubles?"

Carpenter nodded. "I know he had 'em."

"His estate paid a million dollars in income tax—all the money he left when he died. My firm was retained by his daughter to do some work for her and my partner found out that part of the money shouldn't have been paid. He was murdered before he could talk to anyone about it. We have until Friday to file refund claims and we need information —now." He paused. "It's worth plenty to me to know who hired you to fix Wolff's parachute."

Carpenter looked at him through a cloud of cigarette smoke. "If I had fixed Wolff's parachute I'd sure be bright to tell you about it, wouldn't I?"

"We're not after you, Carpenter. We'll fix it so you get off easy. We're after the man that wanted Wolff out of the way. Who was he?"

Carpenter said, "Let me have another cigarette, will you?"

Whit held out the package. The aviator took one and got a light from the butt of his first. He sat and smoked for a while. Whit waited.

Carpenter said finally, "What if Wolff *was* murdered? How do you know it wasn't my idea?"

Whit shrugged.

"I don't, but I'm wrong all the way through if it was. I can't see you and Zimmermann as any-thing but stooges."

He was still watching Carpenter closely and he saw the aviator's eyelids flicker. Whit had mentioned Zimmermann accidentally, because the bookkeeper was linked with Carpenter in his mind, but he knew he had made a strike with the name. He said, "The same man murdered Zimmermann who killed my partner."

It was strike two. The aviator took a long drag on his cigarette, exhaled slowly, and said, "Zimmermann?"

"The bookkeeper at the brewery. It was in all the papers this morning. They found his body last night in old Sacramento."

"Oh, sure," Carpenter said indifferently. "I saw the headlines. Is that why the flatfoot wanted to know if I was in Sacramento?"

"Probably."

Carpenter laughed. "I'd sure be smart to kill somebody and then stick around Alameda waiting for the cops to pick me up."

"I guess you're right."

Whit walked across the cell to throw his cigarette into the corridor, thinking fast. There was a connection between Zimmermann and Carpenter. It could be the wedge they were after, if he handled it right. Carpenter and Zimmermann. Carpenter and Zimmermann. Zimmermann. . . the paroled jailbird whose story somebody knew, who had perjured himself and connived in Wolff's murder because of the threat of that knowledge, and who had been murdered in a dingy front room in Sacramento because of what he knew himself. Carpenter . . . the aviator and ex-gunman. Had he something in his background, as Zimmermann had, that had been held over his head to make him kill Wolff? Why had not the killer finished him off too, as he had Zimmermann? Or was Carpenter the killer himself, and Whit's theory wrong from start to finish?

He stopped in front of the bunk. "Whatever happens, we're going to hook somebody," he said. "Aside from Wolff, Zimmermann was killed, my partner was killed, and somebody took a shot at me the other night. We'll get someone eventually, and if we have to go after you, we'll make it just as tough on you as we can. Why don't you come in with us?"

Carpenter shook his head. "Jesus, I keep telling you you're off the beam. All I ever did was work for Wolff. When he was running beer I rode his trucks and stood off hijackers; when he stopped bootlegging, he hired me to fly his plane. He didn't mean a thing to me except a paycheck, and when he died I was out of a job. Why should I bump him off?"

"All right." Whit turned away. At the door of the cell he said, "The offer still stands. If you give us any information we can use by Friday, there's five thousand bucks in it for you and we'll make it easy on you with the district attorney's office. After Friday, it's going to be too bad. If we can hang anything on you it's your tough luck."

"I could use five grand. If I knew anything, I'd surer than hell tell you."

There were footsteps in the corridor. Webster came into the cell, clanging the door behind him. He said, "Get anywhere?"

"No. He won't talk."

The detective looked at Carpenter sitting silently on the bunk. "I'm getting tired of this," he said. "I kind of think I'll make this bastard give right now." He took three steps across the cell and hoisted the aviator up from the bunk by the slack of his loose leather jacket.

Carpenter was tough, and he saw what was coming. As he

came to his feet he slugged Webster in the belly with his right hand. The detective's grip on his coat loosened, and Carpenter hooked his left fist to Webster's face. It was a short powerful uppercut which would have put the detective out if it had hit squarely, but Carpenter was too close and it missed. Webster caught the aviator's left elbow and held it while he hit him twice in the face with his own left. The aviator's knees sagged. Webster shifted his grip, got him by the coat-front again with his left hand and smacked him twice with his right fist. Carpenter's whole body drooped. Webster let him fall back on the bunk.

Whit said, "You're not going to get anything out of him that way. You could hammer him all night and he wouldn't talk. He's tough."

"So am I tough," said Webster. "I don't like strong-arm stuff either, but what the hell are you going to do? You're the guy that wants action."

"I'd rather get it some other way."

"So would I. But I want to get it, one way or the other."

They watched the man on the bunk. It was four or five minutes before he blinked his eyes and sat up, shaking his head. His chin was covered with blood, and he spat a bloody mouthful on the floor. "You want to talk now, or do you want some more of it?" Webster said.

Carpenter said, "Screw you," and spat again.

Webster lifted him out of the bunk and Carpenter hit him with both hands, but the punches had no steam behind them. Webster held him away to get a free swing. There were rapid footsteps in the corridor and the turnkey and a little man with spectacles stopped in front of the cell. The little man peered through the bars. "Is Frederick Carpenter here?"

"What's it to you?" Webster said. He let Carpenter slide back on the bunk and crossed to the front of the cell. "What the hell do you want? Who are you?"

"I'm an attorney-at-law, Lieutenant, and I am serving you with a writ of habeas corpus demanding the body and person of Frederick Carpenter." He produced a folded paper. "Open up. I haven't all day."

Webster couldn't talk. He took the writ through the bars and the attorney yanked at the door and found it unlocked. He entered the cell and went to the bunk. "Are you Fred Carpenter?" he asked.

"Yes. Who the hell are you?" Carpenter's swollen lips made his words indistinct.

"Never mind that. Let's get out of here." The little man pulled at Carpenter's arm. Carpenter stood up, mopping his bleeding face with Whit's handkerchief. He said suspiciously, "What is this—a gag?"

"I'm your lawyer." The attorney looked at Carpenter's face and turned indignantly to Webster. "I'm going to report you, Lieutenant; this man has not even been charged, and you've beaten him to a pulp. The Commissioners shall hear of this." He pushed Carpenter ahead of him out of the cell and down the corridor.

Webster stared after them, holding the writ in his hand. The turnkey looked at his face and walked quickly away.

CHAPTER TWENTY

THERE were only three chairs in Webster's office. Whit sat in one. Webster's hat was on the second, and the third stood empty behind Webster's desk. Larson diplomatically sat on a table against the wall, and Webster prowled around the room kicking the wastebasket when he passed it.

Whit said, "There were two or three mechanics standing around at the airport when we took him. They saw us."

"What of it?" Webster said bitterly. "We might have been the Berkeley pound for all they knew. None of us was in uniform—we didn't even have an official car. Anyway, no grease-monkey knows enough to get a lawyer moving that fast, particularly a lawyer who never saw his client before. If that shyster ever laid his eyes on Carpenter in his life I'll eat the writ. Harrigan is our man, by God; I had an idea he was pulling a fast one when he wasn't at the airport. I'm going to slap him in the cooler so fast it will make his teeth rattle."

The detective was popping with impotent anger. After Zimmermann's death he had hung his hopes of solving the case on the capture of Carpenter, and there was no doubt in his mind that he would have slammed the information he needed out of the aviator if he could have held him. He had taken every precaution to keep the news of Carpenter's arrest from leaking out, and Carpenter had been sprung anyway. Webster wanted to get his hands on Mr. Harrigan.

Whit said, "Well, if Harrigan got him out, why did he turn him in to us?"

"I don't know. I don't know a thing about anything, but I'm going to jug Harrigan if I lose my job for it. He tipped us off to Zimmermann and Zimmermann was dead when we found him. He tipped us off to Carpenter and Carpenter was out less than three hours after we picked him up. Harrigan has been sucking around me asking questions and playing at being an amateur detective, and every time he has anything to do with the case something backfires. His alibi is full of holes, his stories about getting information stink, and I don't like him anyway. Even if he isn't the man we want he's a goddamn nuisance and the best place for him is in the can." Webster sat heavily on his hat, out of breath.

It was not the time to reason with him. Whit said, "Let me look at the writ. I've never seen one."

The detective took the paper out of his pocket and handed it over. While Whit was reading it the telephone rang. Webster went to the desk to pick up the receiver. "Hello," he said. "You sure took your time getting him, didn't you? Put him on." He waited for the connection. "Hello, judge. . . I'm terrible, thanks. You ruined a case for me this afternoon . . . Fred Carpenter . . . All right, maybe it wasn't legal, but he was a key witness and you've blown me out of the water . . . I won't argue. Who hired the shyster that came in here with the writ? . . . Well, what was his name, then? . . . How do you spell it?" He scribbled on the desk blotter. "Thanks."

Webster put the receiver back on the hook and reached for the telephone directory. He leafed through the book, found the page he wanted, and ran his finger down the column. "Sam Mendell, attorney," he said. "Financial Center Building."

Whit stopped him as he went to take his crushed hat from the chair. "What are you going to do?"

"I'm going to throw the fear of God into Mr. Mendell and find out who sent him to spring Carpenter. If it was Harrigan I'm going to charge him with murder."

"You're too excited to use your head. Do you think Mendeli is waiting for you to drop in on him? Whoever sent him here is going to be damn sure he isn't around to answer any questions."

Webster punched his hat into shape, put it on his head, and took it off to look at it. Whit said, "You can find out for yourself without wasting your time going up there. Telephone his office."

The detective sighed, hung his hat on the hat tree, and went back to his desk. "You do it." He pushed the phone toward Whit. "Tell them your name is Smith or something and you want to see Mendell about getting a divorce. If he is there I don't want to scare him away."

Whit called Mr. Mendell's office, said his name was Peter G. Hemingway, and asked if he could make an appointment to see Mr. Mendell about a legal question. Mr. Mendell's name had been given to him by a friend. Mr. Mendell's secretary was sorry but Mr. Mendell had left town that afternoon for an indefinite period. If Mr. Hemingway would leave his number she would be glad to telephone him when

Mr. Mendell returned. Whit gave her a wrong number and hung up. "Mr. Mendell is temporarily out of town."

"This is my last case," said Webster. "I'm going to resign and raise chickens in Cupertino."

"It's not a bad business. Before you quit the force, let's assume that Harrigan is on the level, just for the sake of argument. Whoever hired Mendell knew that we had Carpenter almost as soon as we got him. How many people does that cover?"

"Harrigan," Webster said viciously.

"And two or three grease-monkeys, and you and I and the Swede. Anyone else?"

Webster turned to look at Larson. Larson said nervously, "I was downstairs pounding my ear all the time you were working on the guy, Lieutenant. I didn't talk to anybody."

"Who the hell asked you?"

Larson said weakly, "I just thought—" The rest of it was a mumble.

The office door opened. Murphy put his head in and said. "See you for a minute, Lieutenant?"

"I'm busy. Come back in a quarter of an hour."

"Yes sir." Murphy closed the door.

Whit said, "The boys at the airport may have had instructtions to do a little telephoning if anything happened to Carpenter. Why don't we go back there and ask questions?"

Webster laughed humorlessly. "One reason is that I'd be picked up for impersonating an officer. I was out of my jurisdiction when I snatched Carpenter across the bay, and those Alameda constables are going to be sore when they find out about it. I wouldn't want to be caught on the wrong side of the fence."

Whit couldn't think of an answer to that. The detective said, "Try again. If you don't like Harrigan, what about the girl in your office? Maybe she blabbed to somebody."

"Miss Kelly?" Whit shook his head. "No. She knows enough not to give out information to anyone who asks for it. Anyway, how would she know we had Carpenter? We didn't even tell her where we were going."

"She could have listened in on Harrigan's call."

"Not with the telephone set-up in my office. You can't cut in on a busy line."

"All right. You didn't talk, she didn't talk, I didn't talk, and the Swede kept his big mouth shut because he was asleep. That leaves Harrigan or someone at the airport, and I pick Harrigan. I'm going to pull him in."

Whit stood up. "You know your business, Lieutenant. I think you're wrong. Harrigan has given you a lot of help."

"He's given me a lot of bum steers. I'll feel better when he's in the tank."

"You're the boss. I'll see you later."

Larson followed Whit out of the office.

Webster went to the window and stood looking at the street, his hands jammed in his pockets. A sparrow lit on the window ledge and began pecking hopefully at spots on the building-stone. Webster watched it for a minute and said, "Get the hell off of there." The sparrow cocked his head to look him over, and the detective made threatening gestures through the glass. The sparrow flew away.

Murphy came in after a while and took the chair opposite the desk. Webster said, "What did you get?" without turning around.

"Nothing."

"How far did you go?"

"I saw everybody within a block of the place. There's a bar in the alley back of the Farmers' Exchange and the windows are right opposite the bottom of the fire escape. I talked to the bartender who was on duty Saturday. He says anybody who would try to go up the ladder without being seen would be just a plain damn fool. I think he's right."

"Then our man went through the lobby. Did you talk to anyone across the street in front?"

"Everybody in the block. They're so used to people going in and out of the building they don't even know it's there. I dug up the newsboy who peddles papers on the corner of Montgomery and he says he unloaded everything he had before five o'clock and went home. The man on the beat didn't see anything, and I worked over both elevator operators again and they didn't know any more than they told you. I just didn't get any place, Lieutenant. The financial district is pretty dead on Saturday afternoon, but there are enough people around so that no one would notice a man going into an office building."

Webster said, "Damn it, he couldn't have walked right in. He had to make sure that the elevator was up before he crossed the lobby, so he must have hung around outside looking through the doors. Somebody should have noticed that."

"He didn't have to hang around the entrance. There's a florist shop right next to the lobby and you can see the elevators through the windows from the street. If he did any waiting he was looking at the flowers. Nobody would pay any attention to him."

Webster stared out the window. Murphy said, "You want me to keep working on it, Lieutenant, or shall I go back to checking the alibis?"

"How are they coming?"

"Swift is out of it. His doctor says he's been paralyzed below the waist for ten years and can't move out of his wheelchair. We dug up a woman next door to Hall who says she saw him in the garden off and on Sunday, but she isn't sure of the times. I've got a man working on DeWitt's trail Saturday night, and another one talking to the people who live next door to Marston. Maybe we'll get something, maybe we won't."

Webster looked out at the street without speaking. Murphy said finally, "I've got an idea I'd like to work on, Lieutenant, if it's all right with you."

"What is it?"

"I talked to the owner of the Buick that was lifted the night Whitney was shot. He says he had it parked in front of a bakery on Telegraph Hill about an hour before the shooting, and I can't see any reason for a couple of gunmen to walk up the hill to pinch a car. Seems to me it would be a lot easier to lift one down at the bottom—unless they were on the hill to start with."

Webster turned around to look at him. "You're using your head," he said grudgingly. "Whereabouts was it?"

"Union Street, almost up to Kearny. It was probably the first loose car they saw and they piled in. I'd like to spend a little time looking around, the hill, if picking up those gorillas means anything to you."

"It means plenty," Webster said grimly. "If I could get a lead on those boys—" He shook his head. "What do you want to do?"

"Suppose I go over and talk to all the women on the street? There's usually a crowd of them hanging out the window in the evening, and if these punks were local gangsters somebody may have recognized them."

"If they're local boys no one will talk."

"There are a lot of feuds on the hill, Lieutenant. The Spaniards hate the wops, the wops hate the Portuguese and the Portuguese hate everybody. If I have any luck at all I'll pick up something inside of twenty-four hours, and if I don't I'll give it up."

"You might as well try it. There's nothing to lose."

"Yes sir."

Murphy was half-way to the door when Webster said, "Wait a minute," Murphy stopped. The Lieutenant kicked at the wastebasket a couple of times before he spoke. "This isn't an ordinary case, Murphy. If it was different we'd take a lot of time, run every lead down to the end, and sew the case up right. We haven't the time now."

Murphy waited for him to go on. The Lieutenant was building up to something.

"If we break the case by Friday, it will be because we're lucky enough to hit on the one lead that will do something for us. We have to take chances to find it. The biggest chance we're taking is that there will be more shooting in the next forty-eight hours, and if there is I think the same torpedoes who tried to knock off Whitney may be doing it." Webster moved the wastebasket with his foot. "If we pick them up now somebody will blab, they'll have a lawyer bailing them out in ten minutes, and we'll be stymied."

"You want me to forget about it?" Murphy was puzzled.

"No. I want you to locate them without letting them know it. They're a lot more valuable to me on the loose."

Murphy smiled faintly. "If I pick up their trail I can sleep in the same bed with them and they won't know it."

"All right, then. If you find them, hang on their tails but don't make the pinch. Get in touch with me and I'll send somebody to give you a hand. Don't tell anybody what you're working on—nobody at all. There's too much leakage around here. If you need help I'll give you some men I can trust to keep their mouths shut."

"Yes sir." Murphy turned to go.

"If you slip you'll get yourself bumped off," Webster warned him. "Don't take any chances."

"I won't slip," Murphy promised. He left the office.

Webster had turned off the light and was fixing the catch on the door when the phone rang. It was Whit, and he was mad. He said, "Have you seen the papers?"

"No. What's up?"

"I take back everything I said about Harrigan. He's either the man you're after or he's too dumb to be wandering around loose. The only safe place for him is in solitary confinement."

"What are you talking about?"

"Buy yourself a newspaper." Whit hung up.

Webster said, "Now what the hell?" and went out of the room.

It was getting dark in the street. A newsboy in front of the building had an armload of papers. The detective bought a Call and opened it under the street-light. On the front page was a smiling picture of Harrigan, and underneath it the story read:

AMATEUR DETECTIVE ASSISTS POLICE

San Francisco, May 22, 1940—Edward Harrigan, retired East Bay businessman and former associate of the late Harald Wolff, local brewer, today stated to reporters that he had led the San Francisco police to their first arrest arising from the murder of George MacLeod, local accountant. MacLeod was killed last Friday while engaged in the preparation of a claim for income taxes which had been illegally collected from Wolff's estate (story on page three), and the police have been at a loss to solve the mystery of his murder. Harrigan, who was a close personal friend of Wolff, has been carrying on an independent investigation of his own. He stated that he had succeeded this afternoon in locating Frederick Carpenter, a former employee of Wolff who is alleged to be a key witness in the case. Said Harrigan: "The police have taken Carpenter into custody, and I am confident that as a result they will soon apprehend MacLeod's murderer."
At a late hour this afternoon no confirmation of Harrigan's statement could be obtained from the authorities.

The paper had been on the streets at three o'clock that afternoon, more than an hour before Mendell arrived at the police station.

CHAPTER TWENTY-ONE

KITTY MacLEOD was sitting at Miss Kelly's desk boring herself with a back issue of The Journal of Accountancy when Whit came into the office to telephone Webster. Kitty looked beautiful in a silver fox cape and a hat with a nose-veil, but Whit was too angry to notice it. Larson wasn't. He thought Mrs. MacLeod was pretty hot stuff, and dressed up to go to town she could have his badge any time. Next to Marian Wolff she was his favorite woman.

Whit cooled off a little after he had talked to Webster. He was still mad at Harrigan's stupidity or chicanery or whatever it was, but not too upset to be surprised at finding Kitty in his office at six o'clock. He said, "You look like Mrs. Astor's plush horse. What are you doing here?"

"Waiting for you. What were you being so grim about on the phone?"

"Harrigan." Whit handed her his newspaper. "Look at that. He's either the biggest damn fool in California or he's the murderer. I'm not sure which."

Kitty read the story. "What's so bad about it?" She asked. "I should think you'd be happy that you've caught Carpenter. Wasn't he the man you were looking for?"

"We lost him." He told her what had happened, expecting at least her moral support to his indignation. She said, "Whit, you're wearing yourself out. You haven't done anything but stew over this since Saturday, and it's not good for you. You won't accomplish anything by damning Mr. Harrigan. Why don't you relax and forget about it for a while?"

"Forget about it?" Whit's voice rose. "How can I forget about it when we had the whole case sewed up tight and a dim-wit like Harrigan kicked it out the window? I'm trying to find the murderer of your husband, and you sit there—"

"Don't be melodramatic," Kitty said calmly. "Lieutenant Webster will find him sooner or later. You're interested in Marian Wolff's money, and it's too much of a strain on you. I've decided that you need a little distraction. You and Mr. Larson are going to take me to the movies."

"Now that's what I call a real good idea," said Larson.

"Out of the question," Whit said firmly. "Even if I didn't have four or five gunmen looking for me I wouldn't go out tonight. The day after tomorrow is Friday and I have work to do."

"Anyone who wants to shoot you can do it here as easily as he can in a movie," Kitty said. "And stop talking about the day after tomorrow. It's a long way off. I've been waiting here since five o'clock for you to come in. You're going to take me to Chinatown for dinner and then we're going to see the Marx brothers, so stop arguing."

Larson grinned at Whit. "I think you're outvoted, chum."

"Positively not," Whit said. "I'm going to stay right here and work."

They went to Chinatown.

After three old-fashioneds at the Imperial Dragon Whit began to forget about Harrigan, and after the fourth he stopped looking nervously over his shoulder every time someone came into the bar. When they were all pleasantly tight they went to a restaurant around the corner and ate quantities of *fan kai ngow yuk* and egg-flower soup in a booth that Larson selected because it could not be approached from the side. For dessert Whit ordered a bottle of something strong and sweet called *ng ka pe* and they drank it out of tea cups. It was quite a party.

Halfway through the dinner Whit found himself wondering again about Kitty and her feeling toward him. He had drunk enough so that he was sure a little heart to heart talk was desirable; after all, he and Kitty were old friends and they ought to be able to discuss things rationally.

His opportunity for the *tête-a-tête* came when Kitty looked at her wrist-watch and decided to call the theatre and ask what time the feature started. She was sitting between Whit and the wall of the booth. He kept his seat when she tried to get out.

She said sweetly, "Would you mind moving your hulking self?"

"Larson will phone. What theatre are we going to?"

Kitty made another futile attempt to get by him and then sat down. "The Paramount."

"Be a pal, will you, Swede? Find out when it starts."

Larson said, "You know what the Lieutenant said about me taking my eye off of you. Anyway, it doesn't matter where you start with the Marx Brothers. Let's go when we get ready."

He was reaching for the bottle when Whit kicked his shin.

"Mrs. MacLeod wants to know when the movie starts. You can keep your eye on me from the telephone booth."

"Oh. Sure, I'll call them." Larson squeezed out from behind the table. Whit said, "Call up the other theatres and find out what's showing. Maybe there's something better than the Marx brothers."

"I was thinking of that." Larson went to the telephone booth and closed himself inside.

Whit filled Kitty's cup and his own with the liqueur. He was pleased with himself for being so clever. All he had to do now was persuade Kitty to answer a few tactful questions. He said, "Marian Wolff came in to see me today."

"Oh? What did she want?" Kitty was only mildly interested.

"Primarily, she wanted to know if you were trying to spike her chances of getting her money back, and if so why." Whit felt that he had phrased it nicely; no shilly-shallying but still plenty of tact.

"What did you tell her?"

"I told her I thought you were and I didn't know why. I wish I did."

Kitty wiped her fingertips with her napkin. "If we're going to see that picture we'd better hurry."

"We have plenty of time." Whit decided to abandon the tact. "Let's come out in the open, Kitty. What have you against Marian Wolff?"

Kitty said, "For heaven's sake, Whit. I haven't anything against anybody. My only reason for wanting you to stop this detecting is because I don't like to see you involved with people who shoot at you on dark streets. You're not a policeman and you have no business chasing murderers. Whatever you might get from Marian isn't enough to be killed for."

Whit was squarely up against a question that was not easy to ask, tactfully or otherwise. He tried subterfuge.

"Marian seemed to think you must have a pretty big interest somewhere in the case if you felt justified in trying to prevent her from getting half a million dollars. I couldn't answer that either."

Whit scowled at the liqueur bottle. Things weren't going right. He wished he hadn't been so clever.

Kitty was silent. Across the room Larson looked at them through the glass of the phone booth and pawed through his pockets. He was out of nickels. He dialed a number at random and listened to the buzz of the dead line in the receiver. If Whit wanted privacy Larson was willing to cooperate.

Whit was still waiting for Kitty to say something and still looking at the bottle. When she didn't answer him, he blurted it out. "Why did you kiss me the other day?"

She said indistinctly, "I didn't. You kissed me."

"The idea was mine, but you carried it out. I want to know why."

Kitty picked up her purse from the table and said, "Let me out." Whit got up and she slid out from behind the table. He looked at her then. Her face was red. He felt like a fool, but he was stubborn. He said again, "I want to know why."

"I don't know." Kitty was furious. "I think it was a mistake and I won't do it again. If you want to get yourself killed because of that blonde bitch you go right ahead. It's your privilege." She walked away.

Whit said, "Wait a minute," and followed her across the floor between the tables. He caught her arm before she reached the door, and she whirled and slapped him a stinging blow across the mouth. He let her go at that, and she went through the door without looking back. The Chinese eating at the tables looked up incuriously for a moment and went back to their rice.

Larson had come out of the telephone booth when Whit got back to the table. He said, "What happened?"

"She's mad about something."

"I could see that. What about?"

"How do I know, god damn it? I'm no mind reader. She's just mad. Let's get out of here.

"There go the Marx Brothers," Larson said regretfully. "I was all set to go to a movie, too. You going back to your office?"

"I'm going home and go to bed," said Whit. "I feel terrible."

~§~

At eight o'clock Murphy had covered half a block on each side of the bakery and was ready to quit. The last building was a three-story flat at the corner of Union and Kearny. He decided to have one more try before he gave up. On the ground floor the door was slammed in his face when he suggested that the occupants needed insurance and he would be glad to sell them some. At the second floor he got a better reception from an old couple who invited him in for a glass of wine and nodded at everything he said. They spoke only Italian, however, and he left after he finished the wine.

On the third floor he got his break.

The door was opened by a fat woman with a black mustache.

Murphy said, "Good evening," and held out a card which introduced Mr. Robinson of the Atlantic and Pacific Insurance Co.

"May I come in?"

The fat woman bellowed over her shoulder, "Ramon, *ven aquí*."

Murphy held his hat across his bosom and waited.

Ramon came to the door in a pair of dungarees and a singlet. He looked Murphy over.

"Whadya want?"

"May I come in?" Murphy asked politely. "I have a message of great importance to you from—"

"Whadya selling?"

"Automobile insurance. Do you drive a car?"

"Yeah. I don't need no more insurance." The door started to close. Murphy said hurriedly, "You can't have too much insurance at present low costs. Just the other day a car was stolen right in this block and my company has already settled for the damage. The owner recovered the full price of the car within twenty-four hours after it was located. The rates—"

Ramon said, "No fooling? The black Buick that got hooked down the street?" The door opened wider.

Murphy put his foot across the sill. "That's the one. My company even located the thieves; a couple of schoolboys from the Mission. Can you imagine high-school kids coming all the way over here to steal a car?" Murphy shook his head. "It shows how important it is to have enough insurance, doesn't it?"

Ramon said, "Come on in and siddown. What makes you think they were high-school kids?"

"Thanks." Murphy came in. The fat woman was in the kitchen and there seemed to be no one else in the flat. "Why, they were identified. We found a man who saw them get into the car and drive away. They denied it, of course, but we had the witness."

"You're screwy," said Ramon. "Hey, maw. C'mere."

Maw came in from the kitchen wiping her hands. Ramon told her a long joke in Spanish, and she answered him at length and waved her arms at Murphy. Murphy looked indifferent.

Ramon said, "Jeez, that's a laugh. Maw saw the guys that pinched that Buick, and they weren't no high-school kids from the Mission, either."

"I guess your mother must have made a mistake," Murphy said patronizingly. "We caught them."

"She didn't make no mistake. She was hanging out the window when that can was lifted."

"Well, well. How can she be so sure? Did she recognize the thieves?"

"Sure she recognized them. Couple of wop bastards that live right around the corner." He snorted. "High-school kids, my fanny."

Murphy said, "That's very interesting. If we've made a mistake we'll have to correct it. Do you know the names of these men?"

Ramon became cautious all of a sudden. "No, sir. I ain't saying. I don't want to tangle with those boys."

"You won't tangle with anyone. Let me know their names and you can forget all about it. We'll take care of them."

"Nope." Ramon had no doubts about it.

"There's twenty dollars in it for you."

"Nope." He was not so sure but still sure enough. Evidently those wop bastards were bad medicine.

Reluctantly Murphy reached into his pocket and hauled out a badge. "All right, son. Police business. Better let me have the names."

Ramon was scared. Maw couldn't follow the conversation but she saw the badge and began to scream Spanish at him.

He shut her up and said, "What the hell is this?"

"Just let me have those names. You won't get into any trouble."

It took fifteen minutes of bullying and the twenty dollars before Murphy got what he was after. Maw didn't need an interpreter to understand legal tender. She and Ramon clashed over who should get it. Murphy left them yelling at each other.

The fog was coming in when he got out in the street. The address Ramon had given him was half-way up the steep Kearny Street hill beyond Union. He toiled up the grade and looked the house over carefully as he went by. There was no garage to the place that he could see and no car parked in front of it, although lights were on inside. He had a hunch that the wop boys borrowed a car only when they needed one on business.

He went over the top of the hill and turned down Filbert Street.

On Grant Avenue he found a drugstore and called headquarters. Webster was not there. Murphy tried his home, with no better luck, and left the store. He didn't like the idea of sitting up in the fog all night on Telegraph Hill without a relief, but Webster had told him what to do and Murphy was not going to cross him. Besides, the Lieutenant came through for anyone who came through for him. Murphy was ambitious.

At different stores he bought a heavy sweater, a thermos bottle, a pint of whiskey, and three packages of cigarettes. In a restaurant he got a paper bag full of hamburger sandwiches and had his thermos bottle filled with coffee, and with his packages under his arm he went back up Filbert Street. The lights were still on at his mousehole. Across the street from the house was an empty lot surrounded by a board fence. Murphy looked around, clambered quickly over the fence, and pried a board loose so he could see. He put the sweater on under his coat, ate three of the sandwiches, and cooled his coffee with whiskey. When he had polished off half the coffee and a quarter of the whiskey he lit a cigarette and settled down. Once during the night he left his post to telephone, and caught Webster at his home. They had a long conversation. Two men in shabby clothes joined Murphy at dawn.

CHAPTER TWENTY-TWO

THURSDAY MORNING was cold and foggy. Whit woke up late, feeling pretty good for the first time in three days, and continued to feel pretty good until he stretched his arms. Larson came running in from the kitchen in his shirt sleeves with his gun in one hand and a half-eaten piece of toast in the other. When he saw no one to shoot at he said, "Jesus, don't yell like that. What happened?"

"I split myself open." Whit held his side with both hands.

"Is that all?" Larson snapped the safety catch on his automatic and pushed it into the holster strapped under his arm. "I thought you was shot."

"I am shot," Whit said sourly. "What do you think I was yelling for? What time is it?"

"Nine o'clock."

Whit swore and swung his legs out of bed. "You should have called me. I'm supposed to be at work at nine."

Larson shrugged. "I'm a bodyguard, not an alarm clock. Anyway, it's your office now. Who cares what time you get to work?" He put the rest of the toast in his mouth.

"That's right." Whit went into the bathroom. "Who cares if I pay the rent? Scramble me some eggs, will you?"

"There's a nice piece of liver in the icebox," Larson said through the mouthful of toast.

"Scrambled eggs!" The bathroom door slammed.

The fat doctor who had given Whit up as a bad job knocked on the door while Whit was drying the parts of his anatomy which had been in the tub. Professional interest coupled with curiosity stirred up by the newspapers had been too much for the doctor. He sat on the toilet seat and asked questions about the murders while Whit rubbed a towel gently over his sunburned legs.

Whit answered yes and no until he was tired of it. "I can't tell you any more about the case than the papers. What I'm interested in is having a bath above my navel. How soon are you going to take this bandage off?"

"A month or two." The doctor reluctantly got down to business. "Let's have a look at it."

The hair on Whit's chest was invisible to the naked eye, but there was enough of it to make him wince when the adhesive tape was stripped off. He watched the operation in the mirror. It was the first time he had seen the wound, and it made him wonder at his own fortitude. A deep furrow stretched for six or seven inches along his ribs, narrow in front and widening to a broad gash toward the back. The doctor scowled and prodded the flesh along the cut.

"What have you been doing—tumbling?"

"Take it easy." Whit shied away. "I popped it this morning. Nothing like a good stretch when you wake up."

The doctor sniffed. While he was putting on a clean bandage he said, "You'll have a good stretch in bed if you keep running around pulling the cut open every five minutes. It's clean now, but you can't take any chances. If you get it infected—" He shrugged, pressed down a last strip of adhesive, and closed his bag.

"Thanks." Whit went into the bedroom and took a pair of shorts from a drawer. "I'll remember that. Have some breakfast?"

"No, thanks." The doctor picked up his bag. At the bedroom door he said, "You're a damn fool, Whitney. You belong in bed."

"I have to earn a living." Whit buttoned his shorts.

"So do all the little streptococci. I'll see you tomorrow." The doctor left.

After he had eaten his scrambled eggs Whit telephoned Kitty MacLeod and stumbled through an apology. He tried to convey the impression that he knew he had done something wrong but wasn't sure what it was.

Kitty said, "It's all right." Her voice was not cordial.

"Will you go to the movies with me tonight?"

She didn't answer for a moment, and then she said, "Won't you be busy?"

"Not too busy."

"You're still working for Marian?"

"Yes. Until tomorrow, anyway."

There was another pause. She said, "I'm afraid I can't make it."

"How about tomorrow?"

"I'm going to be busy tomorrow."

It was beginning to seep in. While he was wondering what to say next she hung up.

In the cab that took him to the office Whit said, "Swede, Mrs. MacLeod hates Marian Wolff's guts. I wonder why."

"If you ask me, she's jealous. She likes you, and the blonde has been giving you the eye." Larson sighed. "I wish one of them would give me a play. Either one."

Whit shook his head. "There's more to it than that."

"When a doll is mad at another doll she's jealous of her or she's afraid of her. She's threatened by her. There isn't any reason why Mrs. MacLeod should be scared of the blonde. Think it over."

Whit thought it over.

At the office Miss Kelly was cutting pieces out of the newspaper to paste in her scrapbook, and Tommy Ward was bursting with excitement. He buttonholed Whit as soon as he came through the door. "About that matter we were discussing yesterday, Mr. Whitney. I'd like to talk to you about it." Tommy was taking no chances. The boss had told him to be cautious, and as far as he was concerned the walls were a solid mass of dictographs.

Whit said, "Morning. Morning, Miss Kelly. Lead the way, Tommy."

They went into his office. The Wolff papers were on Whit's desk, and on top of the pile was Zimmermann's list of payments. Tommy had written numbers after the items in the list—some in red pencil, some in blue. The numbers were preponderantly red.

"I may be all wet, Mr. Whitney," said Tommy. Whit could tell from the sound of his voice that he didn't think so. "But it looks to me as if those payments were made to two people. They split fifty-fifty."

Whit said, "They what?"

"Yes sir. Look at these first four items—January twelfth, fifteenth, seventeenth and eighteenth. I've marked them all number 1, in red. They add up to $1384. The fifth payment, on January eighteenth, is $1384. I marked that number 1 in blue. The next six payments plus the eighth, are all number 2, red, and they total $2755. The seventh is number 2, blue, for $2755. The next three—"

Whit felt excitement stir in him as he looked at the long list. "Does it work out all the way through?"

"Right down the middle." Tommy was proud, nervous, and happy. "Once or twice a payment is over or short but it's offset against the next one. For the two years the amounts are exactly half and half."

Whit said reverently, "God, that's it. That's what MacLeod found. He said he thought Wolff had only got half, but he hadn't worked it all out." He clapped Tommy on the back. "Tommy, you're a hero. It's what I've been looking for."

Tommy swallowed and grinned. He couldn't think of anything to say.

Larson said, "What the hell are you talking about? You've got me all excited."

"Look here." Whit took him by the arm. "These payments were all supposed to have been made to Wolff, but Zimmermann split everything two ways. He made four or five payments to one man, probably Wolff—they're marked in red, number 1. Then blue came around for his cut and Zimmermann turned over the other half in a lump. Then he made four, five"—Whit was counting—"six payments to red, marked number 2, a payment to blue, and another payment to red to balance it off." Whit turned to Tommy. "The red must have been Wolff. He was at the plant all the time and Zimmermann would have turned the collections over to him every day or two, Blue came around only once in a while for his slice."

"That's what it looks like to me," said Tommy.

"And blue—wait a minute." Whit turned the pages of the memorandum. "What about the hunting trips? Did blue get anything while Wolff was up in the mountains?"

"I can't tell." Tommy pointed to a slip of scratch paper on the desk. "I called the Fish and Game Commission in the Ferry Building, and they gave me the hunting seasons in 1921 and 1922; Districts 1, 1 ½ , 4 ½, 23, 24, 25 and 26, September 1 to October 15; Districts 2, 2 ½ and 3, August 1 to September 14; District 4, September 16 to October 15. It depends on where Wolff went hunting, and how long he stayed away. Zimmermann didn't make any payments from August 1 to August 10 in 1921 and from August 1 to August 13 in 1922. In both years he made three payments to one man during the two weeks from September 1 to September 15 and paid the other one after the fifteenth. There are other combinations during the season."

Whit was frowning at Tommy's notes. "It would narrow the field if we knew whether blue went on those hunting trips."

Tommy shook his head. "We can't tell from the memorandum. If Wolff hunted from the first of August to the tenth or twelfth, the other man might have been with him. If it was from September first to the fifteenth, blue didn't go along. We'll have to find out when Wolff was away."

Whit said, "Boy, we're finding out right now," and reached

for the phone.

Lieutenant Webster was out. His department didn't know where he was nor when he would be back. Whit left an "urgent" message for Lieutenant Webster to come to Mr. Whitney's office as quickly as possible. The man at the switchboard promised to deliver it when he could.

Whit thought hard about the next step. MacLeod had said that he and Wolff and "a couple of the other stockholders" usually had gone hunting together. The other stockholders in 1921 and 1922 had been DeWitt, senior, Harrigan, Hall, Putnam and Rogers. Rogers and DeWitt were dead, and Putnam was in New York when MacLeod was killed. Either of the others might be definitely cleared or definitely suspect if Whit could find out about the hunting trips. Hall, Harrigan, Hall, Harrigan, *eeny meeny miny moe*. Why hadn't MacLeod known whom he was looking for? If he had gone deer-hunting in 1921 or 1922 he would have remembered who was along on the trip. Had he thought that one of the dead men had been responsible for Wolff's frame-up, and foolishly given away what he knew to the real murderer? Or had Zimmermann's figures been only of negative value to him, showing who could not have got the money but not who could? Or had he been going round and round in a squirrel-cage as Whit was, without knowing what the hell it was all about? Whit had one advantage over MacLeod for which he was grateful—a bodyguard. He took a long breath, picked up the telephone, and called the brewery.

Mr. Hall said, "Yes, Mr. Whitney?"

Whit remembered MacLeod's remark about stirring up the hive. "Mr. Hall, we discussed Wolff's deer-hunting trips once before, but there are a couple of questions I didn't ask. Did you ever go hunting with him?"

"Two or three times. I didn't enjoy it as much as the others and I avoided it after my first experiences."

"In what years did you go along?"

Hall paused for a long moment before he answered. "I don't remember exactly. It was after the war, perhaps as early as 1919 and as late as 1925. I couldn't say."

He had either a poor memory or a quick grasp of a dangerous situation. Whit said, "I see. Who accompanied Wolff regularly?"

"Mr. MacLeod and Mr. DeWitt invariably, Mr. Harrigan and Mr. Putnam less often but frequently. Mr. Rogers felt much as I did, I believe. I don't know whether he ever went along or not." Hall cleared his throat. "May I ask what you are attempting to—ah—establish, Mr. Whitney?"

Whit stirred the hive. "I have an important clue to the murderer. One more question, Mr. Hall. We've assumed that Mr. Wolff went hunting in the early part of August. Do you know for sure that he did? Could he have been away some other time—say in September or October?"

"I'm afraid my memory isn't that good. But you could find out, I'm sure. Ordinarily Mr. Wolff insisted on starting at the opening of the shooting season. If you could ascertain when it began—"

"The seasons vary from place to place, Mr. Hall. Perhaps you could tell me where the party went hunting. I could get the probable date from that."

"Let me see." He thought about it. "I presume you're concerned with 1921 and 1922?"

"Yes."

"I can't say. The first year I was in the party we went up the coast toward Fort Bragg, and another time we spent a week in the mountains back of the Monterey peninsula. Unfortunately I can't remember the years in which we made the trips. Have you thought to question Mr. Harrigan? His memory may be better than mine."

"I'm going to try him next. Thanks for the help. Will you let me know if you remember anything else?"

"I certainly shall."

"Thank you. Good-bye."

"Just a moment, Mr. Whitney. I was going to call you myself when you telephoned. I'd like to see you this afternoon for a few minutes, if I may. I have something to discuss with you."

"Something to do with the murder?"

"Well—yes and no."

Whit frowned. "Can't you discuss it over the phone? I'm going to be rather busy this afternoon."

"I'd rather not. My—I'm in my office. It's personal."

"Oh." What did he have on his mind now? "Could you give me an idea of what it's about?"

"Well, it's—I—hold the line a minute while I close the door." Whit could hear him put down the receiver and walk across the room. He was back in a moment. He said bitterly, "That young fool DeWitt has practically accused me to my face of having a hand in Wolff's death, and I gather he's suggested as much to you. I must see you."

"It's not necessary to see me, Mr. Hall." Buster DeWitt must have enjoyed putting the needle into him, from the reaction he had got. "Lieutenant Webster is in charge of the case. If it will relieve your mind at all, I was not impressed with Mr. DeWitt's theory."

"I'm glad to hear that. But I haven't been able to get in touch with Lieutenant Webster, and I want to correct any misstatements DeWitt may have made before they prove embarrassing. I'll take only a few minutes of your time."

Whit said reluctantly, "All right. When will you be in?"

"About two-thirty? Is that convenient for you?"

"Fine. I'll see you then."

Whit put the phone down. Tommy said, "Any luck?"

"Not much. Find out what hunting districts Fort Bragg and the Monterey peninsula are in and see when the seasons opened."

Tommy made a note.

Whit tried Harrigan next. Mr. Harrigan was out but his houseboy expected him back and was there any message, please? Whit left one. Mr. Harrigan was requested to see Mr. Whitney immediately.

Marian Wolff was also out—at least no one answered her telephone. Whit was irritated. He had practically solved the damn case all by himself and nobody was around to appreciate him. Webster out, Harrigan out, Marian Wolff out. He particularly wanted to see Marian Wolff. The butterflies danced in his stomach when he thought of the previous afternoon. Kitty's kiss had been surprising, but Marian's was an Experience. Of course, she was only interested in getting her money back and the kiss had been a bribe, but it hadn't seemed to bother her. There was no reason why she couldn't be interested in Whit and her money at the same time money wasn't everything.

Whit looked at the clock and took up the phone again. He said, "Miss Kelly, call Mr. Marston, and then send Krebs in to see me."

"Mr. Krebs is out of the office, Mr. Whitney. Shall I call him in?"

"Where is he?"

"He's at Mackay and Company. He went over to help Mr. Prentice with the audit. He'll be back this afternoon."

"When he comes in tell him I want him to check some figures for me. I'm starting to make up the Wolff refund claims."

CHAPTER TWENTY-THREE

MISS KELLY had been wrong. Mr. Prentice was auditing the books of Mackay and Company by himself, and Mr. Krebs was impersonating an officer of the law in an attempt to get information from the doorman at Marian Wolff's apartment house.

They were standing on the sidewalk in front of the entrance. The doorman said, "Yes, sir. About ten-thirty. They went up together and he came down in fifteen or twenty minutes and got into his car. He was pretty drunk. He almost ran into the telephone pole."

"He drove off immediately?"

"Yes, sir."

"In which direction?"

"The way his car was headed. He turned south on Leavenworth."

"I see." Krebs thought for a while. "Yes. Thank you very much." He walked away. The doorman had expected something more tangible than thanks. He made a nasty remark under his breath.

Krebs walked over to Sacramento Street and took a cable-car downtown. All during the ride he puzzled over something. At Montgomery Street he got off and went to the office, still puzzling. Miss Kelly said, "Mr. Whitney wants to see you. He and Mr. Marston are in his office making up the Wolff refund claims."

Krebs was crossing the anteroom. He stopped abruptly. "Have they discovered something?"

"You'll have to ask Mr. Whitney," Miss Kelly said primly. "He wants you to see him right away."

"I shall. Thank you."

Krebs went down the short hall and stopped in front of Whit's office. He could hear voices behind the closed door. He hesitated for a moment and turned to look back toward the reception room. Miss Kelly's desk was placed so that she could not see down the hall. Krebs went into MacLeod's office and closed the door softly behind him.

The dead man's papers and check stubs were still on the desk as Whit had left them when DeWitt came in the day before. Krebs went swiftly through the stubs until he found what he was after. MacLeod had made monthly payments to the Empress Garage; the stubs were marked *"gas, oil, & pking."* Krebs looked up the Empress Garage in the telephone directory, made a careful note of the address, and left the office. The door barely clicked when he closed it. He went quickly out through the reception room before Miss Kelly could say anything.

At the Empress Garage Krebs waited for ten minutes while the floor attendant took care of a driver who wanted his oil changed in a hurry. When the customer had gone his way the attendant came over to Krebs, wiping his hands on a rag. "Anything I can do for you, bud?"

"I should like some information, please," said Krebs. "Is this garage open all night?"

"Yep. Twenty-four hours a day."

"There is a man who works at night?"

"Yep."

"May I talk to him, please?"

The attendant cleaned the oil from between his fingers. "What do you want to see him about?"

"It is a private matter," said Krebs.

"I can't help you, bud, unless you want to tell me what you're after." The garage man put the rag in one hip pocket of his coveralls, took a jack-knife from the other, and went to work on his nails. "What's on your mind?"

He scraped at his nails for some time before Krebs said, "I am trying to trace a man who came here Friday night."

"What was his name?"

Krebs was up against it, and he wanted information badly. He said, "George MacLeod. The man who was murdered last Saturday."

"MacLeod," the attendant repeated. "The fellah who's been getting in the newspapers? Was he in here Friday night?"

"I don't know." Krebs' tone was sharper than usual. "It is what I am trying to find out."

"Hold your water," the attendant said. "I'm thinking. What kind of a car did he drive?"

"A Chrysler coupe."

"A Chrysler coop." He looked up from his nails. "You a dick?"

Krebs nodded.

The garage man folded his jack-knife and put it away. "O.K.,

I guess I know the guy you're after. He brought the coop in Friday night all right. It was all scratched to hell, so don't blame us for it. You want to take it out?"

"Not now. Who was here at the time?"

"I was. I'm on nights one week, days the next."

"I see." Krebs was finally getting somewhere. "When did he come in?"

"About eleven. He came booming up the driveway, slapped on the brakes, and jumped out and went to the can." The garage man pointed to a "Gents" sign. "When he came out of the john I asked him what he'd done to the paint on his car, and he didn't know and didn't care. He was drunk as a skunk."

"Why didn't you notify the police that he had been here?"

The attendant shrugged. "Nobody asked me. Anyway, I didn't know he was the guy that got shot; I've only been on this job a couple of weeks and I didn't know him from Joe Doakes. He was just another drunk who was sober enough to know he couldn't drive, as far as I was concerned."

"We shall overlook it, then," Krebs said. "Now if you can tell me anything that will help me to find where he went from here, I shall appreciate it."

The attendant looked at him carefully. "Is that so? What's it worth to you?"

"This is a serious matter," Krebs said stiffly. "If you have any information I advise you not to withhold it."

"Horse-collar," said the garage man in a friendly manner. "I don't know who you are or what you're doing, but you're no cop. So don't give me that stuff. How would you like it if I turned you in?"

He was smiling. Krebs said, "Very well, I am not a policeman. I want information and I am willing to pay for it."

"Now you're talking." The attendant held out his hand. "Let's feel something and I'll see what I can remember."

Krebs took out his billfold. "Can you give me any assurance that you have useful information?"

"Nope." The attendant wiggled his fingers. "Come on. You never accumulate if you don't speculate."

Krebs was not going to speculate without accumulating first, and there was a stalemate. The garage man said finally, "O.K. What's in it for me if I give you a lead to someone who knows where he went?"

"Five dollars."

The attendant snorted. "I wouldn't tell you the time for five dollars. Twenty bucks."

"Ten," said Krebs.

They settled at fifteen. Krebs opened the zipper on his wallet and took out two fives and five ones. He handed over a five and three ones as a down payment, and the attendant said, "He took a taxi down at the corner. I was watching him because I thought he was going to fall on his puss before he got there. You find the cab driver that picked him up and you'll know where he went." He wiggled his fingers again. "Let's have the rest of it."

Krebs held on to the money. "There are hundreds of taxi drivers in San Francisco. How am I going to find the one who drove him?"

"Kick loose of the seven bucks and I'll tell you."

He was a good bargainer. Krebs handed over the money and the garage man folded the fifteen dollars into a tight wad and tucked it behind a package of cigarettes in the breast pocket of his coveralls. After he had buttoned the flap of the pocket, he said, "He took a Pacific cab; they've got a call-box down at the corner. You go to the company office, find out which one of their hackers checked in from that call-box around eleven o'clock Friday night, and run him down. Anybody would remember a guy as drunk as your pal."

"The Pacific Taxicab Company," said Krebs. "Fine. Thank you very much."

"Same to you." The attendant patted his pocket.

Krebs wanted to say something else, but be wasn't sure how to put it. The garage man grinned at him. "I've already forgotten you were here, bud, if that's what's worrying you. And I'll give you a free tip; don't try that cop stuff no more. You can't get away with it."

Krebs thanked him for the advice and left the garage.

The office of the Pacific Taxicab Company was on the second floor of an old walk-up building on Columbus Avenue. It occupied one room the size of a steamship cabin. Half of the space was taken up by a big switchboard, and a sleepy man with a telephone operator's microphone strapped to his chest and a receiver on one ear held down a chair between the switchboard and a desk that faced the door. He was the only person in the office.

Krebs said, "Good morning."

The tired man said, "Hello," and swiveled in his chair as a call came in on the switchboard. "Pacific Cabs. . . . Yes, ma'am. . . . Yes, ma'am. . . . 117 Nineteenth. Near Lake Street. Any apartment number?" He pushed a plug into the board and craned his neck over his shoulder to look at Krebs. "You want a taxi?"

Krebs had learned something from the garage man besides the fact that MacLeod had taken a Pacific cab He said, "I should like to get the name and address of one of your drivers," and reached for his bill-fold. The tired man caught the significance of the motion right away. "Whose name and address do you call at 117 Nineteenth Avenue one one seven Nineteenth near Lake Street no apartment . . . right . . . whose name and address do you want?" The speech was made half into the microphone and half to Krebs.

Krebs said. "I am looking for the driver who picked up a gentleman on Montgomery Street at eleven o'clock Friday night last."

The sleepy man was looking at the wallet in Krebs' hand. "Take some work. Lots of gentlemen on Montgomery Street."

Krebs took a ten dollar bill from the wallet and laid it on the table. The man at the switchboard looked at it. He said, "Montgomery Street and what?"

Krebs had a piece of paper with four addresses written on it when he left. The Pacific Cab Company's fleet of taxis was a small one, and only four of the drivers had called in between ten o'clock and midnight on Friday from the box opposite the Empress Garage. Krebs' money had been well invested. One of the four drivers had picked up MacLeod.

The first address on his list was a boarding house on Clay Street. Krebs was directed to a room on the top floor and rapped for two minutes before he got a response. The boarder had been asleep for only three or four hours and did not like being wakened by any goddamn nosy. His answers to Krebs' questions were no, no, and get the hell out and let him sleep. Krebs thanked him for his help and left.

His second call was at a cheap new house in a subdivision on the far side of Golden Gate Park. The taxi-driver had a wife and a year old baby, and he was enjoying the sleep of a man who brings home the bacon. His wife let Krebs into the house but no farther. Her husband had been working until six o'clock in the morning and he was entitled to his sleep. If anyone wanted to talk to him he could just come back in the afternoon.

Krebs said, "Madam, I want to ask your husband only two questions, and I shall not disturb him for more than five minutes. I cannot tell you how important it is for me to see him immediately."

He was convincing. The woman led him into the bedroom, pulled up a blind and gently shook the man who slept in the bed. He muttered in his sleep and she shook him again. He rolled over and opened his eyes. She said, "I'm sorry, dear. This gentleman wants to speak to you for a minute. He says it's terribly important."

The man in the bed was still half asleep. He said irritably, "What do you want?"

Krebs said, "Did you pick up a gentleman on Montgomery Street at eleven o'clock Friday night? He was about fifty or fifty-five years of age, heavy-set, well-dressed, and very drunk."

The man in the bed did not change his expression, but he was no longer half asleep. He looked at Krebs for a long time. "What do you want to know for?"

"Do you know who he was?" Krebs asked.

"No.

"George MacLeod. His picture has been in the newspapers for two or three days."

"The man who was murdered?"

"Yes."

The taxi-driver sighed. "Well, in that case—"

Krebs got what he wanted and went back to the office.

CHAPTER TWENTY-FOUR

WHIT and Marston were still working on the refund claims when the noon siren screamed from the Ferry Building. Whit sent Tommy out for sandwiches and coffee and they finished their computations by one o'clock. If only half of the loot from the bootlegging had gone to Harald Wolff, his taxes had been overstated by $131,826.59 for 1921 and $160,648.22 for 1922, and interest paid four years previously on the overstatement had amounted to $239,405.42.

Whit put in a decimal point and drew a careful dollar sign. "Five hundred and thirty thousand dollars as of May 24, 1936." He handed the computation to Marston and picked up his paper coffee cup.

The lawyer looked at the figures. He said, "Don't we get interest on it for the time the government has had the money?"

"That's being greedy." Whit put his cup down and took the paper. "I don't know about interest on the interest, but we may be able to collect on the tax. Four years at six percent—Tommy, what's twenty-four percent of two hundred and ninety thousand dollars? Quick like a flash."

Tommy scribbled on a scratch pad. "Sixty-nine thousand, six

hundred."

"Grand total, six hundred thousand dollars," said Whit. "Will that satisfy you?"

The lawyer's eyes wrinkled at the corners. "Every little bit helps. What do we do now—sit back and wait for the money to roll in?"

Whit was lighting a cigarette. He shook his head and blew out a streamer of smoke. "Don't you believe it. We've got enough out of Zimmermann's memorandum to file the claims, but we're a long way from convincing the Secretary of the Treasury that he ought to write us a check for six hundred thousand dollars. Before there's any cash paid out, Uncle Sam is going to want one question answered; if Wolff didn't get the money, who did? He'll be asking us to tell him."

"That's Lieutenant Webster's job. We're all through now. It's up to the police to find the murderer."

Whit picked up his cup. "Well, I hope they hurry up about it. I'm still afraid to walk up an alley."

Marston said thoughtfully, "I wonder why you haven't been shot at again. Whoever wanted to kill you seems to have given up the idea."

Larson had lost interest in income taxes an hour before and was standing at the window watching the traffic in the street. He said over his shoulder, "I'm one reason."

"Is that so?" said Whit. "I kind of remember you were with me Monday night. Or am I thinking of someone else?"

Larson looked out the window.

"I'm curious," Marston said, "With all respect for Mr. Larson, it seems strange that anyone who wanted you out of the way badly enough to try to murder you wouldn't have made an attempt to finish the job."

"Maybe those gangsters thought I was someone else." Whit felt his side tenderly. "Maybe they just ran out of bullets. Whatever happened, I'm grateful. I don't like being a bull's eye, even for Marian Wolff, and if I were going to pick anyone to be shot for I'd take her."

Marston said, "Yes, of course," without any inflection in his voice.

Whit decided that the time had come to ask the lawyer some questions. He said, "Tommy, take those figures out to the adding machine and check them from hell to breakfast. If they're all right I'll dictate a statement to go with the claims and we'll get them out this afternoon. When Krebs comes in tell him I want him to give you a hand."

Tommy gathered up the papers and went out with his arms full. As he was going through the door Whit said, "I haven't forgotten our contract. You just got that raise."

Tommy grinned over his shoulder. "Thanks."

Whit got up and closed the door. "I'm in this thing pretty deep or I wouldn't be nosy," he said, "What's the trouble between you and Marian Wolff?"

Marston lifted his eyebrows. "Trouble?"

"I like to know what's going on. If you and she aren't together in this I ought to know about it. I have to protect myself in the clinches."

The lawyer said, "What are you talking about?"

Whit frowned. "Don't stall me. You and Marian Wolff are colder to each other than a pair of ice cubes. If it has anything to do with this case I want to know what it's all about."

They stared at each other for a moment, and then the lawyer's eyes flickered toward Larson at the window. Whit said, "Do me a favor, Swede. Stand outside the door for a minute. Mr. Marston wants privacy."

Larson turned from the window to protest, looked at Whit, and went out without a word. Whit waited for Marston to talk. The lawyer considered his words carefully before he said, "Marian Wolff is sole heir to her father's estate, and as his executor I am her agent. Naturally your responsibility is to her, and you should act accordingly. Whatever—difficulty there is between us need not concern you."

Whit shook his head. "That's a nice mouthful of words, but you haven't told me anything. What is it all about?"

Marston was stubbornly silent. Whit began to get mad. There was enough mystery in the case without his clients contributing a share to complicate it. He said, "Now look here. Either you—" The telephone bell interrupted him. He picked up the receiver, still glaring at the lawyer. "Yes?"

Miss Kelly said, "Miss Wolff and Mr. Harrigan are in the office."

"Ask them to come in."

Marian had arrived at the right moment. Whit wanted answers to his questions before he worked any longer for the estate of Harald Wolff, and if a showdown was necessary to get them he would call for one. He was feeling belligerent when Larson opened the door for Marian and Harrigan, and then he forgot completely what he was stirred up about. All of a sudden he knew that he had gone overboard for Marian Wolff.

Marian smiled at him as she came in. "Hello," she said. "What's the matter? Is my nose shiny?"

Whit closed his mouth. "Oh, hello. Come in and sit down." Strange things were happening to his adrenal glands.

"Good afternoon, gentlemen," Harrigan said cheerfully. He was his usual natty self, with a boutonniere, spats, stick and a panama. "Operators X-9 and X-10 reporting. We've been detecting over at the brewery and the well is dry. Even my money and Miss Wolff's glamour combined couldn't get any more information."

"You'd think that if there were any gentlemen in the place they would have invented a clue for us," Marian said. "For heaven's sake, Whit. What are you staring at?"

"Oh, I—nothing. I was just thinking."

Harrigan said, "I see Carpenter is free again. Did you learn anything from him?"

Whit came back to earth. His pulse was normal when be didn't look at Marian, "He's free, all right. What did you do—take the reporters along with you to the airport?"

"What do you mean?" Harrigan's feelings were hurt.

"You gave everything away with your newspaper story. There was an extra on the streets an hour after we got back from Alameda, and a lawyer came around with a *habeas corpus* before Carpenter opened his mouth. Lieutenant Webster has a cell waiting when he finds you."

Harrigan said indignantly, "I can't see that it made any difference because I helped the reporters out. They have to earn a living. All I did—"

"I'm just quoting Webster, Mr. Harrigan. He had no police power in Alameda and he took a chance that he'd get into trouble by arresting Carpenter illegally. He had to keep it quiet until he could get him to talk, and when you told the papers that we'd picked Carpenter up it was all over town in five minutes. I think if we could have held him we might have solved the case."

It was a little more brutal than he had meant it to be. Harrigan went to a chair near the window and sat down without speaking. Marian said flatly, "Does that mean that you're not going to be able to get the money back?"

"Oh, we're not entirely licked." It was Whit's big moment. He paused to get the proper effect. "We've solved Zimmermann's memorandum. Your father got only half of the beer money, Marian. You have about six hundred thousand dollars coming to you."

Marian looked at him blankly for a moment and then took a deep breath. Before she could speak, Marston said smoothly, "Six hundred thousand less eighteen thousand for me and approximately sixty thousand for Mr. Whitney." It was the first time he had spoken since Marian entered the office. "I think we should be accurate in these matters."

Whit had been waiting for Marian to tell him he was wonderful, and the lawyer's interruption made him mad—so mad he said what was in his mind without thinking first. "The claims will be filed for six hundred thousand dollars and we can worry about splitting it later. The question is whether Mr. Marston should represent you, Marian. As executor of the estate he would ordinarily be the proper person, but be seems to be antagonistic to you. I think it would be better if we arrange for you to act for yourself."

Marston smiled and said nothing.

"Damn you, Frank." Marian's voice was desperate. "What are you trying to do?"

The lawyer was the only self-possessed one of the three. "My dear, I am eager to help you recover your money." He looked at Whit, still smiling. "I'm sorry you feel as you do, Whitney. I think perhaps your emotions are too strong for you. However, I am the executor of the estate, I am going to continue as such until I receive the eighteen thousand dollars due me, and in my capacity as executor I am the only one who can sign a valid claim. You should know that."

There was an uncomfortable silence. Marian looked at the lawyer, turned away without speaking, and sat in the nearest chair.

Harrigan tried to clear the air. "It sounds fair enough to me. Why don't you get the claims out first and argue about the rest of it afterward?"

"Is he right, Whit?" Marian's voice was under control.

Whit nodded. His anger had gone and he knew he had made a fool of himself.

"The executor represents the estate. If he hasn't been discharged from his responsibility or won't give it up he must sign the claims."

"Then we have no choice. Let's do whatever is necessary."

Marston still smiled. "Very sensible of you."

Someone rapped at the door. Whit said, "Come in." It was Krebs. He said, "Mr. Whitney, may I—" and stopped when he saw who was there. "I beg your pardon. I did not mean to interrupt. When you can spare a moment I should like to speak to you."

"After a while. You know everyone, don't you?"

"Yes. Miss Wolff, Mr. Marston, Mr. Harrigan, Mr. Larson." He bowed to each one.

Whit was thankful for the interruption. "Get yourself a chair from across the hall, Krebs. We're making out the Wolff claims and I want you to listen while I dictate a statement. You can go over some computations with Tommy afterward."

Krebs left the room without comment. Whit followed him, called Tommy from the next office, and went down the hall to get Miss Kelly. She was gathering up her pencils when Mr. Hall entered the reception room.

"Good afternoon," he said. "I'm afraid I am early, Mr. Whitney. Are you busy?"

"A little. I'm working on something that will interest you." Whit opened the gate in the partition. "Come in and listen. We can talk in a few minutes."

"My time is yours." Mr. Hall preceded Whit down the hall and into his office. "What are you doing which will interest me?"

"Making up some refund claims. Do you know everyone here?"

Mr. Hall looked around. "I think so. How do you do? The—ah—Wolff claims, I presume. You must have made considerable progress since we talked last."

"I have," said Whit. "Swede, will you get a chair for Mr. Hall?"

Finally they were all seated. Miss Kelly put her handful of pencils on the desk and opened her tablet. Whit said, "Everyone here knows something about this case, and if I make a misstatement of fact I am open to correction. Miss

Kelly, this is a statement to accompany claims for refund of 1921 and 1922 income taxes of Harald Wolff, deceased. Type six copies."

Miss Kelly made quick marks in her book.

"During the years 1921 and 1922—" Whit stopped. He had thought of something else. "Don't take this, Miss Kelly. I suppose you all know that Lieutenant Webster has one or two of you on his list of murder suspects. Personally I think he's wrong, but if he isn't I want to point out that having me killed to shut me up is no longer worth attempting unless everyone here is also killed. The statement I am going to dictate will set forth everything I know about the Wolff case."

Someone laughed uneasily. Whit said, "I'm not joking. Miss Kelly, take this. 'During the years 1921 and 1922, the taxpayer was engaged in the illegal manufacture of beer, in violation of the National Prohibition Act. Prior to 1921 and subsequent to 1922—' "

Miss Kelly's pencil moved rapidly over the tablet.

CHAPTER TWENTY-FIVE

GINO'S TAVERN on Telegraph Hill was run by a law-abiding citizen, and the law said that within the city limits of San Francisco no drinking place was permitted to display advertisements of its wares unless the advertisements were small and inconspicuous. The sign over Gino's place said B——R ON TAP in neon letters three feet high.

Directly across the street from the sign Lieutenant Webster, Murphy, and a couple of plainclothesmen squatted on the floor in an empty flat and watched the tavern through holes in the window blind. Gino's big plate glass window was painted black from the street-level to shoulder height, but from their position on the second floor the detectives could see over the paint into the barroom. Murphy's two wop boys sat at the bar and chewed the fat with the bartender, and a third man was trying to beat a pinball machine in the corner. No one else was in the place.

Webster looked at his watch for the seventh time in a quarter of an hour. It was twenty-eight minutes of three. He said, "Are you sure you got the time right, Murphy?"

"Ask Jack," said Murphy. "He picked it up. Three o'clock is what he told me."

Jack was one of the plainclothesmen. He said, "That's right, Lieutenant. Three o'clock on the corner of Mission and Twenty-Second."

Webster grunted and looked through his peep-hole. "I'll bet you got it all wrong. I don't see why the hell you couldn't have tapped the telephone wire. Then you'd have known who called these monkeys and who they're after and everything else, and we wouldn't be sitting here on our tails hoping you heard what you thought you heard."

"We was afraid to try it, Lieutenant." Jack had been proud of a smart piece of work until he reported to Webster. "The damn wires came out on the front of the house and run to the pole across the street. If one of those guys was to look out the front window and see us working on them we'd of been sunk. Anyway, I had the microphone stuck right up against the wall a yard from the phone, and I heard everything the wop said. Whoever called him wants something to happen to someone on the corner of Mission and Twenty-Second at three o'clock."

"You think." Webster looked at his watch again. "I'll bet you didn't even get the time right. If those guys are going to get to Mission and Twenty-Second by three they'll have to get off the dime. Where's their car?"

"Right under us," Murphy said. "You can't see it from here. Another Buick. The little fellow heisted it down on Columbus in front of that big market. It was a neat job. Those boys know their business."

"Better than some. Did you get our men spotted?"

"There's a carload out on Mission waiting for the fireworks to start, and one man with the Ford down in the alley to pick us up. I left my car around the corner for Ernie. He wants to be in on the pinch."

"I think Ernie's asleep." Webster was at the peep-hole again. "God damn those punks. I wish they'd start moving."

The four men looked through the blind for a while. Murphy said, "Why don't we take them now, Lieutenant? We can grab off anyone who turns up on Mission without a couple of gorillas to lead us to him."

"What'll we charge them with—vagrancy?" The Lieutenant had his face against the blind. "We can't identify them as the men who shot Whitney, and unless we have them cold—"

"There goes Ernie," said Jack.

Ernie was the man at the pinball game. He suddenly got mad and began to hammer at the machine with his fist. The bartender said something threatening, repeated it, and started around the bar to pin the customer's ears back. The two Italians were ready to leave, but they stayed to watch the fun. Ernie got into a hot argument with the bartender.

Webster said, "Let's go. Murphy, you pick up Ernie in your car, drive like hell out to Mission, and tell them we're coming."

"Yes sir," said Murphy.

They all left the room.

~§~

Whit paused at the end of a paragraph. Miss Kelly picked up a fresh pencil. Mr. Hall said, "Perhaps I'm being captious, Mr. Whitney, but I think your last statement is not strictly correct."

"If it's wrong I want to know it," said Whit. "Read the paragraph, Miss Kelly."

Miss Kelly read. "The amounts paid over by Zimmermann comprised net proceeds of the illegal activities of the brewery, after disbursements made by Zimmermann for quote protection unquote and similar payments which were necessary because of the nature of the activities. Claimant concedes that the decedent received one-half of such net amounts, and concedes further that such one-half of the net amounts constitute taxable income. However, from the very nature of Zimmermann's memorandum, as analyzed hereinabove, it is apparent that at least one-half of the payment was made to an individual or individuals other than the decedent."

Whit looked at Hall questioningly. "What's the matter with that?"

"Do you know for certain that the—ah—protection payments were made by Zimmermann, rather than by Wolff and his—ah—accomplice after they received the money? I am questioning your positive statement of fact, Mr. Whitney; I am inclined to think you may have difficulty in substantiating it."

"He's right, Whitney," Marston said. "Even if the statement is correct, we're calling unnecessary attention to the fact that the figures shown in the memorandum were less than the gross receipts from beer sales, and the Government might want to collect on the gross amount. I'm no tax expert, but I don't think bribes to prohibition agents are allowable deductions for income tax purposes."

"I guess you're right. Take that paragraph out, Miss Kelly."

Miss Kelly ran her pencil over a page. Whit said, "It is conceded—"

~§~

The Buick crossed Market Street at New Montgomery and turned up Mission.

Half a block behind it, Webster, Jack, and the other plainclothesman followed in a rattletrap Ford sedan. The second plainclothesman was driving. He got too far behind, and at Eighth Street the traffic signal dropped between him and the Buick. He slammed on the brakes. Webster, in the rear seat, said, "What are you trying to do, lose them? Watch your step."

"Yes sir," said the driver nervously.

The signal changed. The Ford picked up speed in second. At Tenth Street it was only thirty feet behind the Buick. Webster said angrily, "God damn it, don't run them down! Take it easy, you dummy!"

~§~

"In conclusion, there can be no question but that the decedent was taxed on at least twice as much income as he received. Accordingly, claim is made for overpaid tax and interest as computed herein."

Miss Kelly finished writing and looked up. Whit thought for a while. "Paragraph. This claim is attested by decedent's executor. A certified copy of letters testamentary evidencing the executor's power to act for the estate is attached. That's all." He turned to the lawyer. "Have you copies of the letters available?"

"Yes."

"Then we're all set, unless I've left something out."

"You've covered everything we know." The lawyer looked at Marian for the first time since Whit had started dictating. "Does Mr. Whitney's statement meet with your approval, Miss Wolff?"

Marian did not even bother to turn her head toward him. "I leave everything up to you, Whit. Do whatever is necessary."

"Has anyone any suggestions?" Whit looked around the room. No one spoke. "All right, then. Miss Kelly, type that immediately, and copy Zimmermann's memorandum to go with it. No, wait." He turned to Tommy with the memorandum in his hand. "You can run a typewriter, can't you?"

"Sure."

"Use the one in the back room and make six copies of this while Miss Kelly is typing the statement. Transcribe your numbering by hand."

"Yes sir." Tommy took the memorandum and went out to the back room.

Whit said, "Krebs, look these computations over while we're waiting. Tommy has checked the arithmetic, so you needn't bother about the detail. Just see if our theory is correct—interest, tax rates, statute references, and so forth."

"Yes sir." Krebs moved from near the wall to the chair at Whit's desk. "I—wonder if I might speak to you for a minute, Mr. Whitney?"

"After a while, after a while." Whit was irritable. Marston had made him eat crow and it still bothered him. "The Collector's office closes at four-thirty and it's three o'clock now. We have no time to waste if we're going to file these this afternoon, and I want to get them off my mind."

~§~

At exactly two minutes before three o'clock Fred Carpenter came out of a rooming house on Twenty-Second Street and walked down to Mission. He had changed from his leather jacket and was wearing a dark suit and a snap-brim hat pulled down over his eyes. His lips were still puffy where Webster had hit him, and a scab had formed at the corner of his mouth.

At Mission Street he stopped in front of the corner drugstore, looked around, and took an Ingersoll from his breast pocket. It was one minute before the hour. He put the watch away and lit a cigarette.

The Buick crossed Twenty-First and came toward the Twenty-Second Street intersection in the inside lane. The Ford sedan was fifteen feet behind and outside of it, on the car tracks. When the Buick was halfway to Twenty-Second a big brown touring car pulled out from the curb and fell in alongside the Ford, directly behind the Buick. The three cars reached Twenty-Second without changing their relative positions.

Across the intersection Murphy sat behind the wheel of a car at the curb and watched the rear-view mirror. The man who had been bucking the pinball machine at Gino's was with him. Murphy said, "Here they come," and started his motor.

Webster held a gun in his lap and waited for the break. When the Buick was halfway across Twenty-Second he saw the aviator standing in front of the drugstore. He said,

"Jesus, it's Carpenter!" kicked open the door of the sedan, and jumped into the street. Immediately the driver of the Ford blew his horn. The Buick was opposite the drugstore, and as the gunman in the rear seat leaned forward to shoot at Carpenter the brown touring car speeded up and hit the Buick's rear bumper. The bullet shattered the drugstore window two feet beyond Carpenter. The aviator pulled a gun from under his arm, fired twice at the Buick, and ducked back around the corner. He was running diagonally across Twenty-Second Street when Webster took careful aim and shot him in the leg. The heavy slug knocked Carpenter to the street, and the gun fell from his hand and skidded into the gutter. Webster beat him to it when he crawled over to pick it up.

The driver of the Buick had shifted into second and was pulling away from the touring car. The man in the back seat smashed the barrel of his pistol through the rear window and let go at the car behind, and one of the men in the touring car leaned out of the side and emptied his gun at him. The gunman collapsed. The Ford pulled up alongside of the gangster's car, and the driver of the Buick steered with one hand and tried to shoot with the other. He got in one shot at the Ford before he smashed into Murphy's car, which Murphy had pulled out at right angles from the curb to block the road. The crash turned Murphy's car over on its side but the Buick stopped. Its driver's head hit the windshield. He was unconscious when the men from the touring car put handcuffs on him.

Pedestrians were still running in all directions when Murphy crawled out of the wreck and went back to Twenty-

Second Street. He met Webster turning the corner at a run. He said, "We got them, Lieutenant. One dead, one asleep. As soon as he wakes up—"

"To hell with him!" Webster said exultantly. "I've cracked the case!"

Murphy had to run to keep up with him as he went into the drugstore. The clerk was on the floor behind a counter. Webster said, "Where's a telephone, quick?" and the clerk pointed, getting to his knees.

Murphy said, "Who is it, Lieutenant?"

Webster told him as he dialed a number. Murphy said stupidly, "Well, what do you know about that?"

The Lieutenant had the receiver to his ear, waiting. "Tell Jack to get an ambulance for Carpenter, and you go turn that touring car around and pick me up. As soon as I find out where this killer is, we'll be moving fast."

~§~

Marian said nervously, "How long will it be before everything is typed, Whit?"

"Fifteen minutes. Don't worry, Marian. We have plenty of time—another day if we need it. The notary is on her way up here now."

"We'll need the letters testamentary," Marston said. "Shall I have them brought over here or do you want to stop at my office to pick them up?"

"Get them here," Whit said. "The less stopping we do before those claims are safe with the Collector, the better I'll feel." He motioned to the telephone and turned to Marian. "Well, we've done it. How do you feel?"

"I can't tell you how I feel now," Marian said softly, looking up at him. "I shall—later."

Whit's head began to swim.

The telephone rang as Marston went to the desk to make his call. He answered it and said, "Yes, he's here." He held the phone out to Larson. "For you."

"Me?" Larson left the window and suspiciously took the phone. "Hello."

It was all he said, except "Yes," once. When he put the phone down he seemed completely dumbfounded. Harrigan said, "Why, what is it, Mr. Larson?"

Larson shook his head. "I'll be goddamned." He reached deliberately inside his coat for his gun and pointed it at Marston. "Stick your hands up. You're under arrest."

Nobody moved. The lawyer stared at him. His hands were in his pockets and he kept them there. He said incredulously, "What?"

"You heard me." Larson jerked the muzzle of his pistol upward. "You murdered—"

A gun went off with a flat crack. Behind Larson the glass door of the office fell in pieces. Larson stood perfectly still for a moment until his knees buckled, and then he fell on his face. Marston took his hand out of the pocket holding a light automatic—a twenty-five. He said, "The rest of you put your hands up and keep quiet."

CHAPTER TWENTY-SIX

THE BROWN TOURING CAR roared across town, wide open. Its driver kept one hand on the horn. Webster had to bellow to make himself heard.

"—trying to blackmail Marston out of more than Whitney offered him. He was going to meet him at three o'clock for the pay-off only Marston sent his boys instead."

Murphy yelled over the noise. "Was Marston bootlegging with Wolff?"

The Lieutenant nodded his head violently. It was easier than shouting.

"How did he get to Sacramento to shoot Zimmermann?"

"Didn't stop to find out," roared Webster. "Get the bastard in the tank first, worry about how he did it later."

A siren sounded behind them. Webster turned to look back, put his arm out of the side, and waved it forward. A prowl car pulled alongside. One of the two cops in it shouted angrily, "Pull over to the curb! What do you think this is, a—" He saw Webster. "Hey. What's up, Lieutenant?"

"Get out in front and give us some interference," Webster bawled. "California and Montgomery."

"O.K." The prowl car forged ahead, its siren screaming. The

two automobiles swung into Market Street, dodging in and out between street cars. Webster yelled suddenly. "Never did like him anyway. Too smooth. Hope the Swede uses his head."

~§~

Marston had picked up Larson's gun and was ready for Miss Kelly when she ran back from the reception room to see who had broken Mr. Whitney's door. He motioned her into the office and stepped into the doorway in time to see Tommy making for the fire-escape. Tommy had been smart enough to guess that something was wrong when he heard the shot from the next room, but he had waited too long. The lawyer said, "Come back." Tommy looked at the gun and came down the hall with his hands up.

Miss Kelly's face was green. She stared at Larson's body on the floor and the stain spreading on the carpet. Whit thought she was going to faint. He made a movement to attract her attention from Larson.

"Keep your hands up," Marston said quietly.

Whit lifted one arm higher.

The lawyer motioned with the gun in his right hand. "Both of them. Up."

"I can't." Whit felt a strain on the wound even with his left hand at the level of his ear.

Marston raised the twenty-five until he was looking directly into Whit's eyes through the sights. His teeth showed in a smile. "Lift them."

Whit lifted. Something tore loose in his side.

The lawyer said, "That's better," and backed against the far far side of the hall opposite the doorway. He was as calm as he had been before Larson's telephone call. "Now come out of there. All of you. Go down the hall and into the vault. If anyone stumbles or drops his hands I'll shoot."

Nobody moved. Marston twitched the muzzle of the twenty-five at Whit. "You first."

Harrigan said calmly, "What are you going to do with Larson—let him bleed to death?"

"Quiet. Come out, Whitney."

Whit went into the hall. Broken glass from the door cracked under his feet. Behind him the others followed, one at a time. Marian was crying angrily, and tears rolled down her cheeks. Mr. Hall kept clearing his throat, and Miss Kelly had begun to sniffle. No one spoke. At the vault door Whit stopped. Marston said, "Get in."

"You know we'll suffocate in five minutes, don't you?" said Whit.

"Get in."

Whit went into the vault. Somewhere in the distance a siren was screaming bloody murder.

~§~

The police car skidded to a stop at the corner of California Street. Its siren choked off in a snarl. The touring car took the corner on two wheels and stopped in the middle of the street opposite the Farmers' Exchange. Webster, Murphy and the driver jumped out and ran into the building. The two cops from the police car hurried down from the corner and caught up with Webster as he sent Murphy and the driver pounding up the stairs. An elevator was discharging its load in the lobby. Webster and the cops piled in. The detective said, "Eight. Quick!" The doors slammed, and the car shot up to the eighth floor. Webster said, "Come on," to the cops and ran for Whitney's office, taking out his gun.

The reception room was empty. Glass from the broken door lay on the carpet in the hall, and Webster groaned when he saw it. In Whit's office he found Larson's body on the floor. He said viciously, "You dumb blockhead! I knew you'd bitch it up," and jerked a finger at one of the cops. "Take a look at him." The cop knelt beside Larson.

Webster and the other man slammed doors open and looked around. Opposite the vault they heard pounding. The detective tugged at the handle of the door, motioned the cop back, and began firing at the combination dial. Bits of plaster and lead fell in the hall as the bullets ricocheted from the iron. The fourth slug broke the dial loose. Webster knocked it off with his gun-butt, jammed the barrel of the gun into the locking mechanism, and twisted. The tumblers fell apart. He yanked at the handle.

Whit and Marian were last out of the vault. Whit had his good arm around Marian's shoulders. Her face was streaked with tears. Miss Kelly was building up to a case of hysterics, and the others were pale and silent.

Webster ignored everyone but Whit. "How much of a start has he?"

"Two or three minutes." Whit kept his arm around the girl. Webster said, "Well, come on if you feel like it," and ran back down the hall, followed by the cop. Whit looked at Marian and tightened his arm before he took it away. "I'll see you later." He went after the detective.

They met Murphy and his man coming into the reception room. As he went by them Webster said, "Stay here and take over. Call an ambulance for the Swede."

Murphy looked disappointed.

In the elevator Whit put his hand under his coat. His side was bleeding steadily. He said, "Is Larson dead?"

"I don't know. He ought to be if he isn't. What happened?"

"He stuck Marston up. Marston had a gun in his pocket."

Webster cursed. "If that bastard gets away, I'll—I'll—"

"You telephoned Larson?"

"Yes. I wanted to make sure Marston was here and wouldn't get away. I should have known better than to trust the Swede to stop him."

"He tried," Whit said.

"Hell of a lot of good that does."

The elevator doors opened. Webster led the race across the lobby with Whit and the cop at his heels.

The siren, the running policemen, and the automobile standing empty on the car tracks had attracted a crowd. People were jammed around the building entrance. The traffic officer from the corner was threatening and pushing to clear a space on the sidewalk. "Get back there, you. Move along." He shoved at the nearest man. "What's going on, Lieutenant?"

"Finishing up a case." Webster raised his voice and yelled. "Anyone see a man run out of here four or five minutes ago—brown face, grey hair, well-dressed, forty-five or fifty?"

Nobody volunteered. The traffic cop put his shoulder down and heaved. "Come on, break it up. Would the guy be driving a big La Salle, Lieutenant?"

Webster said, "He might be. A blue sedan?"

"That's it. He beat it down California Street just before you got here. He could hardly wait for the light." The traffic cop tried threats on the crowd. "Break it up, now, before I pinch somebody. You aren't going to see anything. Move along."

"He's heading for the Bay Bridge!" Webster gave quick orders to the traffic cop. "Send out a call to pick him up at Berkeley. Frank Marston, wanted for murder. He has a gun and he's dangerous. Better have all the roads out of town blocked."

Whit said, "Two guns. He knows how to shoot them, too."

"Yes sir." The traffic cop pushed his way through the mob and headed for a call-box.

Webster and the cop from the police car shoved in the other direction and broke through. Whit stayed close behind them to keep from bumping his side. Webster said, "Hurry up, hurry up! We'll take the prowl car."

The siren cleared their path down California. In the car Whit pulled up his shirt to plug his side with a handkerchief. Webster yelled, "Did he get you too?"

"No. Made me put my hands up." Whit had to shout. "How did you get on to him?"

The car turned a corner. The rear wheels skidded and both men piled up on one side of the seat. Webster pushed Whit upright and held on to the door handle. "Carpenter. He had the goods on him. Marston sent his gunmen to meet him and we trailed them. Same boys who shot you."

Whit yelled, "He must have expected trouble. Had his car ready for a getaway."

"He's smart." Webster leaned forward to scream at the driver. "Step on it!"

"Can't," the driver shouted. "It'll turn over. Wait until we get on the straightaway."

They hit the curve of the bridge approach and the tires whined. Webster pounded the driver's shoulder. "Cut the siren! We don't want to scare him."

"Right!" The howl of the siren died away. The car came out of the turn onto the bridge and the driver pressed his foot to the floorboards. The needle of the speedometer crept up to 80. Whit wrung out his sodden handkerchief and put it back against his side, wadding his shirt tail over it. The speedometer needle got up to 90, to 93, and hung there. The driver knew his business. He moved traffic out of the way with short toots of his horn and kept his foot down.

Halfway across the bridge they met a motorcycle cop going toward San Francisco at a comfortable fifty. He swung around behind them, and the exhaust roared as he let his machine out. Whit bellowed, "Reinforcements." Webster grunted and peered anxiously at the road ahead. They were almost to the toll gates on the Berkeley side when he seized Whit's arm and pointed to the far side of the gates. "Look!"

Whit looked. "That's it."

Webster tapped the driver on the shoulder. "The blue sedan. Give her the siren and we'll go through. He's staying under the limit. Get him quick before he lets it out."

The siren wound up to an ear-splitting shriek. Men moved quickly at the toll-gate and a bar across one of the entrances swung away. The driver hunched his shoulders and took a fresh grip on the wheel. Whit looked at the narrow passageway between the concrete pillars of the gate and closed his eyes. The siren howled, the car bucked suddenly, and they were through. Whit swallowed and opened his eyes again. He looked back to be sure the gate was in one piece, and saw that their reinforcements had doubled. Another motorcycle had joined the first.

Ahead of them the La Salle was picking up speed. The distance between the two cars closed, held even, and began to lengthen. Webster yelled, "Open it up, open it up, for Christ's sake!"

"All she's got," shouted the driver. "He's going to leave us."

The blue sedan was pulling away. The road curved in a wide sweep to the left and then lay straight before them for miles along the bay shore. Webster said bitterly, "God-damn," and bent forward. A rifle hung in a sling on the back of the front seat. He pulled it loose, pumped a shell into the breech, and braced his feet.

Whit yelled, "He'll never live through it at that speed."

"Maybe not. I'd rather take him alive, but I'll take him in a basket if I have to." Webster leaned out of the car and put his cheek against the gun-stock.

The siren had cleared the road ahead. Cars on both sides of the pavement were pulled up along the side. The La Salle had a free track and was making the most of it. Webster fired at Marston's tires, shooting when the prowl car hit smooth stretches of pavement. The La Salle continued to gain. Webster missed three times. At the fourth shot he lifted his head. "There she—"

A tire flopped on the blue sedan. The car weaved, swayed once from side to side, turned suddenly broadside, and went over. It left the pavement, hurdled a five-foot parking strip which separated the eastern and western sides of the roadbed, bounced once on the far side, and splashed into the bay.

"—goes," said Webster. The driver put on his brakes.

The motorcycle cops bore down, their sirens whining. Whit sat wearily on the running board of the prowl car while Webster explained the situation and argued a question of jurisdiction. The argument was still going on when the ambulance and a wrecking car arrived.

Marston's La Salle was half out of water, embedded in the mud of the tide flats. A man from the wrecking car got a chain hooked to its axle hut his truck did not have power enough to budge it. The ambulance crew waded out to get Marston's body and brought it back under a sheet. When it was stowed away, Whit got up off the running board and walked over to the ambulance. He said, "Any room for another passenger?"

The driver looked at the stain showing through Whit's coat and extending down his pants leg. "Sure. Climb in, if you don't mind the corpse."

"I don't mind anything if it's peaceful," said Whit, He climbed in.

CHAPTER TWENTY-SEVEN

THE ASSEMBLY Friday morning was held in MacLeod's office. Whit's own room was out of service until the carpet could be washed and the door repaired.

Marian arrived in another blue dress which exactly matched the color of her eyes. Harrigan was there, curious as ever, and Krebs and Tommy abandoned the pretense of doing anything and came into the office as soon as Webster showed up.

Miss Kelly brought in the typed refund claims and laid them on Whit's desk. Whit read them over carefully before he gave them to Marian for her signature. She said, "How do I sign them, Whit? Just my name?"

"That's all. You're the heir. Incidentally, you're the only one who could have filed them. That's why Marston was so anxious to sign them himself."

"That had me licked," said Webster. "I couldn't figure out why he was going ahead with it. What was he trying to do?"

"He was putting sand in the gears. The estate was closed when the money was all paid out, back in 1936. Wolff had been cautious enough to provide in his will that his executor had to post a surety bond. When there was nothing left in the estate Marston wound it up and petitioned the probate court for a discharge so he could release his bond. I don't know what kind of fake papers he was going to attach to the claims, but the court had given him his discharge and he couldn't act for the estate any more than the man on the street corner. The claims would have been worthless, and after today we couldn't have filed others."

Marian blotted her signature and returned Whit's pen with a smile. "But he would have had to explain it away afterwards, wouldn't he?"

"He wasn't worried about explaining. All he wanted to do was keep valid claims from being filed so he wouldn't have the Government investigating the case. If you signed them, the whole Treasury Department would have been on his neck. If he signed them they were just waste paper."

Harrigan said, "I hope someone else is good at explaining." He looked at Webster. "Lieutenant, I have mentioned before that I'm a curious man. Would you mind filling in some of the blanks?"

Webster grinned. "It's simple as pie. I thought everyone had it all figured out."

"I haven't," Marian said. "I want to know who shot Whit."

Tommy said, "How did he get to Sacramento to kill Zimmermann?"

Krebs said, "Was Carpenter working for him?"

Webster leaned back in his chair and locked his hands behind his head. He paused longer than he needed to. "Pure deduction was what did it. First of all—"

"Hold it," said Whit. "If you're going to start explaining, I want a record of it. Miss Kelly, will you get your book?"

Miss Kelly had never hurried so fast in her life. When she

was back with her tablet and pencils, Webster said, "There are still some holes in it, Whitney. Are you after the bare facts or do you want the gaps filled in with guesswork?"

"Your guess is as good as anyone's. Go ahead."

"O.K." The detective settled himself in his chair. "Here goes." Miss Kelly poised her pencil.

"Whichever one of them thought up the idea, Wolff and Marston went into the bootlegging racket together. I suppose they thought the combination of a good brewer and a slick lawyer was too good to pass up, with beer worth thirty-five dollars a barrel.

"Marston had practiced law in New York." The detective looked at Whit. "I got a lot of this from Carpenter. He opened up plenty when he knew Marston had double-crossed him. He kind of thinks maybe you'll give him that five thousand dollars, too."

"Maybe I will."

"It's your money. Well, Zimmermann was one of Marston's old clients who hadn't been able to beat a grand larceny rap. He came up for parole in 1920, when Marston and Wolff were getting set for their racket, and he wrote Marston to ask for a sponsor to help get him out. Marston wanted to stay in the background as much as he could when the bootlegging started. He was a crook himself and I guess he didn't trust Wolff any further than he could see him. When he saw a chance to put his own man in on the ground floor he jumped at it."

The detective took a couple of crumpled telegrams from his pocket and laid one on the desk. "I got these last night. Exhibit A. Wire from the warden at Sing Sing. 'Zimmermann paroled 1920 to Frank Marston attorney San Francisco stop promised employment stop parolee has no subsequent record stop.'" He put the other telegram on top of the first. "Exhibit B. Putnam's wire. 'Zimmermann recommended by Frank Marston attorney for Harald Wolff stop have no knowledge re Carpenter present or past.'

"Marston could have put Zimmermann back in the pen anytime by withdrawing his sponsorship and framing a little theft charge, so I guess Zimmermann did what he was told. Anyway, Marston recommended him to Wolff, and Wolff put him in the brewery to handle the receipts.

"Marston was the under-cover man. Wolff made the beer and Marston kept them out of trouble with the law. At first things went pretty smoothly and they coined money. When competition moved in and the going got too rough, they quit. They had split about a million dollars and they must have thought it was a good idea to take it and run before someone bumped them off." Webster looked at Whit. "You can go on from there."

"Not yet. What about Carpenter? Was he Marston's man, too?"

Webster nodded. "Oh, sure. He was a local gunman. Marston pulled him out of trouble a couple of times and got him a job with the brewery so he'd have another man on the ground floor. When the brewery went legitimate again, Marston knew it still wouldn't hurt to have a couple of his own men around in case anything went wrong. So he talked Wolff into giving Carpenter a job. He had Carpenter working for Wolff and Zimmermann at the brewery. Everything was hotsy totsy—until the government moved in. It's your turn, Whitney."

Whit said, "Mine's mostly guesswork. The Treasury Department got hold of Zimmermann in 1935. They must have grabbed him before he could get rid of his memorandum book. He was either afraid of what Marston could do to him or he thought he could hold him up for a slice of the profits. So he hung everything on Wolff. All Marston had to do then was shut Wolff up before he talked too much."

Webster said, "Wolff probably knew what had happened when he got the government's notice. That's why he was in such a hurry to go to Washington; he didn't want to stick around town where Marston could get to him. His only mistake was in trusting Carpenter. Go ahead."

"Well, Wolff was killed. Marston was still his executor, and everything would be lovely if he could pay off Wolff's taxes so the government would close the case and forget about it. He didn't dare let go of a million dollars of estate funds without putting up a struggle because he had to submit reports to the probate court and no judge would overlook deficiencies of that size if they were paid without even a protest. He waited until the last minute and then called George in, so George never had a chance to do anything but rush through a protest without really digging into things. When the protest was rejected, George had to recommend that the tax be paid because as far as he could see they didn't have a chance of winning the case." Whit turned his head toward Marian. "I suppose Marston was careful not to have an opinion, one way or the other."

"Yes. He pinned George down until George had to tell me he thought the money should be paid." Marian made a face.

"I always distrusted Frank Marston. He was so—so— smooth."

"Did you?" said Whit.

Marian looked at him in surprise. "I certainly didn't like him."

"I suppose not. Well, he was sitting pretty after the taxes were paid, except that George still had a copy of Zimmermann's memorandum in his files. If he ever really looked at it he'd see what it showed—what I overlooked. Tommy saved the day for all of us on that."

Tommy grinned and blushed.

"The Treasury Department had the original, but they weren't going to be interested in it after they got their money unless they had to pay some of it back. Marston must have tried hard to get the copy away from George."

"He did," said Krebs. "He attempted to get it from me once when Mr. MacLeod was not in the office. I told him I should be glad to return it after I had made a copy for our records. He said it did not matter very much and that we could keep it if we wished."

"He was afraid to attract too much attention to it," said Whit. "I guess he just had to take a chance that the statute of limitations would expire before George discovered anything. If the refund claims had outlawed most of his worries would have been over, because the Federal Government would have had a closed case. When George told him that he was going to file claims, there was only one thing to do." Whit nodded his head at the detective. "You'll have to go on from there. Are you getting all this, Miss Kelly?"

Miss Kelly said, "Yes," without looking up from her book. She was working hard.

"I'm guessing now," said Webster. "Your partner thought that Wolff had split with one of the other stockholders. He arranged the meeting at the brewery either because he suspected one of the men who were still alive and wanted to see how they would react when he told them what he had found, or because he thought one of the dead men was responsible and he wanted to gather information. Or he might not have known who it was but had the guts to go after what he wanted. His mistake was in telling Marston what he knew. Marston made an appointment with him for seven, got here early, sneaked through the lobby, and came up the stairs.

"MacLeod probably found him here when he got back from dinner. I suppose Marston was too anxious, and MacLeod got suspicious and wouldn't take the papers out of the safe. They had a fight and Marston shot him. He worked on the safe as long as he dared but he couldn't get at the papers, so he closed the vault, went back down stairs, waited until he could cross the lobby without being seen, and rang for the elevator. You know the rest of it."

"I do not," said Whit. "Why did he give up trying to have me killed?"

"I guess he was only worried about you at first, when he read that story I put in the newspapers. You remember he telephoned to find out what was up and we stalled him off. He didn't know for sure whether we were lying to him when we told him the story was a fake, and he couldn't take a chance. He was afraid to try to get you himself, but he had defended some of the local gangsters in court and he hired a couple of them to put you away. Lucky for you they missed. He found out later that the newspaper story was really a phony, so he called them off. I guess he planned to keep you alive until you got really dangerous."

Tommy had been quiet as long as he could. "Lieutenant Webster, how did Mr. Marston get to Sacramento? He killed Zimmermann, didn't he?"

"Oh, sure. Carpenter flew him. Marston still had Zimmermann under his thumb, but he was afraid of him. He knew Carpenter was tough enough to keep from talking but he wasn't sure of Zimmermann. I suppose he had kept track of him just to be safe, and he decided to put him out of the way before we found him. He booked a student's flying lesson at the airport under a phony name. Carpenter went up with an empty plane at ten o'clock and set it down behind a row of trees in a field next to the second fairway at the country club. Marston knocked a ball over the trees, ducked off the fairway, got into the plane, flew to Sacramento in about half an hour, shot Zimmermann, and was back in plenty of time to play a couple of holes before he went back to the club-house. He had no one to worry about then."

"Except Carpenter," Whit said. "I suppose he sent Mendell to get him out of jail."

"That's right." The detective turned to Harrigan and shook his head. "You certainly did your best to ruin us when you talked to the reporters, Mr. Harrigan. I almost swore out a warrant for you."

"It was stupid," Harrigan confessed. "I was so proud of myself for locating Carpenter I had to tell everyone. Pride is a terrible thing."

"It was this time. Marston was lucky enough to see the papers. He got Mendell to spring Carpenter and Carpenter hid out. Marston probably thought that Carpenter would keep his mouth shut because he had a record and he could have been saddled with Wolff's murder. When Whitney told him we would give him the breaks if he talked, he saw a chance to hold Marston up for some real money. Marston said he'd play ball and made an appointment for the payoff, only he sent his gorillas instead. We were there. Carpenter spilled the beans when he found out that Marston had double-crossed him. That's when I called Larson—like a damn fool."

Marian said, "How is he? Was it a serious wound?"

"No. He was lucky that Marston was using those steel jacketed bullets. The slug went right through his lung, clean as a whistle. He'll be in the hospital for a while, and then he'll be good as new—whatever that is." Webster shook his head disgustedly. "I made my big mistake when I told him not to let Marston get away. I wanted him to sit tight and stall until I got there, and he decided to be a hero and make the pinch himself. Marston was too much for him."

Miss Kelly caught up with her writing. Whit said, "I guess that's everything, Miss Kelly. Make a transcript and put it in the file."

"Yes, Mr. Whitney." Miss Kelly was a little awed. For one thing, Mr. Whitney had been getting a lot of publicity, and for another he was particularly serious this morning. Maybe it was just the dreadful happenings of the past few days, but he didn't seem like his old self at all.

She turned to leave the office. Whit said, "Wait a minute. I have an announcement to make. I want you all to meet my new partner, Mr. Krebs. We drew up the papers this morning."

Everyone said something congratulatory. Krebs said, "Thank

you," several times and left the office as soon as he could get away.

The meeting broke up after that. Marian and Whit took a taxi to the Federal Building. In the cab Marian said, "What are you so morose about, Whit? Aren't you happy that it's all over?"

"Sure."

"You seem awfully gloomy."

"I am."

They rode the rest of the way in silence. Whit looked at the floor of the cab. Marian watched him, frowning.

The claims were filed before noon. The clerk who took them whistled when he saw the amounts involved and the dates of payment. Whit had brought extra copies of the claims, and he had the date and time of receipt stamped on them. One receipted copy of each claim he gave to Marian. The others he put in his pocket.

When it was over and they stood on the sidewalk in front of the building, Marian said, "Now what, Whit? Do we celebrate? I'm a rich woman now. I'll buy you some champagne."

"No, thanks. I don't feel like celebrating."

Marian's smile faded. She said, "Whit, for heaven's sake what's the matter?"

He was looking at his shoes. "Nothing. I have some things to do. I'm leaving on a vacation tomorrow."

"Oh." Marian didn't know what to say. "Well, I—how long will you be gone?"

"Oh, I don't know. Some time."

She said angrily, "You mean you don't want to see me again."

He lifted his head to look at her. "That's right."

"Why? What have I done?"

"You and Kitty MacLeod were pretty good friends before Friday night, weren't you?"

She stared at him. He said stonily, "George spent Friday night with you. He never could keep his mouth shut, Marian. Saturday morning he bragged to Krebs about what a devil he was with the women, and Krebs ran down the cab-driver who took him back to your apartment after you sent him out to hide his car so no one would see it parked there all night. George bribed the cab-driver to suck your doorman away so he could get in without being seen."

Marian said nothing. Her face was white.

"George didn't mean anything to you. He was just someone who could do something for you and you paid him off in advance." Whit smiled without humor. "By God, I've just figured out why Marston was sour on you. I suppose you got him to give you that eighteen thousand dollars the same way you got George to make up a ten dollar tax return."

She still said nothing.

"Was that it?"

"Think whatever you like." Marian's voice trembled with anger. "You're so smart. Work it out for yourself."

"I have." Whit lifted his hat. "Your claims are filed and you'll get your money back. I'll send you a bill for ten per cent. Good-bye."

There was a bar around the corner from the Federal Building. Whit stopped for a drink. He stared at the whiskey for five minutes, and then he put the glass down and walked out. At the corner he took a cab and went to call on Kitty MacLeod.

Kitty was surprised to see him. They went into her living room and he sat on the davenport where he had slept Saturday night. Kitty stood by the fireplace. She was wearing a long crimson house dress and red slippers with high heels. She said, "Is everything finished?"

"The claims are filed."

"That's good. How does Marian feel?"

"I don't know. I don't care how she feels."

"Oh."

Neither of them spoke for a while after that. Finally Whit said, "How did you find out that George spent the night with her?"

Kitty looked at him quickly and then at her fingernails. "He bragged to me on the phone Saturday morning. He didn't tell me who it was. I guessed it when I asked Marian if she knew where he had gone when he left her. She's a poor liar. How did you know?"

"George told Krebs he had a new woman. Krebs checked up on his own hook. He thought Marian had something to do with the murder, but he didn't want to make a mistake."

Kitty said, "I'm sorry, Whit."

"You're sorry? What for?"

"You liked her, didn't you?"

"Oh, sure. She was cute. That's all."

Kitty looked at her fingernails again. Whit said, "Well, I've made Krebs a partner. I'm going to finish my vacation now."

"Where are you going?"

"Mexico. I think I'll—" He stopped. "Kitty, answer me one question, will you?"

She examined a nail closely. "What?"

"Did you try to get me to quit Marian Wolff because you were mad at her—because of her and George?"

Kitty bent her head over her fingers. "No. George didn't mean anything to me. I told you that."

"Well, why was it?"

Kitty said nothing. Her cheeks were getting red.

Whit said, "I'm going to get my face slapped again, but I want to know something. Why did you kiss me?"

"Don't be a fool." Kitty's face was almost as red as her dress.

"All right." Whit stood up. "Will you go to Mexico with me, Kitty?"

She looked up quickly and left the fireplace to meet him. He said, "Look out for my ribs, now."

Coming soon from
Bruin Crimeworks...

David Dodge's
To Catch a Thief

Immortalized on film by Alfred Hitchcock, *TO CATCH A THIEF* is a classic crime caper with a decided romantic twist. This timeless story of love and honor unfolds amidst a high stakes game of cat-and mouse. Out of print and scarce for many years, Bruin Crimeworks is proud to make it available again.

Now Available from Bruin Books Originals

CARDINAL BISHOP, INC.

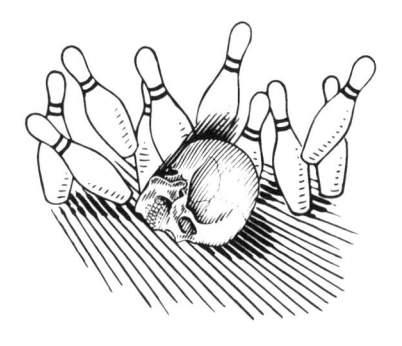

BY JONATHAN EEDS

A FALLEN HERO. . .A JADED GIRLFRIEND. . .

A MISSING HEIRESS. . .AN EVIL RELIC. . .

CARDINAL BISHOP IS OPEN FOR BUSINESS

A STORY OF LOVE, MYSTERY, TIME TRAVEL. . ..

AND A REALLY PISSED-OFF PIGEON

What readers are saying—

"Not since 'Hitchhiker's Guide to the Galaxy' have I read such a humorous book…made me laugh out loud."

"…a likable scoundrel whom I could not help but cheer on."

"The dialog is wonderful…"

Now available from Bruin Crimeworks:

No Orchids for Miss Blandish

James Hadley Chase

Widely recognized as on of the top thrillers of the 20th century, NO ORCHIDS FOR MISS BLANDISH set the standard for crime fiction and has gone on to sell over four million copies worldwide. A kidnapped heiress becomes a helpless pawn in an underworld of sexual perversion, murder and mayhem.

Flesh of the Orchid

James Hadley Chase

A raucous thrill ride of a novel and sequel to the classic crime novel, *NO ORCHIDS FOR MISS BLANDISH*. The story bristles with crazy plot twists, edge-of-the-seat suspense and a cast of intriguing low-life's who mix it up for an immensely enjoyable read.

A city rocked by rape and murder

KNOCK THREE— ONE— TWO

FREDRIC BROWN

Printed in Great
Britain
by Amazon